Advance Praise

Still Come Home, is a stunning and deeply lyrical tour de force.
The tension and interplay between three alternating voices—an
Afghan woman, an American soldier, and a reluctant Taliban
recruit—allow us to understand the characters' struggles in
a way that no single perspective could, and Schultz's ability
to enter into their radically different lives is nothing short of
breathtaking. There is tragedy here, but also humor, moral
blindness along with deep courage, and the desert holds it all.
The sand and dust and changing sky of this novel are, like the
prose itself, like the story Schultz gives us, at once devastating
and gorgeous and utterly mesmerizing.

> —Abigail DeWitt, author of *News of Our Loved Ones*

Still Come Home is personal, global, tender, brutal, and deeply
introspective--in short, a powerhouse of a book. Katey Schultz
has written one of the finest works of fiction yet to come out of
the Long Wars, and she offers more than a few sharp clues as to
why these wars, eighteen years and counting, are still with us.
'So much gone wrong in the name of something right'—the
wrong and the right of it, the mercy, the love, the blood-letting
and profit-making, Schultz captures it all in this splendid novel.

> —Ben Fountain, author of *Billy Lynn's Long Halftime Walk*
> and *Beautiful Country Burn Again*

Katey Schultz's debut novel *Still Come Home* is a remarkable book, impressive in its breadth and depth of story, engaging with its finely-drawn characters, and breath-taking in its pace. I know of few authors writing about war these days who can so skillfully balance both sides of the conflict with equal grace. Katey Schultz gives true heart and dignity to both the so-called 'enemy' and the 'friendly' forces of the American troops. *Still Come Home* made me think long and deep about how we humans all too often lose sight of our humanity during war. The characters in these pages remind us how complicated and anguishing decisions can be on both sides of the battle-lines.

—David Abrams, author of *Brave Deeds* and *Fobbit*

Still Come Home

Still Come Home

To Caroline,

Katey Schultz

Katey Schultz

Apprentice
House Press
Loyola University Maryland

First Edition

Hardcover ISBN: 978-1-62720-230-5
Paperback ISBN: 978-1-62720-231-2
Ebook ISBN: 978-1-62720-232-9

Printed in the United States of America

Design editor: Lillian Lane
Acquisitions editor: Keelin Ferdinandsen
Copy editor: Dani Williams
Promotion editor: Kelly Lyons

Cover art by Marianne Dages and Amze Emmons, "June," letterpress on paper, 2013. https://www.mariannedages.com/

Published by Apprentice House Press

Apprentice House Press
Loyola University Maryland
4501 N. Charles Street
Baltimore, MD 21210
410.617.5265 • 410.617.2198 (fax)
www.ApprenticeHouse.com
info@ApprenticeHouse.com

This book is dedicated to my Number One,

Brad Quillen,

and to the quiet beauty of Mercy Me Hill
where many of these pages were written.

Excerpt from

"A Dialogue of Self and Soul"

by William Butler Yeats

A living man is blind and drinks his drop.
What matter if the ditches are impure?
What matter if I live it all once more?
Endure that toil of growing up;
The ignominy of boyhood; the distress
Of boyhood changing into man;
The unfinished man and his pain
Brought face to face with his own clumsiness;
The finished man among his enemies? --
How in the name of Heaven can he escape
That defiling and disfigured shape
The mirror of malicious eyes
Casts upon his eyes until at last
He thinks that shape must be his shape?
And what's the good of an escape
If honour find him in the wintry blast?
I am content to live it all again
And yet again, if it be life to pitch
Into the frog-spawn of a blind man's ditch,
A blind man battering blind men...
I am content to follow to its source
Every event in action or in thought;
Measure the lot; forgive myself the lot!

Day One

1

Taking Flight

It's market day, and the streets of Imar beckon. There may be nuts, fresh bread, produce—an apricot—and there it is, a craving for fruit seeping from Aaseya's mind to her mouth, her taste buds springing to life. It would taste like candied moisture, a wet slice of sunlight in the mouth. But imagining is hardly enough, and what is a life if not lived fully? She wants the fruit. She wants her freedom. She wants to do everything she shouldn't. She shoves back her purple headscarf and walks to the open window of her small, second-story apartment. She sticks her torso out and leans, hanging her head upside down. Her hair dangles like a black flag in the breeze. Positioned like this, she won't have to look up the street at the remains of her family compound. She won't have to wish she'd died in there three years ago either.

She hoists herself upright and sees sun splotches. A molten feeling fills her skull as blood drains downward and rights itself throughout her body. She leans against the windowsill and looks toward the sky.

The taste is still there.

An apricot.

Sweet and earthy.

Warm.

Amazing how a single thought can bloom like a saffron crocus, infusing the body. Her body. Seventeen years old and no

3

one would have guessed this life for her. Not her father, not her mother or her siblings. All of them gone, leaving only an obstinate Afghan girl in a rushed marriage to Rahim, a desire for fruit, and a village the size of a flea.

"Silly woman!" a child's voice taunts from below.

A different child giggles. "She's the dishonorable one. The one who's shameful."

Aaseya rights her headscarf and studies the two boys standing across the narrow street, their brown eyes as wide as grapes. Behind them, a smaller boy with a dense crop of hair crouches against the corner of a building, examining the dirt. The sun throws light across their bodies in a wash of pale yellow, illuminating their black-topped heads into little, golden orbs, somewhat like desert flowers. But there's nothing lovely about these boys and their accusations.

Ba haya.

Shameful.

"Go home to your mothers!" Aaseya shouts. "You're useless to me!"

The two bigger boys cackle and run quickly out of sight. The small boy remains, engrossed in digging. "If you think you've got something to say to me, you might as well get out of here too," Aaseya shouts. "I won't hear any of it."

The boy stands, his face soft and thin. A desert flower, after all. His eyelids blink slowly open and closed. He looks about six years old and sickly, covered in dirt. For a moment, she remembers the communal bathhouse where her mother scooped water over her head and sang: *Aaseya comes from the village of sun / my dearest, my jewel / my shining smart one.* But here, she faces a barrage of insults. No cushioned embrace. No clean, white steam and sweet melodies or even the basic company of another woman who believes in her.

She barely believes in herself anymore, what with her naive hope for an education. Her petty obsessions about the past. Her private, pitiful habit of pinching her own arms until they bruise purple.

Everything in life feels like a bargain between impossible choices. Just as soon as desire surfaces, forces larger than the desert rise against her. It makes her impatient, quick to judge. It's easy to think everything is insufficient.

But some good always remains.

It has to.

Even outside her window. Even in the middle of a war. Even in a village that insists on the wrongness of her life.

The boy looks at the ground, hair flopping in front of his face, then quickly snatches something from the hole and walks across the street to stand beneath Aaseya's window.

"Well," she says, "which is it—are you starving or homeless? Or both?"

She thinks of her younger brother Alamzeb, perhaps the same age as this boy before he died. But Alamzeb never looked so sheepish or frail, so starved.

"Muuuuh," the boy grunts. He holds a small object toward her. It's indecipherable at first, but as the boy twirls it in his fingertips, metal catches the light and sends a beam outward like a flare.

"Put that away!" Aaseya scolds. It's a brass shell casing, and by the look of the boy's pockets, there are more. War scraps are a common sight, but these casings are shiny. Recent.

The boy closes his fist around the brass and frowns, yet there's still a query in his gesture. Some need to know.

"You can't sell it, if that's what you're wondering. It's worthless. It's toxic. Boys used to get in trouble for playing with things like that. You want something to play with? Hold on."

She turns from the window and dashes toward her chest of belongings inside. An old carved cup. A swatch of fabric. A stick of incense. As she rummages through her thin collection, it strikes her that there's nothing here a boy would want. She unfolds and refolds a sweater. The smell of wood smoke and old sunlight rise from the soft fabric. There's not a single item here worth saving. The chest has been coveted and tucked away, but is effectively empty. She returns to the window, but the boy has disappeared. There's only her ruined former home up the street—the one she thought she'd live in forever—and the sun, stretching across the sky in its slow climb. Her father Janan used to tease her about that, asking whether the sun chased the moon or the moon chased the sun. Though the war has continued since his death, Imar is the same. Loyalties still shift from block to block, day to day. Family feuds and Pashtun decrees still trickle down; it's inconceivable to imagine a world where destiny doesn't reign. Whether commanded by the sun or the moon or the heavy hand of Allah, life is endured.

Thinking of her father, Aaseya feels a sudden bolt in her chest as though a bird tugs at her heart, beckoning outward, toward the street. She dresses quickly in her burqa before caution objects. On her way out, she grabs the empty water pail and curls a fistful of *afghanis* into her pocket. The bazaar awaits. Maybe some chai, some chickpeas, some raisins for a sweet delight later this week. Maybe even an apricot.

Outside, the heat clings to Aaseya in an instant. The air feels soupy, three-dimensional. It envelops everything around her—gray buildings, crumbled walkways, tangled rebar—and fills the vacant lots with thick, pulsing space. She shifts the fabric of her burqa to create a cave between her eyes and the cloth where the breeze from her movement can eddy. She vaguely remembers when women didn't have to wear burqas in Imar, though most still chose to. Fabric tangles at her calves as she walks briskly, hoping she'll go unnoticed. A useless water tap stand sits at the edge of the street where the alley meets the pathway. The American military installed it years ago, trying to befriend her parched community—300 people largely cut off from outside contact. Within a few months, that tap stand was as dry as the well her mother's aunt had thrown herself down in despair.

A scent of spoiled rubbish wafts from one of the crumpled homes. Aaseya steps onto the street, passing a block of clay shacks with crooked roofs and sparse window curtains. It's the walking more than anything that pleases her—the suggestion that she could just keep going. Growing up, her father, Janan, spoke of large cities like Kabul or other countries where women ran businesses, earned degrees. He even had a crank radio for a time, and the family would gather to listen to broadcasts from the BBC. Aaseya's playmates said her dreams were far-fetched, on par with fables the elders liked to tell. But within the walls of her family compound, Aaseya felt as free as a skylark. Today, the bazaar will have to be enough.

A few blocks along, she approaches Rahim's sister Shanaz's house where she'll leave the water pail outside the compound gate. Shanaz's sons fill it for Aaseya each day, walking an impossible distance over the ridge and back—a half day's journey and heavy load. It's no small kindness. Aaseya tried to thank her in-laws once but was only met with stony condemnation. "Don't bother me with your overtures," Shanaz had said. "If you really want to do good, you'll give my brother a child."

But there was more to it than that. Aaseya's unaccompanied forays to the bazaar were like a continual slap across their faces. *Ba haya.* It's not as though she doesn't understand what's expected of her. Around her elders, she acted one way. A few years ago, to avoid notice from the Taliban, she acted another. As far as the Americans, if she saw them, she took what she could get and turned her back on the rest. But even these maxims didn't save her family, and now, they're hardly enough to make her stay inside. Remain obedient. Never dare to want anything and most especially to leave home without a man to protect her honor. Aaseya isn't persuaded by any of it. What's honorable about entrapment?

She sets the pail outside Shanaz's gate and picks up her pace. One blessing of her burqa is the narrow window it provides at this juncture in particular where she can spare herself the view of her old family home across the street simply by steadying her gaze straight ahead. Everyone knows about her early wartime tragedy, the hurried marriage to her father's cousin, Rahim, at the age of fourteen, sparing her from orphanhood. That she can't bear children is another story making her worthy, perhaps, of execution—had she any elders left to humiliate. Now, Aaseya behaves dishonorably, an embarrassment. Neighbors avoid her like a contagion.

A playful cry breaks loose from within Shanaz's courtyard, followed by a gaggle of children laughing. Through the melee, Shanaz barks instructions. Brief silence and then the *wind-whisp-thwap* of a switch across skin. Feet scuffle, and a child cries softly, then whatever game was interrupted seems to pick up again. Aaseya hears it all—young boys and girls roving within their family courtyards, a few older women directing children this way and that, and, of course, Shanaz, her voice loud and thunderous, hovering over them all.

"Aaseya!" Shanaz shouts.

Aaseya turns around to see the woman's hooked nose pressed through the grate of the courtyard gate. She feels immediately sandwiched, condemnation on one side of the street and a horrible stain of loss on the other. Could the ground simply open up right here? Swallow her away? She'd likely let it take her, but then there's Shanaz. Such righteousness. Aaseya won't stand for it.

"You get back here!" Shanaz shouts again.

"I don't have time," Aaseya says. There might be bread left if she hurries. Maybe some ghee. Then again, she might only find maggot-riddled cucumbers. She hates the uncertainty, hates the apricot. Her foolish optimism. It would be easier to dispel hope entirely.

"If you're going to the bazaar, my brother should be with you."

Aaseya blushes and retreats to Shanaz's gate. The woman stands squat and square, fists punched into her soft hips. Folds of skin gather around her jowls, contrasting with her tightly set headscarf. Several grown daughters have joined her inside the gate, carrying with them the scent of cumin and fresh mint. Their hands look greasy and charcoaled, marked by effort.

"Rahim's working the creek beds. You know as much," Aaseya says. She folds her arms across her chest and waits for what may come.

"Just look at you," Shanaz says, "letting the heat of the day spoil your womb! Walking around unattended! What next?"

Aaseya holds herself steady. Admonition or otherwise, attention of any kind provides an odd balm. If it weren't for Shanaz, Aaseya might feel invisible most days. When no further insults come, Aaseya nods bitterly at the remains across the street. There it sits, a historic stain marking her as a Western sympathizer. Piles of rocks avalanche onto the sidewalk—the only reminder of her childhood home. Seeing it always feels like another explosion. So much had been lost, though Aaseya remembers finding part of the radio afterward, sifting through the rubble. Sometimes, she imagines that if she could get it to work again, she could tune in and hear the voices of her family, their laughter.

But she can't bring them back. She can't piece her parents together out of pebbles and mud. Here, her father with his wide palms. There, her mother's soft face. Alamzeb's dusty knees. Her cousins, aunts, uncles, reconstructed from chalky remains. She'll never know why she was spared but certainly not just to be subjected to Shanaz stomping her foot or the ridiculing stares of her daughters aimed like arrows at Aaseya's throat. Certainly not to spend the rest of her life in Imar, a place weighing on her like so many stones over a grave.

"Well," Aaseya says, growing brave, "look at it!"

"I look at it every day," Shanaz says. She takes in a sharp breath. "But you should know, Aaseya, there are worse things than losing your family."

Aaseya studies Shanaz's face—how suddenly slack it appears. The old woman's cheeks burn with color. The only thing worse than death is shame, but what would Shanaz know about that? Aaseya has felt her share of shame. Someone had tipped off the Taliban, certain Janan was colluding with the Americans. True, her brother, Alamzeb, had angered a squad one afternoon, but he was so young. True, Janan had welcomed soldiers into his family compound but only for cultural conversation. Could kindness get you killed? An Afghan prided himself on hospitality and good impressions. Janan modeled that—perhaps too much. Many nights, Aaseya lies awake trying to guess who might have spread the rumor. Sometimes, she even imagines it was Shanaz, whose meddling authority extends from block to block, surrounding their homes. There's an odd logic to it—the way one family can bring down another, though there was never anything afoul between Janan and his neighbors. Trying to pinpoint blame in a village that's at the mercy of history and culture seems about as effective as praying for rain. Aaseya hustles away from the gate, and already, Shanaz has turned her back, a dark cloud in retreat.

Aaseya reaches the crossroad and knows she should turn around. Leaving the water pail with Shanaz is a necessary exception— even Rahim grants her permission. But it wasn't so long ago she left her burqa at home and walked in public with her father. Now, to remain outside the home unattended, Aaseya should shrink at the thought. She's one of only a few women who still pushes this boundary in Imar. It's not in her nature to hold anything back. Not hope. Not fear. Perhaps most of all, not ambition.

She turns down the main thoroughfare where a few rusted cars are parked haphazardly, half on the pedestrian pathway, half in the road. A blue scooter lies in a ditch, its kickstand mangled. She crosses the street to avoid its path; no one has dared go near it for years, the prevailing rumor being that it was planted with a bomb. Imar had only seen two such ambushes in Aaseya's lifetime, both manned by a suicidal mujahideen on a scooter aiming for Americans who patrolled the village frequently during those early years of fighting. Seeing the scooter sets Aaseya's suspicions reeling again. She's heard about fellow villagers swapping allegiances throughout the war. Her father was resourceful enough to outwit such dishonesty, though in the end, what did his skill matter? The abandoned scooter—in a village with no gas stations, no electricity—only confirms one thing: betrayal and indignation share the same bed in Imar.

The neighborhood itself remains quiet today. Hardly a hint of human occupancy other than the occasional tails of smoke rising from courtyards. Like little prayers. So many women tend those fires amidst various daily tasks. Most of them never knew Ms. Darrow, the visiting English teacher who came about the time the tap stands were installed. Most of them weren't born to such a worldly father. Most don't look at the horizon and see a line to follow either. Aaseya longs to have classmates again, or at least another girl with whom to share her dreams of progress. She can't afford to let go of hope, its private comfort like the lead thread in an embroiderer's hand. Lose that and the entire pattern gets disrupted. So much gone to waste.

A few blocks ahead, Aaseya hears the cries of animals for slaughter, sons bargaining on behalf of their mothers. It's a spectacle of activity: the smell of dung, the dry taste of the desert, people coming and going—enlivening the mud-cooked pathways in flashes of teal, maroon, sun gold, deep purple. Men loiter, scuffing their dirt-coated sandals against the ground. At the edge of the bazaar, beggars wait.

"Food?" a girl pleads. Her bone-thin back presses against the corner post of a bazaar tent. The girl stares at Aaseya and whimpers her incantation, "Allah. Allah. Allah."

Behind the girl, narrow rows of tents and tables form a humble economy. Aaseya remembers studying her father as he bargained kindly but firmly, Aaseya often the only young girl in sight. Walking arm-in-arm with Janan through the bazaar, she thought then she might marry a man like him. Someone who is respected and lives openly, escaping ridicule. Someday, she might even command as much independence herself.

"Please," the begging girl speaks again. "Sister, *please*."

Aaseya brushes past, unnerved. The girl's voice rings like a threat in her ears. Where are those English teachers now? Where are any teachers for that matter? No one cares to educate girls in Imar anymore. Finding water. Raising boys. Hatching rumors. Exacting revenge. These things matter. An orphan girl is just another kicked up rock along the road.

Aaseya tries conjuring the bird in her chest. Its gentle tugging and sweet song. *My shining smart one.* With the bird, she can draw herself out. She can press her heels into the warm skin of the Earth, open her lips to the sun, and keep walking—*ba haya* be damned. She can make purchases or trade. She can even wander home the long way just to remind herself that another way is possible. One step at a time. Block by block. Like verbs forming at the tip of her pencil, lead pressed hard into the pages: *ran, run, ran, run, run.*

She placed her hand over a particularly ripe apricot when she saw them. Both stand nearly six feet tall, lean and limber as the cougars rumored to patrol the nearby slopes. How many years has it been since she has seen Taliban fighters in public? They're even laughing as though one fighter has just told the other a joke. It's not so much their ammo and weapons as their iron stares and meticulously draped turbans that give them away, black kohl ringing their eyes. Both men have bundled their turbans at the top, swooped them below their chins, then swaddled them across their faces, leaving only a slit for the eyes. She doesn't dare look directly, but that tiny opening of fabric, that suggestion of identity makes her feel fused to its possibility. If given the chance to show only one thing about herself, what might she reveal?

The fruit vendor *tisk-tisks*, and Aaseya feels a slap across the top of her hand. So few vendors will sell to her—this un-right, supposedly Pashtun woman wandering the streets—and certainly not this vendor, not now that she's lingered too long, coveting the apricot immodestly. She turns from the booth and crosses to the other side of the path. Here is Massoud. Maybe he will sell to her today. The naan smells so fresh she can almost taste it, and she's drawn to its doughy, charcoaled musk. She reaches out to select one of the toasted loaves. Of all the people she suspects could have started the false rumor about her family, she has never considered Massoud. His daughters also went to Ms. Darrow's language lessons. He even speaks to Aaseya sometimes if there's no one in line, and he can busy himself with tasks as they whisper. But Massoud has spotted the fighters too, and as quickly as Aaseya approaches, he turns his back. She angles her body closer to his table display as if the loaves of bread might stand in for her family, but Massoud offers no indication that he's going to help her.

From the corner of her eye, she sees the fighters make purchases several booths away. The apparent leader moves deftly, his hands bloodied at the knuckles. He selects cucumbers, dates, and a satchel of almonds. Only a portion of the exchange is visible through the screen of Aaseya's burqa, and she shifts on her feet to bring a different view into focus. Money flashes—crisp, green US dollar bills—passed like poison seeds from the fighter to the vendor. Two-days walk from a US base, a handful of years since any occupation, and here—an Afghan vendor taking American dollars without pause? She hasn't seen *that* currency since Ms. Darrow showed the schoolgirls her purse one day, all the womanly items it contained. Such a treasure then. Now, the image sends shrapnel through Aaseya's chest. The money can mean only one thing: the Americans are coming, and if the Americans are coming, these Taliban will be waiting. Imar will become a mere backdrop to their battle with one inevitable outcome.

Aaseya wouldn't believe she has even seen the bills if it weren't for what happened next, the vendor casually making change and the little boy from outside her window rounding the corner at top speed, running into the fighters, and knocking the currency to the ground.

"Pest!" the leader kicks at the boy tangled in the fabric of his *dishdasha*. Several more bills drift through the air, and coins tumble from his pocket.

"You dog!" shouts the other fighter. Both grab for the money.

The boy stands and dusts himself off. In the scuffle, a fresh date has fallen from his pocket and rolled into the dirt. He reaches for it but not quickly enough.

"What's this?" the Taliban fighter says mockingly. He swoops down and takes the date. "Looks like we have a thief here."

The boy's eyes widen.

Aaseya leans toward Massoud's booth. "Do you see this? Friend, you have to do something."

"Get," Massoud says, barely a whisper. He won't look at her.

"I'll leave," she says. "Just forget I was here. Go help that boy."

"You get!" Massoud says again. "Get back and away. I refuse to let you endanger me, you dishonorable whore."

The fighters look up, curious, and Aaseya's breath escapes in a wave. She rushes toward the boy.

"There you are!" she says, grabbing his bony shoulders. She looks at the ground, addressing the fighter humbly. "I'm sorry. My son was only doing errands for me."

"Muuh-uuuh," the boy blathers. He empties his pockets— shell casings, old springs, a broken pair of sunglasses, a plastic button. The stash tumbles from his hands as he tries offering it to the fighters.

"Over here," Massoud calls. "One free loaf for any servants of Allah, the most merciful, the most powerful."

The fighters look up, and with that, Aaseya and the boy are gone, slipped behind the nearest booth, between the side flaps of tents, past the hookah stand and the butcher's table, through a small huddle of goats, ducking under a display of headscarves, pushing through the line for the kebab vendor. And then it's just Aaseya—the anonymity of her burqa, the stifling air, the bird in her chest beating its wings.

Where did the boy go? Disappeared again, as elusive as water. She knows he made it through the butcher's station where they both slowed down to dodge hanging carcasses above the slippery ground. Maybe he hid amidst the scarves and *keffiyehs*.

Aaseya looks for him briefly, then hurries out the far end of the bazaar toward the dead end of town where the old schoolhouse looms like a bad memory. It hurts to think how many days she spent believing Ms. Darrow would come back, certain studying was not only her privilege but her right. Beyond the schoolhouse, an overflow block for vendors' booths and tents opens up. It's quiet now, more like a park or garden space for nomads. At the end of the park, the tight walls of mountains forming either side of the Imar valley meet in a U-shaped trap. Aaseya has heard that another village lies not too far beyond that ridgeline, though nobody she knows ever traverses the upper slopes. Imar has always been described as cut off, physical isolation a part of her daily existence for as long as she can remember. But before the upslope begins its steep climb, the loop road arcs along the base of the valley and back around the bazaar, paralleling the edge of town and wrapping round to the entrance of the village. She meets the road and walks steadily, occasionally checking over her shoulder to see if she is being followed.

Before long, the loop road ends and opens toward the wider road leading out of the valley. It's a junction Aaseya knows well, occasionally allowing herself to walk this far from the apartment. From here, the view widens down the length of the valley and outward to the uninterrupted desert, and she can imagine how it will be when they first arrive—tails of dust, the reek of gasoline, the strangeness of some of them with pink skin and a different language. Do the Americans know what's waiting for them? How little it takes to disrupt a life? There's no stopping whatever those dollars have set in motion.

She studies the view one last time, considering. She's never stepped past this point, but she imagines it would be the beginning of something better. Somewhere in the near distance, Rahim must be digging in the creek beds, his makeshift job of forming bricks only possible in the wake of war's destruction as families slowly rebuild. Somewhere else nearby, there must be Taliban too. She recoils at the thought, as if something is being pulled from her grasp and sucked into a vacuum of cold. She turns her head from one side to the other, letting the panorama of horizon in through the screened view of her burqa. Some mornings, the sky here fills with pink and orange tendrils that unreel like spools of yarn, stretching from north to south. But now, the sun sits mid-sky, the world hyper-saturated in blues and browns. Aaseya folds her arms and pinches the flesh where her forearms crease at the elbows, a slight twinge across her skin. She pinches again and thinks of the apricot. How promising its texture. Hardly a spot of mold. She pinches again, recalling Shanaz's admonitions, the possessive timbre of her voice. Heat blooms across her forearms, and she pinches again, so tender. She imagines sinking her teeth into the apricot, holding the pit in her mouth. How she would clean the sweet flesh away with her tongue and find the pit in the center. She can see it clearly—that apricot pit like a missile careening from her mouth through the screen of her burqa with piercing speed as she yells every curse imaginable in the face of those Taliban. Those imposters. Those loathesome creatures riddled with more lice than the roadside carcass of a dog. She's lucky she survived. That's what Rahim always tells her. That's what Shanaz wants her to believe. Just as surely as Aaseya imagines that apricot pit zeroing in on its target, Aaseya feels the skin across her forearms break beneath her fingertips, bleeding into clarity.

There's no denying it: Shanaz is the one who tipped off the Taliban. And the Taliban must have believed her, mistaking Aaseya's family compound for an American hideout. The Taliban reduced her fate to one moment of dust and vibration that stole everything from her but her own heartbeat. They hurt Ms. Darrow, hurt everybody, and although the Americans may be coming soon with their own measure of fate, it's too late. It's not enough. Aaseya has her own explosions to carry out, and now she envisions Shanaz with black kohl around her eyes. She wants the Taliban to rape Shanaz, to kill her, but then Aaseya's vision shifts, and her enemies turn to face her. Warmth moves across her fingertips—blood is the only proof she's still alive—and as her accusers point their fingers at her mockingly, the apricot pit explodes on target. Body parts pepper the open desert like so many seeds of war.

As Aaseya approaches her apartment, she hears the sound of bare feet not far behind. How bad will it be if the fighters followed her? She sees herself tossed onto the ground, legs spread. Sees them spit on her, burn her hair and her eyes. Maybe it's her due—catching up. She never should have survived the blast. Rahim and Shanaz might even be grateful if she died now, released from association with her disobediences.

"What is it?" she says and turns to face her follower.

The boy must have stayed close, after all. Feeling floods her limbs, and she looks at her burqa, noticing a few small dots of blood where the fabric sticks to her arms. She almost rushes to him in relief.

He points to the tap stand near Aaseya's apartment steps.

"There's not any water," she shrugs.

The boy crosses the street, and Aaseya marvels at his little brown calves, as flat as kebabs, his twiggy arms hanging from shoulders that jut outward like wings. There's some measure of peacefulness about him or, at least, possibility. Maybe it's his innocence she finds charming—his age alone permitting unawareness of what's headed their way. He moves the pump slowly, tiny frame working hard against the pressure, but nothing comes. He looks at her again, untrimmed hair flopping around his eyes and ears.

"What's your name?" she asks, and when he points with excessive gestures toward his chest, she understands that he must be mute.

"Oh. *Zra?*" she asks, pointing at her heart.

He shakes his head, then points back and forth between his heart and his mouth.

"*Shpeelak*," she says, meaning *whistle*.

Wrong again. The boy moves his hands from his lips to the air in front of him, as if pulling something from his mouth.

"*Ghazél*," she says at last, quieted by the irony—a mute boy named "song."

He nods enthusiastically, then does a little dance in the street, his face opening into a charming grin.

"Wait here."

She heads toward her apartment and up the stairs. And so it begins—Aaseya tossing down a stuffed date and Ghazél catching it skillfully, the two connected mid-air by an invisible thread.

2

Blister in the Sun

The call center on base is nothing more than a dented double-wide lined with makeshift cubicles and a few wobbly folding chairs, a fine coating of sand over everything. Second Lieutenant Nathan Miller walks to the back corner and sits down. A boxy, push-button phone and dusty desktop fill the narrow space. He dials the unending stream of numbers for home and waits. On the computer screen, a cursor flashes in the blank Google search field, keeping time. A framed photo of President Obama hangs on the wall above, but it might as well be Ares, these Middle East wars so unending that entire generations have already come of age.

Tenley's voice crackles across the static of 7,000 miles, delayed. "...and then the school counselor called after that, and I just, Nathan, I just. I don't know what to say. Cissy's angry."

He waits, absorbing. Their daughter is only six years old. Tenley is a good mother, but lately her phone calls have turned into emotional rants, and Nathan resents it. He resents the resenting. Then he feels like a dirt-bag husband and absent father, and, before he knows it, all he wants to do is hang up because it feels like the most loving thing he can do.

But Cissy? *Angry?* He sits up in his seat, trying to think clearly. "What did the counselor say?"

"The counselor said if Cissy hits another child, the school will be forced to expel her. It's district-wide policy. Nathan, where else is she going to go? We'd have to move. We'd have to sell the house. We'd have to…"

"Hits *another* child next year?"

And then he remembers the emails he hadn't read all week. The ones he thought were school newsletters and automated messages about attendance. The ones that should have caught his attention, but it's a joke these days, trying to complete a single thought without interruption. His mind hops, jack-rabbit style. Add in his other life, his other self, the other side of the globe? Forget it.

"…and then there was this thing about Host Nation Trucking, and they had this talking head on there who said the Americans are straight-up giving cash to the Taliban in Afghanistan."

"Who? Who said that?" Nathan reaches for the keyboard, typing a few search terms into Google.

"They're setting you up to fail. Just get yourself home. Come home. I love you too much for this."

"It's going to be OK, Tenley. Ten? Try not to worry."

A page of links appears on the screen the same time static cuts him off. The phone line goes dead. He scrolls through the pages. *The Guardian*. NBC. *The Nation*. CNN. The headlines send a spike to his gut.

How the US Army Protects Its Trucks—
by Paying the Taliban

US Trucking Contracts Fund Taliban,
Source Says

It's all over the news. Isn't it just peachy when the military screws itself, then tops it off by stealing the ten minutes Miller has to talk with his wife about his homecoming? They were going to discuss their dream vacation in the Keys, Cissy's favorite bedtime story, the latest episode of *Breaking Bad*. Anything. Anything but this.

The trailer door kicks open, and Private First Class Folson enters. "Yo, LT Miller!" he says, pointing to a clock on the wall beneath Obama. "Game time!"

"Be there in a few," Miller calls. "Don't wait on me."

Folson closes the door, and Miller is alone again. He looks up at Obama. As much as he'd like someone to blame, the only common denominator in war is a string of impossible decisions. There's no god of war presiding, no black-and-white definition of good and evil either, and it strikes him then that if anything can be called "commander in chief" of these twenty-first century wars, it's the almighty dollar. He reads the articles in a rush. Of course his country is double-dealing. Of course he's a pawn. When has he ever really believed otherwise? Proof doesn't change the fact that he's still in Afghanistan, decidedly not home, not with his wife or daughter, not even sure what family should feel like anymore. He's had enough—of news, of sand, of failure, of phone calls, of himself, of whoever that self is these days. He closes the web browser and heads out the door. Gotta sweat this one off.

It's all in good fun, these pick up games on Forward Operating Base Copperhead on the outskirts of Tarin Kowt, Afghanistan. By landscape and amenity, the multi-national base could almost be in southern Nevada, eastern Oregon, or any place dry and bleached and American with too much of what you don't want and not enough of what you need. Taco Bell? Check. Burger King? Check.

Tube socks, Kraft Mac & Cheese, Facebook, Double Stuf Oreos? Check. And football, of course.

Two plays after kickoff, an Alpha Platoon linebacker slams into Miller's ribcage, and it feels like a blessing. A crisp smack and thud. Miller falls to the ground the only way gravity allows. His side hurts, which is good because if it hurts, he's alive—exactly what he must be in order to keep everyone else alive. He lets loose a grunt as the play moves past, then presses his palms into the grit to get up. This is what he does: try and try again. He's the leader with a reputation for meticulousness, effective decision-making. Nearly everything his career has brought him to so far has given him the chance to prove himself in this way, again and again. But what if perfection is its own kind of failure? He's so close to finishing the tour and getting back home. A muddy centerline, the cool slap of cleats on wet grass, the freedom to fuck up. For now, home is miles out of reach, light years. So when Miller rises from the makeshift field and feels a heat-laced head rush pulling him down as though someone roped sandbags over his ears, he knows this is all that remains: to stand up anyway, even as his own country tries to push him back down.

The game is in Spartan Platoon's favor now, PFC Folson hustling downfield with the ball clutched to his chest in a manner not unlike the picture pinned above his bunk. Miller has seen it: twenty-two-year-old Folson cradling his infant daughter right before their first goodbye, the wife frozen sternly in the background. The photo appears both unique and unoriginal, a sad foreshadowing played out more times than Miller can count. A letter addressed to Folson is waiting on Miller's desk right now with a return address that suggests divorce. Folson might have some clue of what's coming—he's acted lackluster lately. Slacking on weapons maintenance, missing meals, even turning up late once for a division-wide meeting with the company commander. But Miller can't be sure how Folson will react, and the Spartan Platoon sergeant has been too fed up to bother dealing with Folson's misdeeds as he should.

Twenty yards downfield, the Alpha linebacker tackles Folson, and they tumble into the dirt. Miller hustles to catch up, tornadoes of dust rising with each step. If a devoted father like Folson is screwing up, what might be said about Miller? He and Tenley already worked through one scare, shredding divorce papers together over a toast to new promises. He'd stop trying to protect her from the details of his experiences on tour. He'd answer her questions straight; he owed her that much. She'd stop blaming him for being gone. Stop being coy as he tried to find his way back into routines each trip home. That was three years ago. Now it's 2009, and he's four tours into this mess. No one would guess that he stockpiles pills just in case he can't hack it anymore. That the letters are already printed—one for Cissy to read when she's older, and one for Tenley that, he hopes, explains losing Sergeant Mercer and why everything changed afterward. This tour is Miller's final chance to find his cool again, forget he ever drafted a suicide note, and land softly back home, back into marriage, composed and capable as ever.

Blind spots. That's what Miller heard someone call those unforgivable missteps from the past once. Like thinking you can see the folds of your own asshole simply by turning on the high beams. But nothing works that way this tour, what with his National Guard unit attached to a bro-bra army division that has bigger things on its mind. Nothing ever works—not night vision goggles, not spark plugs, not good luck charms, and certainly not high beams. Even the interpreters supplied by an on-base branch of the Afghan National Army seem to come up short—if the

Spartans are lucky enough to get one for a mission. Miller simply hasn't found a way to fully see what's coming yet, and today's headlines about US funds are just one more example. Abdul-Bari Gawri, the Oruzgan district chief Miller's negotiated with for the past six months, has been rolling in US dough all along. Now, Miller knows Gawri's cash supply directly correlates with the unending stream of trucks delivering to Forward Operating Base Copperhead. The soldiers on base have clean water, electricity, PlayStations—freaking Facebook out here—and all of that is because no one's blowing up Afghan supply trucks contracted by the US Department of Defense. Yet anytime Miller's platoon tries to bring aid to people in need, they're at risk of getting shredded by a roadside bomb. This week will bring what Miller likes to think of as final harvest: a trip to the remote village of Imar and back—Spartan's last mission outside the wire. Then, blind spots or not, Miller can call it done. In the bag. Trimmed and tied. All of the Spartans can. Every last one of them rip-roaring ready for home, alive and lusting for the long legs of the women who love them.

"Hey, hey, hey," somebody shouts. "Chill out, Folson."

Miller closes the distance on the huddle of shirtless bodies centered around Folson and the linebacker. The heat of the day almost immediately suffocates him, the sun pinking his skin into a perma-burn. It's as though he's a lobster, the light a buttery condiment of death. Is there any relief on this tour? Miller would be hard-pressed to say yes. Except, perhaps, in moments like this next one, where he'll get a read on Folson and try to help fend off the quake. This is what he does best. All of them, even the opposing Alphas, would give him that. He elbows his way into the middle of the pack.

"The hell?" the linebacker says. His voice squeezes through blocky muscle and bone.

"You heard me," Folson says and slams the ball into the ground. It bounces off the dirt and pings into someone's shins. "Tackle me around the neck like that one more time, and I'll stuff your nutsack down your throat!"

"Dude, it was a fair tackle. All shoulders," one of the Alphas offers.

"Just drop it, Folson, would ya?" Specialist Rachmann says. He's with Spartan, a know-it-all. The kind of guardsman that makes it easy for army fuck-sticks to poke fun at Miller's unit. If it were possible, Miller would have duct-taped Rachmann's mouth shut for the duration of their tour.

"Hey, Folson?" Miller says. He gives Rachmann a stay-out-of-this look. "PFC FOLSON!"

And there it is—that brash confidence, that heady bellow. Miller's voice makes for an odd pairing with his creaseless skin and boyish, button nose. He would have laughed out loud if someone played a recording of this to his teenaged self ten years back. Now, it's a voice that upholds his standing, embodying the dependability everyone counts on. "PFC Folson, you'll respond when I address you."

"Yes, LT. However, I've got a problem here," Folson waves his hand in the direction of the linebacker, as if shooing a fly. For a moment, the sun catches the glint of his wedding band, though everyone has warned Folson he's better off noosing it around his neck with his tags.

"We do too. We'd like to keep playing," Miller says. "So cool down or walk off."

"And what problem is that?" the linebacker asks. He squares his hips and shoulders to face Folson, a pit bull reflex.

"The problem is, I've promised to stuff your nutsack down your throat, but studying you now…" Folson scans the linebacker one more time, "it's not clear you really have one."

The linebacker lunges, and the two momentarily vault, then hit the ground.

"Tackle low enough for you, shitbag?" the linebacker asks. They grapple chest to chest, and he pins Folson into the dirt with admirable efficiency.

"Get off of me, you faggot. Get off!" Folson bucks in useless defense. Pressed into the ground, he appears utterly small and flailing, his sunburned face reminiscent of a newborn's—scrunched, helpless. In one humph and exhale, the linebacker rises to his feet. Both teams stare for a moment as Folson writhes in the dirt.

"Who's the faggot now, Spartan?"

Miller moves in, offering Folson a hand up. Face-to-face, they could be sunburned siblings at a beach party, matching brown buzz cuts and blistered ears, the booze and heat getting the better of them. But, of course, there's rank. There's experience. Miller has both. He's also got bad news to deliver to Folson, and there's no more putting it off. "My office," he spits. "1900 hours."

"Yes, Sir," Folson responds. His affirmative sounds like defeat. Typical, for this half-bro-bra/half-teddy-bear soldier whose personnel file reads nothing like Miller's three years in the army after high school, including two deployments. When Miller got out, he joined the National Guard to pay for college—not that he graduated—and now, with tour three under his belt and number four almost wrapped up, he's the 2LT every grunt dreams will take him outside the wire. More experience than his rank suggests, without the ego, which is why he knows it's best to give Folson the letter from the divorce attorney privately, sparing him the humiliation at mail call.

But there's more to Miller's confidence than experience. Back in his room, showered and shaved, he thinks about the locked filing cabinet in his office. The bottom drawer of pills. Six bottles of Ritalin. Another two of Percocet. It's comforting, knowing they're there, like a rich man who never spends a dime. Mercer would have understood that—the dignity in death over failure. Trying to lead the Spartans has felt like reaching for something dropped into a pool, then watching how quickly it sinks away. Knowing how easily he could down those pills, Miller thinks— or how he could mishandle his own weapon or put himself in harm's way outside the wire to end it quickly—gives him more than confidence. It gives him permission to do whatever it takes to keep his men alive and his sense of pride, at least outwardly, intact. During his third tour—the Korengals, Mercer shot dead while Miller targeted the wrong man—Rachmann served on the same fire team. Now, Miller is superior to the one person who saw just how clearly he failed.

If he stayed true to his promise, Tenley would know all of that. But how could she understand? He hasn't been able to tell her. Can't even give her the chance to love him the way he needs it most, and perhaps that, more than anything, is what makes him consider ending it all. He'd seen ground zero on a debate team trip in high school. He'd visited the Grand Canyon, the old growth forests out West. He's a father, a husband. He'd held his daughter the day she was born. A lot for one life, if you considered the big scheme of things. Can he say he's lived well? Would Tenley say as much? He likes to think so, and if Rachmann dares to suggest otherwise, dares to even mention Mercer, that locked drawer is within arm's reach.

Strange to realize the last time Miller felt such desperation, he'd been falling in love with Tenley, now his wife of six years. It was a different kind of desperation, but the core of it—the burning hot middle of wanting something so badly you'd hurt yourself just to get it—felt one and the same. It's been four tours and almost as many years away since he first felt that burn for her. Miller is hardly familiar with the house they bought in Tenley's home state of North Carolina just a few months after tying the knot. Still, Tenley waits through tour after tour, tied to her Appalachian roots with stubborness. What has Miller been doing all these years away? He can hardly name it, the war fanning in countless directions, each mission a drop in a leaky bucket. Waiting is about the only thing he and Tenley have shared these past years. Meantime, she's racked up $5,000 in education loans (and counting) starting an online degree program in social work. "Just because you're stalled, doesn't mean I have to be," were her words, and Miller had to admit, the military itself, the machine of it, had never felt like it would take him anywhere.

He remembers how good the Guard looked back when life growing up as an Indiana farm boy didn't. In high school, Miller was impressed by the recruiter who came to the assembly hall and gave a presentation about signing bonuses and education benefits. The bell rang, and half the graduating class stayed put, lured by the idea of something bigger than all the cornfields in Indiana combined. "But you're valedictorian," his art teacher had said. "You got scholarships…" she wrinkled her forehead and suggested he belonged elsewhere. The recruiter's requests felt reasonable: work hard, follow rules, and get paid. It was an equation that never manifested in farm country, where hard work and harder work meant a government subsidy, his father's breath held as tightly as a clamp over the dinner table. Finally, someone understood the injustice of that basic lie and offered Miller a way out. Seventy-eight days to graduation, a summer job in North Carolina as a camp counselor before boot camp that fall, and as the husk-scented air whisked around Miller on that graduation stage, the sun burnishing his skin to a young, hornball perfection, he grinned—button nose to the sky—and tossed his cap into the air with a fat wish and a fuck-it smile. It was very likely the last cap and gown he'd wear, the commission from National Guard Officer Candidate School his junior year of college too strong to turn down.

Eight years since that graduation stage and Miller believes that fuck-it smile will get him through these last days on the FOB leading Spartan Platoon. Through the paperwork, the homecoming. It's a good enough smile. It has gotten him this far. Just one more mission.

3

Stars & Stripes Forever

...The arrangement for moving supplies throughout Afghanistan, known as the Host Nation Trucking contract, began in May 2009. There are eight companies handling the work. The full $2.16 billion contract covers the movement and transportation of 70 percent of the material needed for US troops in Afghanistan. Security guards hired by the trucking companies funnel that money to the local warlords or the Taliban to ensure the supply truck convoys get to their destinations unscathed...

Miller sinks into his chair, reading on his Army-issued Dell PC tucked into the back room of a stripped down trailer. Drywall panels barely set straight. No paint or decor to hide the fast-paced construction demanded in wartime. Even his desk, a large piece of plywood lofted by milk crates, is hastily gathered. The discomforting irony isn't lost on him; everything in this room came from someplace else. Everything has a price.

Folson's letter rests atop a small pile on the center of the desk. Stacks of *Army Times* and kid-signed "Dear Soldier" letters cluster around a burgeoning wastebasket on the floor. A box of lotion Puffs sits on top of the filing cabinet, pills locked below. Tenley had sent the tissues when Miller caught a cold, though by the time they arrived, the virus had moved on. What he could really use is a tube of ChapStick, his papery lips constantly cracking and peeling, little lines of dried blood like cosmetics. The front door to the trailer opens, and the drywall shakes when the door slams shut. Three swift clomps of a soldier's boots across the hollow floorboards and a knock on the office door.

"LT?"

"Come in, PFC."

Folson enters and salutes.

"Sit down," Miller says.

Folson's reflex appears slow, but he manages to sit, and in those few seconds, Miller makes a quick study of his soldier: shoulders sagging like a wet poncho over Folson's frame, eyes half-lidded. Miller can't help but think: *Ativan? Klonopin?* There's a different air about Folson tonight, like static before a lazy summer storm. They've all had to rely on an upper or downer before. There's an unspoken protocol: do what needs doing, and keep it to yourself. Better yet, locked in a drawer. Whatever Folson has swallowed since he sulked off the field, it was too much of the wrong thing.

"All right, Folson. I'm tired. But I'm not too tired to walk you through this, so I need you to listen up."

Folson keeps his gaze down, staring at his feet. He fingers his wedding band, turning it round and round. The shuffling of his boots across the concrete interrupts the quiet. "The heat got the better of me out there."

"You think I care about a fight on the playground?" Miller says.

Folson has always responded to slight condescension. He raises his gaze, eyes settling on the letter. His lips part slightly, a wheezing intake of breath. Slow as sunrise, a look of disbelief dawns across his face.

"Sir?" he says. He reaches for the letter. "Sir, is that…?"

"Now, listen…" Miller swipes the letter from the top of his desk and looks at the label.

Folson withdraws his hand, and his eyes, suddenly tightening, finally meet Miller's. "Sir, that letter says Esquire."

"Yes, it does. This isn't going to be easy."

Miller hands Folson the envelope. "But I've seen you go through much worse in combat."

"Lewis Fontineau, Esquire, & Sons, Divorce Attorneys at Law, Gatlinburg, Tennessee? Urgent response required?" Folson looks torn. "No," he whispers. "Just—*hell no.*"

"Hold on a minute here because where I come from, this could mean there are still options."

"She actually meant it!" he shouts and stands. "Can you believe this? Can you even *fathom* what kind of polar-fucking-vortex bullshit this is, coming from a woman living in a house I'm paying for by busting my ass against the hajis, while she's streaming Netflix and painting her nails?"

"No, PFC, I can't. Let me take it to the Echo Company lawyer. They've got him camped out at the TOC all day, twiddling his thumbs. He can at least translate the thing for you."

"There's nothing to translate," Folson says. "I know Becca. She doesn't do anything halfway. Jesus. And the girls. What about my girls?"

He kicks the metal wastebasket, and it slams into a corner with a loud, snare-drumming clap. Its contents spill out like guts.

"Look," Miller says, "you'll be stateside in no time. You two have made it this far, Folson. She's got to know that."

"You can't see it, can you?" Folson shakes his head. "Just the same as you can't see a cheap tackle on the field or the Band-Aid missions we've been sent on all month."

Miller stands. "If you want to talk logistics with me, you can wait until you're promoted, though you and I both know that's a long way from the direction you're headed now," Miller shakes his head. "We can shout about this, or we can be civil. It's your call. In either case, I won't have you trashing my office."

Folson retrieves the metal wastebasket as if to set it back in place, but instead, he throws it across the room.

"You've got to be kidding me..." Miller says. He moves from behind the desk, ready to scruff Folson by the collar.

That fast, Folson punches the dent in the wall where the wastebasket hit. The plaster gives way. A small cascade of chalky drywall lets loose, and Folson dashes out the door.

Seeing how quickly things can turn, Miller can only think of Cissy's tantrums. Everyone has their own version. Folson punches. Cissy hits. With only two elementary schools in the county and Cissy already kicked out of one, could he and Tenley survive the stress of a move? When they shredded their divorce papers, the promises they made to eachother felt giddy but conditional, as if marriage was some sort of currency measured on the exchange. He certainly hasn't kept his end of the bargain, and the more Cissy heads down this track of disruptive youth, the more Miller hates himself for the suffering his absence must cause her. It doesn't exactly make him want to arrange a tell-all with his wife in which he'd have to confess that he failed at the one thing his job requires above all else—to keep his men alive—and besides, he's 7,000 miles away. He's here. Now. A soldier under his charge getting eaten alive by a woman equally far away. The trajectories his family and Folson's family are on seem impossible; Miller can't even touch them. Absence makes the heart grow something, but he's not certain that it's fonder.

Outside the trailer, daylight fades to a dim, orange belt that parallels the horizon. It's the only hour during which FOB Copperhead could be called beautiful, and Folson appears determined to crap all over it. Miller scans a few alleys between trailers, then jogs toward the main pathway opening to the rest of the base and looks for something awry. The base unfolds in front of him like a gigantic Monopoly board—sandbag-lined barracks and coalition offices to one side, the infirmary and dumpsters dotting the opposite. Separate offices for the ANA, of course, who seem under constant harassment to "use their own assets" for Afghan troop casualties or wounded civilians. In the distance, the chow hall and PX sit near rows of Porta-Johns, their fecal-soup scent a nearly constant tickle under his nose. From there, it's not difficult to spot Folson, what with a cluster of soldiers gathered around the flagpole next to the chow hall and a high-pitched holler hitting Miller's ears the same moment his brain finally makes sense of what his eyes are showing him.

Miller arrives at the flagpole breathless, having sprinted the 100 yards full-bore, passing articles of Folson's desert camis along the way. First the uniform blouse. Then one combat boot. Another. Impressive, considering the cumbersome laces. Folson's ripstop pants and undershirt came off last in what looked like a tumble to the ground, though quickly recovered, and there he is, nearly thirty feet in the air, straddling the flagpole, wearing nothing but boxer briefs and white tube socks. The piercing sound hits Miller's ears again, and he sees now that it's coming from Folson, wailing like a baby. A handful of onlookers holler up at him, partly out of concern but mostly out of annoyance. They've come for the nightly flag lowering and instead discovered a crazy motherfucker flexing his muscles to the sky. Miller herds the soldiers aside, though most stay close to witness the reputed 2LT in action. Miller squints upward again, trying to draw a line of clarity. This may well be one of the strangest, most fitting sights produced by the war: a trained soldier sobbing in the dying light, the bold stars and stripes of the American flag thwapping him across the chest.

"Hey, man, let's get you down from there!" Miller cups his hands around his mouth and shouts.

Folson looks down, and one of his legs slips free, causing him to nearly lose balance before latching on again.

"Just keep your gaze level," Miller calls. "Just hold on up there."

"Sir?" Folson yells. His voice is a mishmash of rebel teen and muscle man, teetering between tears and brawn.

"Yeah, PFC, I'm right here," he edges closer to the bottom of the flagpole, though he knows any position he finds is futile. If Folson lets go, there's no stopping the inevitable.

"Sir, I need you to burn that letter."

Miller stares up at Folson's face, astonished to see surprise, then relief in quick succession. "Consider it done," he says, cupping his hands to project his voice once more. "Now tell me about how the Vols football is looking for next season."

"Fuck that, man. Fuck the entire fucking state of Tennessee. I *am* a 'volunteer,'" Folson's voice sounds steadier now, a bit less in conflict with itself.

"You got that right."

"And back home, they're sucking down Mountain Dew and swiping Sudafed, hulking around in their bright orange football jerseys. You and I both know it. Our country is full of shitholes, Sir. Shithole, after shithole, after shithole."

"Not the whole country," Miller says. "I went to California once when I was a kid. Dad squeezed us all into a camper for a week. The ride sucked, but those old growth trees, man. I'm telling you…Nothing shithole about 'em."

"I bet you my neighbor back home drinks more Mountain Dew in a week than a goddamn tree sucks water in a year."

A slight breeze rolls across the FOB, and the ropes clatter and tangle along the flagpole. "Sir, my arms are shaking."

"Mine would be too. Why don't you come down?" Miller says, and now he knows. Folson has scared himself. Plain and simple. Climbing a flagpole is one way to do it. Miller suspects the feeling is at least a little better than whatever Folson felt looking at that letter.

"Just…just…I'm shaking. It's just a lot. There's just a lot of everything, Sir."

"I understand," Miller says.

"Look, I know it's weird, but I need you to tell me about your wife."

"Anything, bro. But why?" Miller asks. To think of Tenley in this moment rattles his composure. He's trying not to fall short. How desperately part of him wants to climb that pole too.

"Because your wife wouldn't pull something like this. You've said it yourself. She's a good woman."

Miller looks down for a moment, stretching his neck. His brain ticks its way through the muck. Do good women always remind you how much you've missed? Do good women say they'll always love you, then grow cold because they're questioning what kind of man they married? Yes. No. Miller could go either way, but what matters has always been the same: he likes who he is with Tenley and Cissy in his life. He has come to depend upon the way they see him. What remains is whether or not they'll keep seeing him that way once he gets back.

"It's not as simple as being a good woman or a good man," Miller finally says. He looks back up and sees Folson's muscles freeze around the flagpole. The soldier's skin appears pale from the neck down, making the array of emotions across his sunburned face all the more dramatic. "I'm not gonna lie to you, man. It's just not that simple. But I will tell you how I screwed up back home last Thanksgiving. How I still have some things I've got to set right."

It stings to think of it, let alone say it out loud. But Folson's situation demands honesty, and Miller isn't above personal exchange when called for.

"Did you take the cheesy bread out of the oven too early? Because that's what Becca always rides me for. The cheesy bread. Can you imagine?"

"Naw, man. It was worse than cheesy bread. But you gotta come down. It's killing my neck to look up that way, and besides, I'm sick of seeing your hairy back. You're fucking Wolverine up there, man. Anyone ever tell you that?"

Folson allows a half-smile. "'I'm the best there is at what I do...'" he quotes. Below, Miller raises his hands into the air, fingers scraping upward like Wolverine's claws. He lets loose an animal growl. They finish the line together, and the shout echoes across FOB Copperhead: "'...AND WHAT I DO BEST ISN'T VERY NICE.'"

4

Worse than Cheesy Bread

Miller and Folson find the rec room completely empty, thanks to a late-night screening of *Full Metal Jacket* on base. A portable generator hums in the corner, parlayed for a Star Trek pinball machine, of all things. No one can get the straight story on who authorized that. The two-player function button is jammed with sand, ruling it out. Delta Platoon sawed the legs off the mail-order air hockey table as a prank on Bravo, and now the game simply gathers dust. Tonight, the pucks are arranged in alternating colors of red and blue, aligned across the face of the gameboard in the shape of the letters OEF. Folson challenges Miller to best three out of five table tennis, and they begin the search for paddles and balls.

"Got one here," Folson calls. He crouches on one hand and both knees, reaching his free arm under a dank, brown sofa.

Miller grabs a ball from a dirty paper cup and wipes it clean.

"So?" Folson says. He stands and pockets the ball, then brushes his hands down his pant legs.

Miller pulls two paddles from the top of a vending machine and hands one to Folson. "So, as I said…last Thanksgiving."

"I'll serve," Folson says. He spins the paddle in his right hand a few times. "My friends call me Forrest…"

Miller slips the coffee-stained ball from his palm and beats Folson to the serve. "Think fast, Gump."

41

"Oh, I see how it's gonna be."

They volley, the hollow *toc-toc* sending a wash of relaxation down Miller's back. He thinks of home—Indiana—the pinging of the ball in his basement to while away winter boredom. Mostly, he played with his older sister, Miranda, the two juking while their mother shuffled around them with loads of laundry. There had been warmth, even then, though high winds pierced the empty nights and whipped snow into long, powdery banks. Home seemed an unquestioning embrace—one he now understands he took for granted.

Folson lets out a victorious shout. "One-zero, my serve," he calls. Miller bats a soft one back over the net, forcing Folson to stretch across the table, just barely tapping the ball in return.

"So, we've had the turkey dinner," Miller says, "and the pie…"

Folson smacks a direct shot across the line and scores a quick point.

"…and it's not even really about all that," Miller continues, "because the shit didn't actually hit the fan until two days later."

"Ha!" Folson paddles the ball hard and quickly, back across the net.

Miller catches it midair. "I can't do this in here. Let's walk."

"'My Mama always said you've got to put the past behind you, before you move on…'" Folson stutters through his best impression.

"Yeah, yeah, Gump. You comin'?"

They drop their paddles and head for the door. Folson tosses the spare ball into the corner on his way out. Miller hocks a sand-clogged loogie into the trashcan. Together, they find the main path and begin tracing the extended loop inside the perimeter of FOB Copperhead, which hasn't been on blackout for over a year. Beneath the security lights and glinting concertina wire, Folson's face still looks haggard, but his demeanor is oddly cheerful. Easing Folson's mind is a task Miller readily welcomes, if for no other reason than the sheer obviousness of what's needed—friendship, permission to be imperfect, a listening ear. These things Miller can give. These things don't cost him anything. Not sleep, not rank, and certainly not a soldier's life, and so there is only the sound of their boots plodding along the far end of the FOB, Folson quietly breathing as Miller opens up.

In North Carolina last Thanksgiving, Miller suggested having another child. He imagined Tenley would let her thin lips burst into a smile. That tears might well, and he would know she had been waiting for him to say it. "Let's try. Let's do this together," he'd planned to say. "I'll do it right this time. I'll be ready."

Maybe Tenley would even beat him to it; maybe the cold air blowing between them since the stillbirth of their second child had less to do with him and more with Tenley, the self-sufficiency she'd been forced to master in his absence.

He took Tenley to Micaville Park at a bend in the South Toe River where the 6,000-foot Black Mountain range abandoned itself to a narrow valley. The park had become their family spot before Miller redeployed, before the stillbirth. Water sang against the rocky riverbanks at the edge of the park, moving slickly and slowly in its long line toward the ocean. Shimmering flakes of mica dotted the river bottom, capturing sunlight. Even the soil in western North Carolina crumbled in Miller's hands, beautiful but unsettling. He carried a piece into the shower once, just to see how each flake peeled back, glowing and fragile in the wetness.

In the muted light of that overcast afternoon, he and Tenley watched Cissy slip down the slide and giggle. Cissy had her mother's hair, pale wisps so blond they appeared white against a certain angle of daylight. On that day, they looked plain, a papery, golden color reminding him of sunrise over the Miller Family Ranch. They cheered as Cissy slid to the bottom of the slide, stepped down, then repeated the dance. It calmed Miller to stand in this open, airy park so rarely found amidst tight Appalachian hollers. Tenley looked at him and smiled lightly. It wasn't the smile he had fallen in love with. A handful of years into marriage and he had given up that fool's gold. No couple stayed like newlyweds forever. Hard enough to imagine newlywed anymore. Miller wasn't even home long enough to try.

Cissy squealed with laughter and raised her pudgy arms as she *whooshed* down the slide. Miller marveled at the simplicity of it, how readily joy came bursting forth. He put his arms around his wife and smelled her citrus shampoo and cinnamon bark perfume. Nothing about her seemed to give. He moved closer, but she felt iron-plated, as if any assurance this short time before redeployment might afford didn't matter anyway. There was so much he wanted to say, even more he'd promised he wouldn't hold back, but she would never understand what it's like to have someone die on your watch.

"I love you," was all he could muster.

For a moment, it almost seemed to be enough. But when Tenley pulled away, Miller forced himself to look her in the eyes. It was then he saw that her tightness stemmed from decisions she had come to in his absence. He recognized something fierce and bolstered there, and it occurred to him that she'd been fighting too, slow and steady on the homefront. He had waited to tell her about going to FOB Copperhead in person because the bonus and promotion would set them ahead for the future, for their family. But he didn't tell her it was also a chance to prove himself capable again, the ghost of Mercer biting at his every thought. Studying her in the park, he knew waiting had been a mistake.

"Baby, let's go sit down," he said. "We can watch Cissy from our spot."

He tried to guide Tenley to the park bench, but she insisted on walking a half step ahead of him, refusing to be held. He looked at her petite shape, the way the smooth curve below her ribs widened at her pelvis. The way her legs held her upright so infallibly. The war had done that to him, making him keenly aware of how entwined flesh and bone really are—likewise, how readily they betray one another. But the war also gave the mundane back, offering the simplest pleasures in Technicolor: drip coffee on an automatic timer, the feel of bare feet across a carpeted living room. The park view expanded outward from where they sat, the horizon circling back as if it started and ended at Tenley. It may have been cliché, but Miller felt it—his world rose and set by that woman— her dimpled cheeks, her tiny earlobes, her Southern drawl that came so softly and sweetly it made him woozy. She was the first woman he ever felt understood that his quiet way came carefully calculated. Others misjudged it for defiance or passivity. But she always held a vision of his highest potential at the forefront. He could feel it just as surely as he felt the mountains around them, holding everything together in this rural Appalachian bowl where Miller had moved his life to prove his love and come around to opportunities just like this.

"Baby, I've got to go back," he said.

"Me too. And I'm sure Cissy's getting hungry by now," she brushed a flyaway hair off her forehead.

"No, Ten. I mean to Afghanistan."

She looked at him, eyes so beautifully blue he felt ashamed. How much more would he take from her? They wanted the same things: stability, family. Getting there, though, seemed another matter.

"I can't...Nathan," she pressed her fingertips into her closed eyelids. It was a strange gesture, as though she intended to claw something out of herself. When she pulled her hands away, she had to blink several times before looking back at her husband. "You can't be serious, Nathan," she shook her head.

"I am, baby, but listen."

"When have I ever *not* listened?" she asked. It wasn't the kind of question she wanted him to answer. Miller heard that much in her tone. "What I want to know is what's so great about it? What do they give you that we can't?"

"Tenley, don't."

"No, I'm serious, Nathan, because there must be something, and it can't be the bonuses. I don't care about that."

"Ten...I don't know. I'm trying to make you happy."

"Happy?" she stood from the park bench and jammed her fists into the pockets of her jeans. "Happy?" she paced in front of him, gaze lasering into the dry grass. Behind her, Cissy played on the slide.

"What I mean is it's all for you. For us. For our family. All this work. All this being gone. I've got to go back and finish right, Tenley. I need this," he said.

"But do you need me?" she asked.

Of course he needed her. Without her, there was nothing to come back to. Without her, he didn't know what to define himself against. Without her, there couldn't be this—the park, the day, their daughter, the world. It all seemed so obvious it never occurred to him to say it out loud. At what point did his own wife no longer believe that? How long would her doubts hang over him? He couldn't fathom the shift, couldn't accept that he tried to do everything right and still ended up wrong. He remembered searching her for some clue he might have missed, but he came up short. He could only see her as he always had—perfect, really—and that's when he knew she never would be.

"What I'm trying to say is that of course I need you. More than you know," he stood from the bench, forcing her to stop pacing. "If you don't believe me, consider the fact that I'm doing all of this because I want to have another child. We can do this. We can do so much."

Her jaw dropped. She tilted her chin slightly, but it could have been the earth slipping from its axis. His wife would never look at him from the same angle again. "You're going to leave us again," she said. Her breath had grown short, almost a pant. "And on top of that, you want more? You want—" she dropped her hand to her abdomen.

Miller could almost see it, the smooth, stretch-marked skin that had held their baby boy. The same skin that looked flat and gray in the empty months afterward. The humble smallness of their child, whom they held only once to say goodbye. He'd been mistaken. Family. The Guard. Home. Marriage. To him, everything connected.

"Nathan, my body failed us. Don't you see that? *Me*. Something inside of me. The one thing I'm supposed to be able to do, *have done* before, and all of a sudden, I couldn't."

Before he could speak, she turned on her heels and headed for the car. As she reached for the door handle, Cissy wailed from the bottom of the slide. Tenley turned and dashed back to the playground, joining Miller in the sawdust. Cissy lay crumpled into a pile of pink corduroy pants and a purple down jacket at the bottom of the slide. She sniffled.

"Daddy's here, Cissy. Can I take a look?" Miller inspected Cissy's forehead and found a small goose egg forming against her skull. "You're my tough girl," he told her. "It'll stop hurting in a few minutes. Are you ready to go home? We could make some hot chocolate when we get there."

He looked at Tenley for a sign of softness, but all he saw was his own ignorance. Tenley *did know* what it was like to lose a life, and she knew it in a way he never could: cellular. He wanted to tell her the stillbirth wasn't her fault, but if he did that, he'd have to forgive himself for Mercer too. The military hadn't given him language for these kinds of sentiments. It had only given him language for leaving, and there was violence in it—this idea of deploying, touring, serving—all just another way of saying *gone*. He had done so much harm from so far away. But coming home had hurt them even more.

Cissy leaned her head against Tenley's shoulder, a few tears drying on her round cheeks. Miller kissed the top of his daughter's head, breathing in her smell of wet Cheerios and that soft, underscent of infants that faded with each trip back. He looked again at Tenley, her eyes watering, waiting. Those promises they'd made to one another growing more and more impossible to keep. Miller hugged Tenley and Cissy, wrapping them both in his arms, then turned toward the car to load up.

A few miles down the road, Miller steered into the driveway. "Tenley, I'm sorry. I—"

But she wouldn't have it. "How could you?" she said, her voice rattling and hoarse. "After everything," she unbuckled her seat belt and got out of the car. "I've got to study," she closed the door and walked briskly inside.

Miller stayed in the car for a long time. He stared at their house. Its white siding. Its rough stone foundation. The over-stuffed gutters. The curtains closed against the cold. He studied it all again, searching for something that made sense. He felt like an intruder in his own driveway. He wanted to feel something other than guilt, but there was only Cissy's sleepy breathing from the backseat, whispering toward an uncertain future.

Twilight has fallen into navy darkness. Miller and Folson are the only two visible on base now, other than a few soldiers on guard in the towers.

"Is there even a way to do this marriage-during-deployment thing right?" Folson asks.

"I may not know what right is anymore."

"I hear that, Sir. I hear that."

They reach the rec hall and complete the loop, Folson fighting back a yawn. They've both made messes they haven't found the edge of yet. So little time remains on this tour, even less energy. "No matter how things turn out with Becca, there is one thing I can never tell her," Folson says.

Miller waits.

"That it's easier here sometimes. All of this—the FOB, the war, Spartans—it's just...*easier*."

"I guess so," Miller nods. "Not in terms of winning but in terms of clarity. The Spartans are all pointing in the same direction."

He won't tell Folson how impossible the senior officers have become. How the army brass seems to give orders for a different war than the one Miller and his men fight outside the wire.

"I need you solid on our way to Imar tomorrow."

"What's the mission?" Folson asks.

"Humanitarian, I know that much. Details haven't been sent over yet. They'll get around to it just as soon as they're done polishing their medals. Should be relatively straightforward. Regardless, I know I'm going to need you at your best. Can you give me that, Folson, for one more mission?"

"Yes, Sir, I can. I can do that."

Folson's look seals the deal, and there it is—the relief Miller had been hoping for. When sleep comes, it's perhaps his soundest in years.

Day Two

5

Nothing in this War

Rahim moves briskly down the stairs from his apartment. Early dawn illuminates the alley in lines of dusty yellow. He grabs his wheelbarrow and angles it onto the street. A shovel and bucket clang like angry bells inside the dented, metal bin. He walks to the edge of Imar, then departs the loop road and crosses a few dry creek beds to access the old two-track leading out of the valley. Onward, past the wrecked Jeep, past the shell casings, past the random patterns carved into the sand by wind and time. Sometimes, the vastness reminds Rahim how utterly small his efforts have become. How little consequence he believes his life carries. Weariness hits him in the chest, and he slows his gait. The day has hardly begun, but he can already feel it—that incessant tug of dissatisfaction. If he could do anything he wanted, this moment, he'd curl into the shade of a gaf tree and pass the day unnoticed. Yet he knows it's a blessing that work gives him a way to survive, his brick-making tools as useless as a peace treaty these last few months. Even Badria, his oddball partner, can grasp the good fortune that's come their way during wartime. No sense making bricks to rebuild houses anymore when the drought that has kept Imar dry for two springs means they're somehow supposed to make something out of nothing.

A few kilometers from Imar, Rahim spots Badria alongside the two-track, leaning into a shallow dip in the land. In the distance, a nomadic clan dots a surrounding slope on one side of the valley. Beyond, Rahim imagines more of the same—only bigger, uninterrupted. The wide open desert a blank canvas warmed by the sun, its constant presence like the only good promise ever made.

Rahim leaves his brick-making tools in the road and follows Badria to a narrow slit tucked at the base of the surrounding slopes. The two men paw at the dirt, sand loosening at their fingertips. Rahim finds the burlap sack first, feeling the weight of the AKs beneath the cloth. He tugs. They divvy the weapons, load the magazines, and almost immediately, a white van comes into view about one kilometer in the distance. Badria hustles toward the two-track, nearly tripping as he hides their digging tools behind a cluster of shrubs. Rahim darts across the road, taking his weapon off safety, then leans his side against the embankment from shoulder to ankle, blending into the land as seamlessly as a scattering of dirt. The desert is amazing like that, the way it stretches and folds across the country like the broad, sloping belly of a giant. The way it holds almost everything a man could ever need, including his shape, until they're practically one.

Rahim fishes a pair of binoculars from the burlap sack. "The driver is white, and the van is marked, but I can't make out the logo," he shouts to Badria across the road.

"White is marked enough for me," Badria says. "How far is he now?"

"Five hundred meters. He's got security. An SUV behind him."

Most of the drivers aren't really white, of course. More like pink. Or a patchy blend of ivory and lavender. Some are even brown-skinned like Rahim.

"Is there anyone else in the van?"

"I can't tell."

Engines rumble, and the sound wafts through the valley in slow waves, as if sluggish from the heat. Rahim loves these moments for their suspended power, those few seconds when he's in the know, and the target isn't. He presses his face sideways into the sand, and a slight breeze moves air through his thin linen clothing. The target comes into focus, easily in range now.

Right here. If Rahim could just hold his breath and never exhale, perhaps this moment would freeze before the complicated threads of his life knot back together.

He hears Badria's first shot in front of the van's tires. Rahim follows up with a few quick bursts parallel to the passenger-side door. Their efforts send the drivers into a flurry—brakes slamming, dust kicking up, the gritting teeth of gears working nervously into reverse. He's seen it before. He'll see it again, his country a revolving door.

With the vehicles out of sight, Rahim joins Badria across the road. They retrieve their shovels and supplies from behind the shrubs. The scent of gunpowder lingers in the air as they traipse to the creek bed and feign their search for water to make bricks. At least it passes the time between ambushes. Occasionally, Rahim scans the horizon. The line where sand meets sky always wavering, never suggesting certainty. The distant, dust-covered shrubs bursting like tiny explosions from the ground. The persistent thickness of the air, the sunlight, the sand between his toes—everything infused with a heat that feels like home. When a second vehicle pops into sight later that morning, it's easy work.

A few weeks ago, it wasn't the Taliban fighters' movements that caught Rahim's attention but their laughter, little jabs of sound punching through the packed heat. Rahim looked up and saw them traversing the slopes above the road. They moved as easily as mountain goats along the edge of distant boulders, and very quickly, they were upon him, demanding that Rahim and Badria climb out of the creek bed.

It's not as if the fighters held them at gunpoint. No one threatened or fired. No one suggested Rahim couldn't back out. The desert simply offered the fighters and their money, pairing them with this sideline opportunity to ambush deliveries and suspicious non-residents. Rahim had wanted to ask about the Americans. They were non-residents, but their firepower wasn't anything two men could take on. Didn't they still patrol here once or twice a year? But he stayed quiet, shocked by the currency the Taliban promised next. The Taliban's instructions were clearly given: deter vehicles just enough to get them to turn around, and prevent them from entering the valley. Five American dollars paid to each man per deterred vehicle—more than a month's income for Rahim and Badria combined. One of the fighters had even waved a bill in the air like candy, chuckling as he incanted, "In God we trust," more laughter. "In God we trust."

All totaled, Rahim and Badria deter four vehicles for today's work—the van and SUV, one sedan, and a rusty delivery truck bearing an unfamiliar logo. French? German? Such foreign lettering, as haphazard as insect trails in the sand. By the day's end, Rahim is more than ready for a break. Soft shade. Warm tea. The ease of letting his eyelids close. With shovels and buckets in tow, he and Badria part ways along the loop road, and Rahim walks the remaining blocks back home.

As he nears his apartment, Shanaz shouts and waves, insistent on a visit. He avoided her yesterday. Today, he relents. She never cares to listen. Rather, to report. It annoys Rahim, if for no other reason than the energy it takes to pay mild attention to her when he'd just as soon be in his own home. Between bursts of pious proclamations, she informs him that Aaseya has been going to the bazaar by herself again. Did he avoid his sister's gaze? Did she even notice? He is so utterly fatigued—by the day, the circumstances, the endless, endless rope of it all. Even years ago, working in the Mirabad Valley, as beautiful and free as it had felt, it still came at a cost. Some sense of fatigue and falling behind Rahim can't seem to shake.

Finally home, he sets his supplies in the alley near the defunct tap stand, its dusty pipe a mockery. Such uselessness. Such waste. He can recall a few years of his forty in this life when Afghanistan wasn't being invaded. But those times are mostly lost to the fog of childhood or delegated to the realm of family lore. Mostly, when Rahim thinks about his life, he thinks about a spiral—always circling toward the same black hole, always seeing what's trying to pull him down, helpless against gravity.

He thuds up the mud steps to his apartment and rests for a moment at the top of the stairs. He fills the entryway from top to bottom, his long, gray *dishdasha* caked in sweat and dust. Linen pants of the same color balloon from his legs. Aaseya glances up from her work slicing cucumbers. Here's the moment he could tell her he's not making bricks anymore. That he's working for the Taliban but not with them. That in fact, right in their bedroom— pressed into a small wooden box—is a hidden stack of US bills, which may very soon be of use. Whether the Taliban pay in *rupees* or *afghanis* or dollars isn't for Rahim to worry about, though if he dwells on it, he knows it means his situation is unsustainable. The money will either run out or bring something bigger to a head. He's seen enough of war to know one of those outcomes is inevitable. For now, he does his job, earns his pay. That's got to be enough.

"*Salaam*," Aaseya says.

A dignified man would probably shove her into the wall. Might even ask his brother-in-law to help plot her execution. But even this thought comes with a wash of fatigue. What can be said of dignity for a man who's had the unforgivable forced on him? Rahim's heart pounds in his throat, and he remembers nights with General Khohistani as a boy. Aaseya nears to kiss his cheeks in greeting, but Rahim feels frozen. He studies the thin, downy hair along her upper lip. A silk forest of grace, perhaps how forgiveness would feel if it were a place. More, the easy curve of flesh above her mouth, the naive hope her youthful body suggests. The general falls from his thoughts and he leans forward, accepting Aaseya's welcome.

"*Salaam,*" he replies.

He crosses the room and reaches for a cup on the counter, then sees the water pail is empty. "What's this?" he frowns. "Shanaz said you've been out again, and still not even any water?"

Aaseya looks at her feet. Her restraint in his presence reassures him of his power, perhaps the only thing that remains his own in a country torn to bits. But in truth, he's never been good at punishment, his thoughts often pulled into poetic frenzy, encouraged by his studies in music and culture as a young boy. All things good and true. All things close to heaven, echoing the divine. He'd just as soon forget the rest and go take a nap. More powerful than any weapon he fires, it's the tiny salvations that keep him from splitting in two. Like a poem finds its form, he too will find his role.

"I'm sorry," Aaseya says. "We were only given a small portion."

Rahim shakes his head, nostrils flaring. He knows the spell his silence casts, the oddity of his own expression with the right side of his nose smooshed slightly off-center—the result of an early disobedience Aaseya would never understand. Does she think he's a fool or ferocious? Most days, Rahim feels too tired to venture a guess.

"Tea will be fine," he says.

Aaseya turns to her small cooking space and jabs at the coals, then sets the kettle on to boil. When the chai is ready, Rahim gulps it quickly. Warm silt slides down the back of his throat. He stares at the empty cup. He'd like more but feels something beyond thirst. A tightness in his gut nags, some days worse than others. Today it feels like a tiny man is working down there, twisting Rahim's gullet into knots. He wonders briefly if anything could actually soothe that kind of pain. It seems too unpredictable to name. An embarrassment, really. A sign of weakness. Not something he would ever complain about out loud. Even if the pain had a name, there's nothing that can be done. He shifts a little with the discomfort and imagines that the tiny man has started to pound pinhead-sized fists into the bottom of his gut. More than water, more than a hot meal, more than a wife, even, he'd love to kill that man and quiet the pain. The first time he felt it, he was ten or eleven as a *batcha bazi* dancing boy. There were nights when Gen. Khohistani dubbed Rahim the most talented. Such a cursed compliment. Rahim learned to focus inward during the humiliation of Khohistani's advances, imagining a rootball in his belly, firey and alive. When he danced for Khohistani, Rahim pretended that the rootball grew, spreading its tendrils upward and out of his throat until his entire body was covered in a knobby shield that protected him from the general's fondling. Most of the time, the mind trick worked. But one night, Rahim's imagination failed. There was only the darkness of Khohistani's office, the way he entered Rahim from behind. Rahim's slow slump into passivity.

Quite immediately, he understood: his body was like his country; it would survive, and it would always be used. But enough

61

of that. The Persian poet Hafiz would say that the past is a grave, the future a rose. Think of the rose.

Aaseya reaches for Rahim's cup, and he feels her fingertips meet the edge of his own. As soft as a petal. As uncallused as polished stone. There's so much she hasn't seen, but for a young woman quickly cast as a wife—and moreso, a young woman raised under Janan's worldly idealism—Rahim knows she's more savvy than most her age. She returns his mug, refilled, and walks to her cooking space. She appears sluggish, her limbs moving heavily as she mixes half-moons of cucumbers with lemon juice and salt. Rahim leans his back against the wall and rests.

Before long, Aaseya carries their meal into the gathering room and sets the tray on the floor. She smoothes the striped canvas *dastarkan* and sits across from Rahim. They eat silently, like isolated leopards startled to find themselves in the same den. Rahim watches her chew. The nervous way her fingers clasp each wedge of bread. The calculated flick of her tongue to collect hummus from the corners of her mouth. She could almost be feral, a helpless cub. But there's restraint in her movement. A careful calculation that Rahim recognizes as a secret withheld. Three years of marriage and she still makes everything so much more difficult than it needs to be. He understands that Aaseya likes his touch sometimes. A firm, hot hand sifting through the folds of her *shalwar kameez*. But other times, he presses into her and asks, "God willing?" the pleasant shock of her lips on his. "God's will is busy," she said twice this week already, her freedom of refusal a rarity in Imar, in Oruzgan Province, in most of her country. He's weary of her dismissiveness, too fatigued to press. If he told her, would she understand? That odd pain in his gut. Liminal, almost. Like a ghost. *Batcha bazi*—dancing boy. Two words he'll never repeat, though they make this marriage what it is. Being courted under the guise of tradition and honor turned Rahim inward, his poetic fancies blooming into elaborate disassociations—the rootball growing, spinning, cinching tightly. As frequently as Aaseya denies Rahim's advances, he has yet to push her into the wall, to grab her throat, to truly punish her. Not after all he's seen.

Daylight fades and with it, the pervasive heat. Something that could almost be called cool settles the dust in their tiny apartment. Rahim rests along a row of low cushions propped against the wall. Every few moments, he brings the lukewarm tea to his lips. His stomach loosens slightly, and he exhales, willing his shoulders and neck to release. It's not like the leather strap of an AK feels so strange. It's not even that so many hours in the sun each day cause more distress than he's put up with before. No, this tightness has the twist of a warning. A tired fable. His work with the Taliban will have its consequences. Meantime, Imar continues to destabilize, its inhabitants growing more and more susceptible to bribes or back-knuckled work. "You know what they say," Badria had told Rahim just last week after the Taliban paid them. "Follow the money to its source."

But dollars can come from as far away as the markets in Tarin Kowt or Kandahar. They can be plucked from dead bodies or filtered through the hands of ANA recruits in training. The source of Rahim's pay could be perfectly legitimate, even if the outcome is not—and what is legitimate when war has its hands in everyone's pockets? Morality is for the privileged; honor codes are for the elderly still remembering a world that never knew Osama bin Laden. Everything feels like a backwards pact. The thought only exaggerates Rahim's physical discomfort at the end of this long day. Needles move up his spine and settle like razor blades underneath each shoulder. Too much movement and he could slice himself in two. Maybe then the tiny man could crawl out. Maybe then the only thing that would matter would be those pieces of himself left behind. Pieces still useful enough to save. And isn't redemption something else entirely? Beyond dollars and roadside bargains? His heart says yes. Hafiz would believe in a world that says yes too.

Aaseya removes the remaining water from the small bed of coals, pours it into a wash basin, and carries it into the bedroom. Rahim sets his mug of tea aside and follows her, settling onto the edge of their thin floor mattress. Slowly, so as not to trigger the tiny man any further, he unwraps his turban and sets it next to himself on the bed. Thick, black hair stands atop his head, tossed like dunes. He stretches his legs in front of him and catches Aaseya's gaze. Eye to eye, they remain silent, assessing. Aaseya is still covered from hairline to ankle, and she snatches a small cloth from its hook, then squats at Rahim's feet with her knees pressed together. There's just enough water left to submerge the cloth. Clumsily, she begins her work.

How did it start—this ritual? Rahim lost a sandal in the creek one day and sliced the bottom of his foot on a piece of shrapnel. He kept digging, and by day's end, dirt filled his wounds to the bone as he wheelbarrowed his hand-pressed bricks down the two-track. The cut festered for weeks, and Aaseya washed Rahim's foot meticulously. In time, it seemed only natural to wash both feet. Eventually the wound sealed. But he still asks her to heat the pail each night. She still obliges.

Rahim lifts his *dishdasha* up his back and over his head. Aaseya stares into the bucket as though avoiding his bare chest, whorls of hair as thick as a rug. His nakedness fills the room, a rustic scent of onions fried in salt and left to sour. Pungent. Older. Twenty-three years older. He looks down at his wife, and her youthfulness has evaporated.

"Why'd you go all the way to the bazaar yesterday?" he asks. He presents his left foot, and Aaseya brings the cloth to his skin. She works her thumbs into his arch.

"Food for our dinner," she pauses. "But I went quickly. I didn't buy anything. There wasn't anything you would have liked."

"You'll have to wait. Wait for me, and we'll go after I come home."

Aaseya offers no indication that she has heard him. She keeps her gaze pinned to the floor.

"That's what you'll do from now on," Rahim insists. How many times has he said this before? He loathes the repetition. The tea stirs in his belly, disruptive. A wife should appease not torment. He stares at the top of her head, the purple headscarf teasing her dark hairline. Her skin is light, the same color as the dirt he used to work his hands through at the creeks, yet he can't shape her. Hafiz surfaces, a voice in his ear: *There are different wells within your heart. Some fill with each good rain, others are far too deep for that.*

Aaseya works her fingers behind Rahim's heel toward the tightrope of tendon, massaging efficiently. Water drips from her palms as she works. Some of it *plinks* slowly onto the floor. Her nonchalance unnerves him, the way she insists on remaining so calm. Aloof. Does anything upset her? She drops the cloth, careless again, and more water spills. A dark, wet line smears across the hard mud floor, then pools toward an unseen place beneath their mattress. Most men would probably kick her in the chin right now, and from this angle, Rahim could easily knock Aaseya backward. He sees in his mind exactly how it might play out, but there's a difference between the image and the action. It's not so much violence that he wants but simply an affirmation that he's been heard, that he's even in the room—breathing and thirsty and fed up.

"You know the dishonor your behavior casts," he says.

The defiance across her face makes him want to close his eyes. He wishes he could put the whole world to sleep. But a wish is only air. Without something to fill it, air remains invisible. Air doesn't have any impact. Maybe it's time for impact. Maybe he really should kick her.

"What do you have to say for yourself? What about this *ba haya?*" saying it aloud stings more than he anticipated. If his wife is shameful, what does that make him? A husband as small and complacent as a mouse. Worse. A means to an end. A role he seems fated to fill, those mujahideen generals like Khohistani ploying the elite with entertainment, *batcha bazi* performances a backdrop to elaborate meals that end in stealth agreements. It disgusts him to know that he'd been passed around as a boy, his cock responding in helpless confusion and how he took it in. How he let them take everything. A wish is only air. He should have fought back, and here he is now, hardly anything to claim as his own but more of the same. Air. Everywhere. The bleakness of it. He stands abruptly from the bed, body ignited, and kicks over the pail.

Aaseya flinches, tight-lipped.

Rahim's nostrils pulse impatiently. "What do you want me to tell Badria? What about Shanaz? The neighbors? What do you want me to say?"

He'd like to kick something bigger, to push. Anything to rise from this stale place. Hafiz was right about so many things. The well is too deep, too parched. Rahim feels his foot already drying against the clay floor. He feels his hands reaching, his fists filling with Aaseya's clothing. He pulls her to her feet, then lifts her slightly off the ground, aligning her face a few inches from his own. She squirms.

"Say something, Aaseya. *Say something.*"

Her breath catches as he holds here there, scruffed like a kitten.

"Sometimes," her voice like a child's, barely audible, "you look like my father. Your eyes are partly the same. I can't stand to see him in you. He'd never approve of this," her throat stretches as she speaks, exposed, and her skin looks so vulnerable. The generals wouldn't have tolerated this kind of back talk either. Her neck like a piece of fruit, waiting to be sliced. Her dangling limbs suggesting a corpse, and what those generals did to the corpses of women too.

Rahim could almost vomit.

He lowers Aaseya to the floor but keeps his fists tight, holding her body against his own so that there's nothing between them but fabric. No space, no light, no air, no power. They are equally beaten.

When Rahim finally speaks, it's only a whisper. "I knew your father for more years than you've been alive. He was a brother to me. He was the only one who respected me unconditionally. He would expect the same of you."

It's at least partially true. Janan and Rahim spent their elementary years in the same one-room schoolhouse. Years after, Janan welcomed Rahim with open arms whenever he visited. Consistently generous, never asking too much.

Aaseya's chest rises and falls against Rahim's body. There's warmth there beneath the fabric. Maybe not love but certainly the heat of flesh, certainly the loyalty of family. That will never be erased. He brings his lips to her ear and kisses the narrow space between her lobe and hairline. Her oily scent disarms him, like sweat and water mixing into the desert. Hafiz probably had a word for it—this elixir. He slides her headscarf partially down the length of her hair and holds her face between his palms gently. He leans farther, aligning his crotch with hers, and as he shifts, a folded wad of US dollar bills slips from his pocket and falls onto the floor.

Aaseya stares at the bills. "How?" she tries to free herself from Rahim's arms. "That's not right."

"I have more," Rahim says.

Aaseya remains locked in his grip.

"Aaseya," he says, and he almost turns toward his hidden wooden box, almost shows her just how much more, "it's not for you to know about anyway."

Her shock forces a line of thinking back into his mind. Money always moves before soldiers. Every Afghan knows that. Now, it seems to be moving everywhere. The dollars are proof this war isn't what it used to be. That the degrees of ignorance grow ever-wider. His work could all be for naught. He and Aaseya would never escape Imar in time to avoid a battle. But he can't share his aspiration to move their lives away from the village, maybe even as far as Kabul. If he fails, the humiliation will be too much.

"I saw Taliban fighters yesterday," Aaseya confesses. They remain standing close together, not quite easily but not as strangers anymore either. "They were using American dollars. Where did you get that money, Rahim? Why do you have it?"

"Tell yourself you didn't see the fighters," he says. "It's best that way."

"But why would they have dollars? Why do you?"

"You aren't even supposed to go past Shanaz's compound. Don't you understand? You should hear what Badria says. You should see how other men mock you. *You*. My wife. You have to be patient. There's no point trying to make sense of it, Aaseya. There will always be something bigger than us."

She shakes her head, as if knocking a thought free. "Oh," she says softly. "*Oh*," and there it is. Her smile—a thing he'd nearly forgotten. "You're working for the Americans?" she asks, and in asking, Rahim hears that she's already convinced herself it must be true. Calmness overtakes her. "Rahim," she says, eyebrows raised, "even when others disagreed with him, my father always said—"

"—that the Americans stand for hope," Rahim completes her sentence. He can't help it, though he knows she is pitifully wrong.

She nods, leaning into his chest.

"Janan always said that to me too."

She stares up into his face, her cheeks as flushed as plums. Such abundance, even here, even as he fails to say anything to her that feels dignified. But this space they share, the promise of it. It can only be Hafiz's deep well. Aaseya is the good rain. She's a blessing. She's a flower. She's this pretty, breakable thing, and Rahim is suddenly so ravenous he could eat her alive. He tastes the skin along her neck. She pulls away, and the space is too much for him, a chasm that threatens to leave him wanting. Money slides beneath their feet as he lowers her to the bed. Her headscarf falls the rest of the way down, and her hair settles around her face, black strands framing her eyes. For a moment, they lie next to one another, breathing loudly. The soft light of sunset falls across the far end of the mattress, and it's as if they both know not to venture there, where everything can be seen. Rahim pulls Aaseya closer, into the gray dark.

"Aaseya," he says.

She meets his gaze.

"Aaseya, I'm nothing in this war. God willing, it will stay that way."

She nods slowly, then places her hands on his hips and agrees.

As they move together, his feet begin to tingle, tightness gathering in his crotch. It's possible that someday Aaseya will respect him. That someday she'll obey. The thought quickens his advances, and she moves with him as he pushes, leans, tongues his way into her mouth. Their bodies find an odd rhythm— something like falling and hovering at the same time. He kisses her again, cupping a hand over her tiny breasts through the folds of fabric. He listens for the subtle quickening of her breath for any hint of fear, but her hands merely rest along his back like branches from a tree, bending with the weather. Her body is a flash of color beneath him, fabric shifting, and that quickly, he's inside.

He only has so much time before memory crosses wires with the present, the ghost of Khohistani pounding into his back like enemy fire. She can never know this; she can never sense the angry, beaten thing inside of him. He slows himself, but the effort is too much, and he lets out a tiny yelp, quickening. Aaseya rises beneath him, her torso lifting as they rock, and whatever this is, it's better than what came before. Rahim moves his hands up her back, shoving her robe over the top of her head. The fabric gathers between them, curling into her stomach. He wants to slow down. He wants to forget. He wants to put water in the well. Their bodies move into the mattress, and he feels her need something from him that he can actually give. So close to finishing. So little air in the room. He opens his eyes and searches: sandy skin, smooth curves, her firm, brown nipple pointing at him like a bullet. He moves his lips to it, and that does it.

6

Should You Choose to Accept It

The screensaver on Miller's desktop loops through a photo album of recent uploads. Here, a shot of the Spartans training ANA forces, Miller in the back row shoulder to shoulder with Captain Kashmala, head of the brigade. They sweated their balls off that mission, temperatures passing 110 while the Spartans demoed standard operating procedure to clear houses. Next, an image of Specialist Baldwin's Humvee, gutted and charcoaled after an IED took every fire team member but Private Caldwell, the rookie from St. Paul. Caldwell survived, the photo emailed to Miller along with Caldwell's transfer from Bravo to Spartan two months ago. What Caldwell couldn't have known when the army division sent the picture over is that his coping mechanism—a near constant incantation of the prayer of Saint Francis of Assisi—had called his mental capabilities into question. Spartan would be Caldwell's last chance. If the young Guardsman couldn't fire straight under Miller's watch, he'd be kept on the FOB for psychiatric review. From there, who knows.

When the screen flicks to a photo of Tenley and Cissy's blond-framed grins at the local fire department picnic, Miller touches the dust-coated keyboard to interrupt the slideshow and pixel his wife and daughter out of sight. He loves the image—sunlight casting Cissy's face in soft hues, and Tenley smiling lazily at the end of a long afternoon. But he could do without the lumbering firemen shown in the background. Perhaps one had even taken the photo for Tenley, saying, "One…two…smile, you're beautiful… THREE!" and pressing his big thumb over the clicker.

The day continues in this vain, ebbing and flowing through the Roy G. Biv of emotions. After reading a few emails, Miller opens the bottom drawer of the filing cabinet and rolls the tiny, round prescription bottles between his palms. "Whenever you need it," Doc had said at the start of this tour, though Miller still hadn't taken a single tablet. He was out of refills, but he had enough. He closes the drawer, momentarily motivated again, and tackles a few more messages in his inbox. Even if deskwork isn't Miller's forte, in the back of his mind, he's thankful for the small sense of accomplishment it can impart. At 1430 hours, he'll meet with Captain Chaffen for God knows what, then strategize. For what an email tells Miller will send him and the Spartans to Imar on "Mission Aqua" less than twenty-four hours from now. They can call in air support at any time, and the road is being cleared by an ordance team ahead of the mission. Twelve emails down, twenty to go. He's going to need more coffee.

The next email gives him pause. It's from Captain Chaffen, the company commander. The subject line reads, innocently enough: "ROE—Rules of Engagement." But Miller knows better, as does every platoon leader on FOB Copperhead CC'ed in the message.

```
DATE: 02 JULY 2009

MESSAGE: Gaining and maintaining
support    from    civilians    must
be    our    overriding    operational
imperative.    We    will    not    win
based on the number of Taliban we
kill but instead on our ability
```

to separate insurgents from the center of gravity: the people. All leaders at all levels are expected to limit the use of force against residential compounds and other locations. Any searches of Afghan buildings will be executed by Afghan National Security Forces with the support of local authorities. No United States forces will enter, fire upon, or fire into these buildings except in self-defense. This is different from conventional combat, and such discipline entails risks to our troops, but excessive force resulting in an alienated population will produce far greater risks. The Taliban cannot militarily defeat us, but we can defeat ourselves.

By the end of the message, Miller feels cross-eyed. His ability to protect the Spartans is merely a street lamp in the Godzilla path of this war's directives. He jabs at the power button on the monitor and shoves his chair back from the desk, bumping into the wall behind him. The hole Folson put in the drywall across the room crumbles further, a small chunk tumbling to the floor. Miller considers making a few holes of his own, imagining the satisfaction of busting the flimsy trailer to bits, but hitting has never been his style. He swivels on his chair, unlocks the drawer, and grabs one bottle of Percocet. Still plenty left, should he need them, though even now—his first time opening one of the prescriptions—he questions his judgment.

Three tablets, chewed and swallowed with a quickness, the bitter sting a welcome distraction. His Ritalin chaser comes with surprising ease, as though Miller is watching someone else's hands do the swift work. The twist and pop. The tapping of pills. He crushes two into powder with the bottom of his stapler and—just like he has seen in movies, at off-base parties back home, on YouTube, even—arranges it in lines, and then it's gone.

A few minutes? An hour? Couldn't be. His mind is so soft, humming white noise and elasticity. First snowfall in a hardwood forest, the daring tracks of rabbits through the powder. First kiss—not Tenley but a girl named Sandra from art class, permed hair and a quick tongue. First finish line, back in his 5K days of blacktop and sprints. First art museum, that traveling Van Gogh exhibit, and he didn't care if it were every other would-be painter's story too. He'd been transfixed. Brush strokes across canvas, across centuries, across his eyelids and then gone. Blinked away with a signature and Guard promotions. First time he didn't stand up for a friend being bullied. First time he broke a girl's heart. First time Cissy cried—not for nursings or at vaccines—but at goodbye, and goodbye, and goodbye, and goodbye. To be a father. To be fathered. First spanking.

The memory forces Miller from his desk to pace the hallway. Age four. Indiana. In the aftermath of a summer thunderstorm, Nathan walked to the end of his long driveway where dirt met asphault, two-lane Indiana State Highway 67 stretching for miles. Here, the ground that only ever seemed to give up corn, gave up something else. Earthworms. Droves of them, writhing across the blacktop as if in pain. Nathan looked left, looked right. The puddled highway heaved with beautiful, slender creatures that—his kindergarten teacher had told him—did the most amazing, inivisible work underground.

He looked left. Right again. Then left one more time. The big rigs would be coming soon the way they did, dozens of them every hour, splashing between one town and the next. The earthworms were helpless in the aftermath of the downpour, turning in circles, already starting to cook as water evaporated from the road. Nathan wanted to save them, every single one. For show and tell, he'd be able to brag about it, explaining how he had done his part to keep the Miller family corn's reputation as best in the county, maybe even best in state. He imagined a vast colony of worms beneath his family's fields, moving through the soil, helping the corn breathe.

He named them as he walked down the center of the highway, placing them gently out of harm's way. *Morris, Danny, Sean.* These names from his cousins. The ones that came to mind first. Then: *Scooby, Grover.* Walk, walk, walk.

And then it came. His father's voice like a mad roar, Nathan pulled by the arm, shoulder whipping back as his head snapped like a knot at the end of a rope. Only fifty yards or so from his own driveway but still over the double yellow line and—*My God, boy, you could have been killed,* his father, breathless, *What were you thinking?* And Nathan felt the sentence on the tip of his tongue, *That I could save them, Daddy. That they could help our crops,* but there wasn't time. Nathan's pants down, bare ass to the sun, a truck blazing past, the whoosh of dust and dirt whipping around them. Was it horns from the semis that rang in his ears or the hurt? The hurt of it, his father's palm hot and fast, making a point so that Nathan never forgot.

No difference, really, between being held back when he could have saved more earthworms and what these new ROE will bring into reality. Except these were human lives. Limbs that didn't regenerate when cut in two. Families that didn't regenerate either. Close-call scenarios and missed opportunities fill Miller's mind as he paces the cramped hallway, tunneling into hyperfocus and nausea: A sniper ducks into position on a rooftop but runs away when the Spartans spot him. Instead of firing, they're forced to watch the sniper take shelter in a family's apartment two stories below, off limits. A suicide bomber approaches along a narrow sidewalk and slips into a shop next to Miller's parked convoy. They can't see him through the curtains and don't have permission to go inside. There's the slight scent of sulfur—a match lit—and the scene shakes, then blackness.

The door to the trailer opens, and four soldiers step inside. "Sir?" one of them says.

Miller stops pacing, startled.

"Sir, we're security detail for your meeting with the company commander."

"We're going off base?" his tongue feels dry, mouth pasty. The soldiers stare at him blankly, as much in the know as Miller, which is not at all. "We're the goddamn Girls Scouts now—has anyone told you that? *Girls Scouts*."

The soldiers look at their feet. "Sir?" one offers, meekly.

"Because of this new ROE, your jobs have officially gone to shit. So has mine. You wanna provide me with security? Find a way to shove a sock down McChrystal's throat, that's what. Find a way to shut this whole charade down."

Miller grabs his cap and charges toward the door.

The move from shade to oversaturation burns Miller's eyes. That dizzying blue sky. That goddamn sun lasering into him. The buzz isn't what he'd expected, but he's not entirely opposed to it either. There's an inner propulsion to his muscles, something both floating and electric, and though his head throbs ever so slightly, minor irritants that usually set him off kilter now and seem laughable. Miller shuffles past the Echo Company Headquarters toward the main gates. Ahead of him, Captain Chaffen waits with his thumbs tucked into his front pockets, telltale posture recognizeable from a hundred yards. A quick salute and greeting, Chaffen's voice like gravel, grating. Paired with the salt-and-pepper hair and aviator shades, the captain strikes a chord somewhere between grandpa and gladiator. They walk quickly, automatically. A brief wave through from the entrance guards who hold Miller and Chaffen's name and rank patches for safekeeping, and they're out, security at their flanks.

It's a short walk to the teahouse, but that sun—so relentless, like a drone, hovering, targeting. Miller makes small talk, soaring on autopilot. Every bead of sweat and patch of heat rash on his body feels ignited. Chaffen tells him they're scheduled to meet Abdul-Bari Gawri, the district chief whom Spartan has worked with for the duration of this tour. Chaffen's presence is meant to assure Gawri that Miller's replacement will pick up where Spartan leaves off. That projects won't halt, and communication will remain open. They've done good work here, Chaffen assures him, and Miller releases the hard knot at the back of his throat, easing back into the euphoria a bit.

"Your men keeping themselves together?" Chaffen asks.

"Absolutely."

He won't say "Captain." Not here, where such esteem would paint a target on Chaffen's forehead. He won't mention the ROE, either, though every cell inside of him teems with questions. Changes like this rarely come paired with satisfactory answers.

"Good because, in my experience, they get squirmy once the end is in sight."

"Understood. I've seen a little of that," Miller says. "Nothing I can't handle."

He thinks of the flagpole. Hopes that Folson really has turned a corner.

A stray dog trots beside them, ribcage like a xylophone beneath flea-scabbed skin. Its lips sag around missing teeth, as though someone took a fist to its jaw. Even the dogs here appear spent from too many years meddling in messes that aren't theirs.

A few blocks from base, they reach the *chai kana* and outdoor patio. About thirty locals sit cross-legged beneath the large awning with dusty, brass trays placed before them. The men talk quietly or not at all. Miller and Chaffen settle at the far end of the patio and cross their legs awkwardly, butts resting on the dusty palettes. Almost immediately, a short, wrinkled server appears and places a porcelain teapot and cups in front of their cumbersome boots. His hands look leathery, dark folds ringed with scuffs of skin, but his face offers a different story. Smooth cheeks and an easy smile. The kind of nonchalant hospitality Miller always marvels at. Even in a war zone, most civilians he has met greet him with the optimism of a new day. Chaffen nods and pays the man with local currency.

The customers at the far end of the patio laugh openly, and Miller deciphers some of the watery, Pashto syllables into words he knows: road, safety, wife, water. And Bush. Always "George Bush," like a corporate slogan cropping up in civilian chatter on every tour. Every so often, a man with a unibrow looks up and stares. Miller can't place an emotion behind the gaze, and it disturbs him—those deep, reflective, brown eyes taking something with each glance, offering nothing in return. An elementary-school-aged boy joins the circle of men for a moment, and Mr. Unibrow whispers something to him, then pats the boy affectionately on his lower back. Just another day in Tarin Kowt, Miller supposes, though he likes to believe that experience has taught him the price of assumptions. There truly is no rest in this life he's made for himself, and it crosses his mind that there's a chance his anxieties will never disappear. That he'll have to change how he lives with them in a way where change doesn't mean the kind of high he feels now.

A wave of banter rises from the far end of the patio, conversation cresting into what sounds to Miller like heated opinion. The man with the unibrow looks again at Miller, then Chaffen, then back to Miller.

Miller sips his tea. Overhead, the burlap awning flaps eerily in the breeze, shooting shadows across the patio. Occasionally, sunlight pinpricks through the fabric like little golden bullets.

In training, they tell you what failure *isn't*, as in, "failure isn't an option." But they don't tell you what failure *is*, or how to live with it. Miller felt smothered in shame after Mercer's death. He can't let that kind of mistake happen again. He looks at Unibrow. Tries to commit the man's face to memory. But Unibrow has shifted slightly amidst his circle of friends, and all Miller sees now is the man's turban wound as tightly as a wasp's nest. The boy returns to the circle and serves what looks like a speciality drink, then sits in Unibrow's lap. The gesture is sexual and familial all at once, and Miller's skin crawls.

Chaffen pours himself more tea, then repositions his back against the wall of the shop, on alert. If Gawri plans to keep Miller and Chaffen waiting like meat for the taking, this meeting is a bust. Slowly, Chaffen begins polishing his sunglasses, eyes crisscrossing the busy street and nearby shops. Just inside the *chai kana*, the soft-faced server tends two samovars, dropping bits of charcoal into copper pipes.

"There's something I need you to hear," Chaffen finally says. "I know there are a lot of other things you'd rather talk about right now, and I can't change what orders come down, but I can change what goes out."

"What goes out?" Miller asks.

"You. Mission Aqua," Chaffen shifts his posture, stiffly crossing and uncrossing his legs. "Half of your men need to stay back to pack up the Conex. The logisticians are picking it up in thirty-six hours for shipment to Kuwait. No more putting it off. It's got to be done. They can inventory while they pack up."

"Fair enough," Miller says. "I'll take three fire teams on Aqua. The others can stay back."

"And you can stay back too," Chaffen says. "Aqua's a humanitarian mission. TBs haven't been seen that deep in Oruzgan Province since '06."

Miller sets his tea down and leans forward, resting his elbows on his knees. The air feels sticky, his head suddenly pounding. "My business is always wherever the greatest threat lies for my men," he says. "That'll never change. My platoon sergeant can stay back, but I'm going outside the wire."

Chaffen offers a half-smile but refuses Miller's gaze. In profile, Chaffen's face could almost be described as chiseled, though the hints of age betray him, a sunburned jawline sagging like a wet wash towel. As with everything else about the captain, it suggests his logic is dated, his outlook antiquated. Paired with the gruff vocals, Miller often struggles to buy into much of anything Chaffen offers. "Might I remind you that your platoon sergeant isn't married, Miller. Might I remind you that he doesn't have a daughter. More to the point, he's not four tours into this war and looking haggard like you."

"My wife and daughter have nothing to do with my loyalties to my men."

"No, they don't. But they have a lot to do with you once you get back home, and I want to make sure you get there. You've done enough. Just ease out of this. For once, give someone else the door to walk through. Going outside the wire this close to the finish line? It's not something I want you doing on my watch."

"I know the feeling," Miller says. "Which is why I can't send my guys on Aqua without me."

Chaffen lets out a small, condescending chuckle and pushes his sunglasses back up the bridge of his nose. "God, I remember that."

"What?"

"Tunnel vision. Ego. Thinking that so much depends on your actions when, in fact, war is a machine so big that very few people, Miller, very few, actually have a sense for its scope. Take the two of us, for instance. For every person you trust, I've got ten more above me that I'm counting on for intel. That means when you don't trust me, you're making it harder for me to do my job. And that's just the beginning…"

Miller swallows a scoff. He can't decide whether to feel insulted or complimented. Miller doesn't need overtures, he needs autonomy. The war he's fighting doesn't wait for paperwork, for permission. The senior officers tug one way, junior officers encounter problems pulling the other. Meantime, soldiers and civilians get killed, while overlords in Washington deposit their paychecks.

"Look," Miller says, sitting up straight, "the Spartans are under my watch. Nothing changes that, even the new rules of engagement."

Chaffen leans toward Miller. "You don't know the shit storm that went down before that ROE made it through to you guys. Hear me out. We've got bigger issues in Oruzgan. I'm only going to say this once, and then we're both going to forget it. Got it?"

Miller nods.

"There's been a media fallout back home because of the reportage about Host Nation Trucking. Things are happening— *fast*. Higher was ordered to pull contracts in Oruzgan as a point of show, and the locals here are pissed about it. Gawri found out last night, and he's taking all the heat."

"What about our supplies?"

"Oh, Copperhead will get what it needs—probably for ten times what the government is used to paying—and it's only a temporary pause anyway. But that's not what has my attention. Word is going to get out among civilians that we have our hands tied with this new ROE. At the same time, an entire network in Oruzgan has been stripped from the payroll. I don't want you caught in the reverb. I already tried to postpone the mission, but the Battalion commander sees it as another PR opp, and maybe he's right. Imar is so remote that it'll be quiet there for a while. Until it's not. You're this close, Miller. Think about it," Chaffen stands, hooking his thumbs into his front pockets and squaring his shoulders. "Look who decided to show up," he nods across the street.

The soldiers on security pat Gawri down lightly. Chatter amongs locals on the patio halts. Unibrow stands and walks straight toward Miller and Chaffen, eyes dark and flat as spilled oil.

Chaffen looks down at Miller, who still sits. "What are you doing down there? Playing with Legos? Stand up, soldier."

Miller rises quickly and kicks the life back into his lower extremities. "Are you aware of the man approaching us from nine o'clock right now?"

"That's Gawri's security detail. Guess he's playing it safe already. But my question is, are you aware of anything else? Because in the ten minutes you've been listening to me and fretting over that guy, an American soldier has died somewhere in the Middle East. I guaran-goddamn-tee it. That's how you've got to start thinking, Miller. In all directions. That's how everyone has to start thinking."

Unibrow sidles up to Chaffen and Miller without a word. Chaffen looks at the man and nods. Unibrow stands still as a heron, limber frame holding firm. Together, they watch Gawri approach. A slow gait, his white robes flowing, a dark beard to mid-chest, and fat lips that part over a row of stained teeth.

"*As-salamu alaikum,*" Chaffen says, shaking Gawri's hand.

"*As-salamu alaiku,*" Gawri smiles, revealing a tiny gap where a lower incisor is missing. He grips Miller's shoulder and nods. "Brother," he says.

"Brother," Miller says. He forces a grin and pours Gawri's tea, letting Chaffen and Gawri sit first. Their talk is light, their tone easy. Gawri clearly ass-kissing, as if Chaffen could reinstitute the contracts with a wave of his hands. Miller calls to mind the directive, its ominous sentiment: *The Taliban cannot militarily defeat us, but we can defeat ourselves.* Like grabbing fistfuls of sand—that's what this war is. Like trying to hold onto the impossible.

7

How Easy It Would Be

Aaseya slips from bed and dresses quietly. She tiptoes through the darkness, headed for the stairs. It feels good to move in her own skin, her body completely hers again. She sits at the bottom of the stairs and steals a glance into the alley. Even at twilight, the air outside feels close, the stars unsettlingly distant through the haze. Nostalgia for her old life pulls at her chest, as if to tow her back to the ruins of her family home down the street. She used to nap in the shade of an almond tree there and often woke with the fresh memory of a dream—riding on the back of a snow-white tiger through a lush forest she'd never seen in real life or building a library with books stacked as high as the clouds. Three generations of her family lived behind those compound walls when the explosion happened and so many more before that. She'd like to say that tonight's stars wink a promise at her. That the half-moon is surely waxing full, but that's a fool's dream.

Even if Rahim's work for the Americans signifies hope and her father would have agreed, the presence of Taliban in broad daylight overshadows this beacon. A street-side battle will only make things worse. Aaseya has seen it before—the way the neighbors shutter their windows for months at a time, and the streets grow quiet, nearly abandoned. She wants to love this village that could make a man like Janan, but it hasn't looked as kindly upon her. Her chest tightens. The vast skies are unreachable, as inconsequential as her thoughts. She turns to go back upstairs and catches a flash of movement. Something darts down the ally, quickly and lightly as a fox.

"Who's there?" she whispers.

Another dash and hustle, moving closer.

Aaseya retreats halfway up the steps.

A small clink and rattle, then silence.

She wills herself completely still.

Another clink. Rattle. Soft steps in the dry dirt.

"Ghazél? Is that you?"

Another clink. Rattle.

It's the sound of a pebble, she realizes, being tossed at the tap stand. "Quiet now. You'll wake the neighbors."

She slips back down the stairs and sees the boy in the moonlight filtering through the alley. Somehow, he has found a pomegranate. He holds it out to her, smiling.

"No," she shakes her head, "you eat it."

Ghazél settles onto the bottom step and picks at the molding fruit. Aaseya sits next to him and watches him work. His shoulder feels bony pressed against the side of her arm, but at least it's gentle, alive. "My brother was a lot like you," she says. "Smart. Curious."

Ghazél fingers several seeds into his mouth, mining the fruit deftly. He looks at her, listening. Alamzeb had sat close to her too, as if she could protect him. As if simply by staying nearby, he'd remain safe.

"I saved him from a lot of trouble once, but in the end, it didn't matter."

Aaseya looks toward the tap stand and sees that it wasn't pebbles Ghazél threw but more shell casings. She retrieves one and squeezes it between her palms.

"Ghazél," she says, "who do you think fired these bullets?"

The boy shrugs. She doesn't want to encourage him to go looking, but even as a mute orphan, he has more freedom than she has to wander.

"Where do you find them?"

He hops down from the steps and begins to trace a line into the moonlit dirt along the alley. He concentrates, drawing and considering—a long roofline, a tall building, and the telltale wide double doors.

"That close?" she asks. "At the schoolhouse?"

The boy nods.

"That can't be right, Ghazél."

Wouldn't she have heard shots if they'd been fired? Wouldn't someone, even Shanaz, have told her if Imar really was that unstable again? But she knows these answers before she can finish asking herself the questions. No one in Imar would tell her anything. Maybe she should warn Rahim, or seek information from Massoud. Maybe then her husband will see the useful information her excursions unearth. Maybe he'll earn even more prestige if he can tell the Americans this morsel of information. Maybe then Imar won't fall prey to whatever battle surely awaits, locking her away for months. She's got to see the schoolhouse for herself. She's got to know for certain.

Ghazél points to the tap stand. He looks at Aaseya and gestures with two fingers, like a figure walking, to indicate that he's willing to find water for her. Always eager to help; Alamzeb had been too.

"It's too far and too dangerous, but Shanaz's sons fetch some for me. You can walk with me to bring them the pail tomorrow."

He raises his eyebrows.

"But you can't bother Shanaz if we see her. She's a liar and a pest."

Ghazél shuffles his feet, ever fidgety. He tosses the pomegranate to Aaseya, then puts his hands on his hips and scrunches his nose. Next, he points and jabs at the air rapidly, as if scolding.

Aaseya laughs lightly. "That's exactly how she looks when she's angry."

She sets the pomegranate back into Ghazél's hands, and he sits beside her. There's so much she wants to say, this new kinship an odd yet soothing outlet. The night might make her desires seem distant, but Ghazél certainly brings a sense of possibility closer. If she can go where he goes, she'll have the answers she needs. He can't be living very well wherever he's finding places to sleep. His toenails are nearly torn off, and dark lines of dirt coat his limbs and face. His floppy hair is matted and clumped. He has so little, yet here he is, foraging for seeds in the middle of the night and finding comedy in the village witch.

Ghazél sets the pomegranate down, half-eaten, and fishes into his pockets. He wriggles side to side as he searches, tightening his red-stained lips with concentration before bursting into a smile. Victorious, he hands Aaseya a miniature plastic figurine with neon pink hair. It's an oddly naked, brown thing with arms and legs and a soft belly, appearing both wild and foolish. A small part of one plastic foot is melted and blackened.

"Thank you," Aaseya says and takes the toy. She combs the pink hair with her fingertips, working several clumps of dirt free. "He needs a bath," Aaseya says.

Ghazél nods.

"And you do too."

Ghazél shrugs.

"Let me help you tomorrow when I have extra water. You help me go to the bazaar, and I'll help you wash. Will that work?"

Ghazél shakes his head, no.

"Well, how about another meal? But the bazaar first. Then you'll come back here with me, and we'll see what I can cook for you."

She's aware of the eagerness in her tone. Can feel herself ready to do whatever it takes. Her father helped her find her voice as a girl, and here she is, using it to bribe a helpless boy. The irony isn't lost on her. Ghazél can't even talk. Between the two of them, could their circumstances add up to a life lived fully? A life that's complete?

Ghazél's lips part to a row of small, crooked teeth, and he nods. He brings his palms together, as if holding water, then dips his head into it like a bathing bird. Gesture complete, he looks at Aaseya with a smile.

"OK, good. But I have to ask—do you have any family?"

Ghazél's smile flattens into a furtive line. He brings one hand up over their heads, maneuvering it like a plane. He forms his second hand into a fist, tucking it underneath the first. "Kerrrg," he stutters. "Kerrrg," then he brings his fist down to the ground, as if dropping a bomb.

"Mine too," Aaseya says. "Except not exactly like that. Not a bomb from the sky. An explosion. One that came from the street. This street."

Ghazel reaches his arms around her neck, twiggy and tender, and squeezes. Aaseya lets him hug her in the stairwell, the motion of sympathy all his. Such tiny might. No one's expressed condolences since her family died three years ago, nor did she think sympathy was something she missed. Company, sure. But sympathy—who had time for that? She swallows the tight sensation in her throat and hugs Ghazél back. For a moment, there's no future up those steps into her dark apartment. No past out on the streets where so much has already been taken.

"So," she says, pulling away. She looks at the pink-haired toy as if asking its opinion. "What do *you* think about our plan?" she asks. "Tomorrow?"

Ghazél nods and squeezes Aaseya's hand, then lets go. He grabs the pomegranate and is gone just as quickly as he appeared.

Inside the apartment, Aaseya studies the small toy. Maybe Rahim will find it in the morning and think it's curious too. The pink hair is certainly something to behold. She's never seen anything like it. She's never seen something carry itself so nakedly either. So joyfully itself. She shapes its hair into a coil and leaves it on the counter, then walks into the bedroom. Rahim has shifted slightly, kicking the sheet free. She lies onto her back next him and stares into the darkness. A gentle snore teases the edge of Rahim's breath, soft and high-pitched, almost feminine. What shook him so thoroughly earlier that night? Aaseya knows her restlessness costs him. But there was something unyielding about his reaction this time. She reaches for a small fan on the floor and waves it side to side, stirring the air. She won't question Rahim again—that much she's decided. He brings money home. That's more than most husbands do. Her impatience is unforgivable in his eyes; worse, it somehow makes him feel useless, risking rage. She waves the fan faster, thinking of the schoolhouse. How dry the world feels. How poised to crack. Each breath as brittle as bone.

Rahim rolls over and flops an arm across Aaseya's middle. She sets the fan down carefully and looks along the length of her body. Two small knolls across her gown, breasts like little lumps of dough. Long hair tangling across her chest. She fingers a few strands, playing with them loosely and tracing the lines of her rib cage. It's a wonder, really. This armature that houses everything she needs to live, to breathe. Why can't it be enough? She drops the strands of hair and props herself up on her elbows. Rahim's hand slides to rest on top of her belly, as if trying to conjure the very thing they can't make together. Slowly, careful not to wake him, Aaseya slides her hand on top of Rahim's and presses, breathing steadily. She focuses. She can see it clearly now. How easy it would be to take the boy into their lives completely—Ghazél asleep in the corner of their bedroom, the soft comfort of another's company during the day. The chance to rise above these stigmas, these shackles, that one little orphan boy can lift from her life entirely.

8

The Spartans

It's another fetid sunset—this one orange, molten—and Miller watches from the high perch of a security tower, sunlight seeping across Tarin Kowt, as if from a wound. He slept off most of the crash from that afternoon's uppers, but something still feels off, the world a little canted. A headache balls at the base of his skull. He watches the city fade into shadows, block by block. Airborne particles of sand catch the sun's rays, Mother Nature's tracer fire. Within minutes, the horizon appears lit by a throbbing Armageddon. Four tours and it has come to this. The night before Miller's last mission outside the wire, Chaffen's voice echoing like a challenge inside Miller's head: *That's how you've got to start thinking, in all directions.* Miller has gotten the Spartans this far, though there's no denying the number of jihadists and civilians blown to bits along the way—a leg, a torso. One time, a man's nose and ear blew right off his face from the force of a blast. *Mr. Potato Head,* Miller remembers thinking, *It's like Mr. Potato Head and his bucket of parts.* That's how the mind works in such moments. Twisted, private humor. A curiosity that makes Miller shrink in shame and feel charged with life all at once. The nose went one direction. The ear went the other. The memory almost makes him laugh out loud for its wrongness. Its rightness. The man had been a civilian, busted up by a roadside bomb. Before Miller could think, he'd found himself applying well-aimed, direct pressure to the wounds, then Doc took over. He stood, wiped his hands on his DCUs, and high-tailed it to the two insurgents his men had just cuffed. He could have killed them—could have killed so many people but didn't—the two of them kneeling at his boots with bags over their heads, one just having shat himself and the other wailing some tinny, syllabic prayer.

Miller moves from the tower, the clap of his boots ringing down the stairs. He crosses the courtyard, returns a few salutes to soldiers in line outside the phone center, and flashes for a moment on Tenley. He really ought to call her back. There was an unspoken superstition about calls getting cut off, phone lines going dead. To reverse the bad luck, all he had to do was reconnect. Just once. Just enough for "hello." But he pushes onward toward the staging area, and there, at the end of a long row of concrete bunkhouses, Miller spies half of Spartan Platoon gathered around their Humvees for a mission brief. They haven't noticed him yet. He can't even hear himself approach, what with the bunkhouse air conditioners humming like spacecrafts, as if this whole war has been an alien invasion. Exhaust swirls in Miller's face, and he walks down the corridor, flashing between slanted bunkhouse shadows and angled light. It could be Kansas. It could be Oz. It could all be about to blow away.

Laughter breaks through the pasty air, and Miller recognizes Pilchuck's snare-drum bray, a natural leader, and the platoon is better for it. Pilchuck. Upchuck. These guardsmen just call him Yak. Around Yak, ten more Spartans wrestle and juke like Olympians before their next heat. The smell of diesel fumes hits him, and his throat tightens. The human body is so needy, so easily rattled. It's all a wonder as he steps through the last patch of shade and into the bright, final seconds of daylight unreeling from that goddamn ever-racing sun.

Spartan spots their platoon leader and comes to center. Behind them: three rigs gussied in desert brown, dark brown, and beige—the difference between shades a topic of unending debate. Bullet holes and veiny scratches of rust mottle the side doors and gunner hatches, lending a vintage look that would give AM General manufacturing an epic woody. Caked, desert gumbo has dried on the undersides of each vehicle in the most invasive places, and stacked high on the back of each Humvee are cardboard boxes of bottled water. Specialist Reynolds stands on one foot in the center of it all, leg outstretched to balance his Kevlar on the tip of his boot. His black mop of hair has been formed into a gelatinous, clipped mohawk, but whether or not this soldier is trimmed to regulation is of no concern. Combat infantry has bigger bones to pick. Miller is not the kind of leader who gets tied in knots about dress code.

Reynolds flicks the Kevlar playfully, and Miller snatches it mid-air. He feels Spartan's energy encircle him, the questions they know well enough not to voice: How long will processing take in Kuwait? When will I be able to take an unparasitic dump in my own bathroom? Anyone else counting down the days?

Miller tosses the Kevlar back to Reynolds. "Home's a hell of a lot farther than a mission away, gentlemen. But it is within reach," he tries to calm them. "Now—the mission brief…" but the Spartans are too amped, their eagerness swarming through the air.

Private First Class Nacho Supreme yanks the Kevlar from Reynolds's hands, boots knocking over his Mountain Dew bottle of tobacco spit in the process. A viscous, brown pool forms in the dust at the center of the hustle.

"Dude!" Reynolds says, grabbing for his Kevlar but missing.

"Go long! Go long!" calls Supreme, whose eyes remain hidden behind a coveted pair of mirrored Oakleys. He lobs Reynolds's

Kevlar over the Humvees and lets out a laugh. Inseparable, these two, one-upping their way through conversations like comedians, and they're just as dependable on delivery. More than once, Supreme and Reynolds have saved a fellow soldier's life.

"I gotsta, gotsta, gotsta get me suh-uh-ome," Yak croons. He sprints around the other Spartans, beanstalk legs and all, and catches Reynolds's helmet as effortlessly as the varsity basketball star the Spartans swear he must have been. He's Miller's right-hand man, so here's where the game stops. All 6'4" of this first sergeant ambling back to the huddle with a grin that says, *Now now, Guardsmen...*

The Spartans don't let up, and conjecture about home eeks out. It's not where their minds should be. Miller should have known better than to begin with its mention, but it was Tenley, really, who was still on his mind, and so, of course, the first word out of his mouth was *home*. Some Spartans aren't superstitious. But others refuse to test chaos: John Boy with the baby face and blond hair that got him his name, or Sergeant Caldwell, the transfer from St. Paul whose entire fire team exploded around him. Their bodies were like trees—that's what he told Miller. Like dead trees that fell on top of him and protected him from the blasts, and then St. Francis found him. Haunted him with prayers. Caldwell's language skills will be an asset on this mission, at least, though none of the Spartans are formally trained in Arabic, Pashtun, or Dari. They'll make do.

"Now, the brief..." Miller repeats, a practiced steadiness. He's got the voice. The one that makes them believe. Likely, some have heard about the media fallout, but there's a lot more they don't know and are better off not knowing. At least Miller is confident that not a single Spartan disputes his own value. Spartan makes them better than they are on their own. Miller has seen as much.

He also takes confidence in this: that beyond Spartan, beyond the military, beyond all of it, are Tenley and Cissy. He thinks of them with every stomp of his boot heels, every gulp of water from his Camelback, every needling grain of sand that cuts his concentration, every cell, every moment leaning closer to them. In this way, he's become something altogether separate from himself: a leader who gets the killing done, keeping silent vigil for life all the while.

Yak rejoins the circle and sets the Kevlar on Reynolds's head, smooshing the mohawk with pleasure. Miller scans the Spartans and nods with reassurance. Not a liability among them—save, perhaps, Private Rachmann—and here, Miller's eyes pause on that stubborn, red patch of eczema staining Rachmann's neck like a hickey.

Supreme and Reynolds stifle laughter.

"It's not what you think, fuckers," says Rachmann. "It won't go *away*."

He scratches impatiently. Rachmann is Rock—as in, he fights as *dumb as a*—and what Rock lacks in battlefield skills, he overcompensates for in par-baked insights that trigger a tightening of Miller's jaw. And, of course, Rock knew what Miller was like before Mercer died. Happy-go-lucky, one might have even said. At ease. "I can't get the skin cream I need until we go home..." Rock continues.

"At least you got a home you want to go back to," says Corporal DeShawn Taylor. He punctuates the sentiment with the smack of Ice Breakers Peppermint Gum—Spartan's favorite flavor. Taylor is average looking, but his superhero shoulders and narrow waist lend a look that begs to differ. "Couldn't they give us all a waiver from the recession?"

Taylor pauses to blow a bubble. Reynolds jabs his finger into the goo, and it pops.

"That's it. That's my platform. I'm running for office when I get back. You all better vote for me too. Got it?"

Taylor folds his arms across his chest and leans against the side of his Humvee. A fat clump of dirt drops from the undercarriage onto the ground. He shakes his head. "Fuckin' foreclose on my ass while I'm fighting the hajis. Man, that's bigger than bullshit. That's like... *T. rex shit.*"

"Dude. Prehistoric dooks," Reynolds ponders.

"I still have two years," a small voice breaks from behind Folson's meaty stance. It's Huang. Bless him. Barely old enough to vote. The youngest of five brothers. Doctors, engineers, and then Huang. Kevlar bobbing over his eyes, a constellation of pimples across his cheeks. Miller has always felt an affinity for this one, like rooting for the underdogs in college football. It would be great, wouldn't it, to see the kid surprise them all? But most Spartans aren't timid like Huang.

As if on cue, Romero swaggers toward the center of the circle, a wide-framed walk. "Yeah, Huang, me too. That means two years left taking ROE from the army brass that ties our hands behind our backs while we're outside the wire with targets on our chests," he says.

Sparco, Romero's typically silent fire team buddy, offers a fist bump in agreement. Taylor blows another bubble with his gum and nods.

"We'll get to those ROE in a minute," Miller says, then clams up.

"Supreme," Romero says, "got any more chew?"

Romero folds and unfolds his deeply tanned arms. Starfish patches of lighter flesh flash across the insides of his elbows, proof he has spent more daylight hours with his arms bent holding a carbine at the ready than not. Supreme spits into his Mountain Dew bottle, then tosses a pack of Skoal across the huddle. Romero catches it deftly.

"'Where there is hatred, let me sow love…Where there is injury, pardon…'" Caldwell mutters to no one in particular, and Miller sees it—the way Caldwell's face appears glassy, distant. He might as well be reciting the Pledge of Allegiance or a Dr. Seuss book—anything, really, to help the young recruit stay steady enough to finish the tour.

"All right Spartans…Mission Aqua details."

Miller opens a map of Oruzgan Province and spreads it across the wide hood of his Humvee, affectionately known as Bean Curd. "We've got one task left, so let's finish strong. You're all familiar with the NGO aid trucks trying to get through Tarin Kowt and deliver to refugee camps in Kandahar, right?"

Yak and Taylor nod, following the tip of Miller's fingers as he draws a long line between the two cities. Huang crouches behind them with a please-sign-my-hall-pass look twitching across his face. Miller's remote control is working now, the mute button unlocked.

"Here's the main supply route," he continues. "These narrow enclaves to the west are working against the NGOs."

He points again, this time to the Imar Valley, where satellite imagery shows a network of makeshift pedestrian paths and traces of roadbed as faint as an erased pencil mark. "The NGOs are getting ambushed out of valleys like this one, and they're not armored, so they're turning around in droves. Without the NGOs reaching those villages, more civilians will take up arms with the insurgency in order to survive. Some of these villages might be harboring the gunmen or even the Taliban overseeing valley operations."

He's got them. Their devotional focus like a die he rolls between his palms and tosses for good luck. Each mission, he bets his life on the outcome. They all do. He steps away from the map and looks at his men. "Our task tomorrow is humanitarian, Spartans. For our last hayride, we'll be delivering water to the village of Imar."

The circle tightens around the map, and Miller backs away. The Spartans study. Yak adds further observations, his long arms and torso a convenient advantage for holding court over such a large spread of land across the map. He counsels the men that it's going to be a lengthy ride, but that's no excuse to get sun-slack. Supreme passes his Skoal around for good measure, though Huang declines. Rock stands to the side, trying to disassemble a perfectly functioning tripod for his semi-automatic weapon—for what tactical reason, Miller can't fathom. A screw slips from Rock's hands and rolls toward Miller's boots. He kicks it back to Rock and shakes his head. Better to focus on the huddle, that buzz of energy now balling around them. It smells familiar, hopeful, like home away from home. These men have completed every task Miller set before them. They're at their best working face to face with civilians, humanitarian efforts a lot closer to what these guardsmen envisioned upon enlisting in the first place.

Yak wraps up the brief, and everything angles true and crisp through the expectant air. For a moment, Miller forgets what the military has taken from him. Forgets about risks and advantages. About dollars and leaders, contracts and deceit. Just look at Spartan, chomping at the bit and ready as ever; Miller loves each inexplicable molecule that makes this moment.

He flips back the pile of papers stacked on his clipboard and steals a glance at the photo of Tenley and Cissy. Their toothy smiles have been pressed onto the clipboard with clear packing tape ever since Miller's toughest tour back in '06. The Korengal Outpost. Those mountains that almost swallowed him whole. In a flash, the Afghan elder's face comes to mind. A hooked nose. Hennaed beard trailing halfway down the elder's chest. Dark wrinkles, folds of skin as tight and weathered as the hills themselves. Then there was Corporal Mercer. The headache at the base of Miller's skull rolls around like a loose grenade.

"It's kind of hard to get it up for this one, don't you think?"

Folson peers over Miller's shoulder at the clipboard. A dark bruise encircles his left eye from the night before where a metal clasp on the corner of the flag whipped across his face.

"Folson?" Miller says and tucks the clipboard under his arm.

"No, not the photo LT. Not your wife. The mission. Busting our asses fifty kilometers across the desert to do something one heli drop could handle in a few hours?"

"You know as well as I do that we can see better when we're on the ground," he says. He wonders what cocktail Folson's on today. "Our eyes and ears out there are priceless. Depending on what we find, the guys coming in after us will be better for it."

"I'd just as soon stay back."

"I'd just as soon see you straightedged by 0530 hours tomorrow morning, Folson. We've been over this. You're good with the kids. This mission has your name all over it."

Miller's headache pulses slightly, like a tiny heart lodged in the back of his brain. It's an all too familiar twinge that, within hours, may overtake his entire state of mind. Or not. This one could still simmer down.

"Humanitarian, my ass."

Miller sets his eyes like a drill bit on the target of Folson's face. "Folson, there's a war going on. A platoon you owe your life to. We've been given orders. Spartans move the way we're told."

Folson packs his shoulders defensively around his ears. "So those horseshit suitcoats change our ROE, and you're just going to lie down and take it?"

Yak looks up from the huddle, and Miller knows he's heard the fight in Folson's tone. Huang stares from the wings, curious. Yak says a few more words to the group, then peels away and begins a calculated approach at Folson's back.

"Are you done, Folson? Because the last time I checked, I had a platoon that backs me up and that I'm proud to lead and—"

"You'd rather send us outside the wire with our dicks swinging and our hands over our eyes than stand up for us!" Folson says. And it's that last part, really, that is so grossly out of line. Miller can only square his shoulders and wait until Folson's steam runs out. His face glows unnaturally pink, the same color as strawberry jam stuffed into an MRE. "Hearts and minds. *Hah!* If I'm going to be helping somebody's kids, I'd rather be helping my own, *thankyouverymuch!*"

Yak stands only inches from Folson's back now, at the ready. Miller focuses on Folson's black eye. The way the puffy flesh rings the blue cornea. The way the edge of the bruise already yellows, but the center looks dark, pitted. It's a black hole, a dark place, a trap he won't fall into. Miller starts to walk away, intent on addressing the Spartans with the remaining mission details, then there's a quick shuffle of boots. He ducks low, dodging a fist, and that quickly, Yak latches onto Folson from behind, locking him into a full nelson.

Miller regains his balance. "You're kidding, right?" he says. His voice is so calm, he's sure it has the effect of an insult. Calm—at a time like this? Yes. Precisely. Calm and a thousand other things that Folson, apparently, is not. "You're seriously out of line, PFC. I've got better men to deal with. Most of the time, you're one of them."

He turns on his heels and walks away. Not a stomp. Not a scuff. Just the cool gait of a leader who knows the right words at the right time. Somehow, Miller has regained that much, *thankyouverymuch*.

"Spar-*tans*!" he calls.

Synchronized, the men turn and face their platoon leader. Yak wrestles Folson from the staging area to cool off.

"It'll be ok, Folson," says Huang, but his voice sounds as small as a pigeon's.

"Fuck off, gook."

"Hey—"

"This is what we're doing, gentlemen," Miller says. "This is why we've been brought together. The people in Imar need us. We're going to be there for them."

The men look eager, not at all swayed by Folson's show. They're not ready for battle so much as they're ready to redeem themselves. Reynolds with his mohawk of avoidances. Supreme and Romero—their stuffed cheeks and brawn-like masks that say "do or die." Taylor and Sparco sidelining the war as if it won't notice them. Caldwell digging a fast grave with St. Francis. Rock with his need to prove. John Boy just trying to keep up. Huang, tiny in a world built for everyone but him. Even Folson, with his victim mentality. Of course, Yak is as cool as ice, a soldier unto himself. Still, all eleven of his men have something they'd like to shake off. This is what Miller wants. He needs them to start fighting for this. After Aqua, they're going to go home, and after that, the only thing left to fight for will be themselves.

"Are you with me?" Miller asks.

"Hoo-ah," the Spartans chorus.

"Good. Let's screw this hog till she squeals."

And with that, the war is theirs. They will fight it for these reasons. Not for freedom. Not for politics. Not for God or country or trucking companies. But for the individual things. The needles of hurt across a spectrum of life.

9

Weapons of Potential Destruction

By nightfall, the bunkhouse sounds like a schizophrenic chorus of snores and guffaws. Some soldiers PlayStation the night away, crammed into rooms with Doritos crunched onto the floor, trash cans overflowing with tissue wads of sandy phlegm. Others twitch and yelp through a litany of dreams. Half-lidded gasps let loose into the night: *Take cover! Goddamn raghead. No…FUCK YEAH! I'm sorry.* Some read or write silently, tucked into stories. Others wait with held breath for a roommate to nod off, earning rare privacy for a midnight session of salami slapping. It's a wonder anyone sleeps at any hour, but Miller's saving grace is this—a bunkroom all to himself these last few weeks. His roommate was sent home on a cancer pass: the mother—her brain tumor the size of a kiwi and unresponsive to chemo.

Miller lies on his bed in the near darkness, the headache arcing like a rainbow up the back of his neck, across the center of his forehead. It ends with a pot of gold at the bridge of his nose. If only. More like a pot of coals, and with each breath he feels the heat rise. The coals sizzle. Smoke fills his head, which threatens to implode. He feels shaky and spent, if not also eager to fulfill these final orders of this tour. He hears a soldier clod down the hallway and enter the room across the hall. Somewhere through the sheetrock, another moans into his sheets. It's almost enough to make Miller hard, the embarrassment of which he long ago forgave himself. Who's to say hearing another man cry out isn't just as thrilling as the thought of Miller's own rigid potential? Though it's not that, exactly, so much as being able to let go enough in the first place. Something Miller hasn't experienced for longer than he wants to admit. His headache glows and smolders, glows and smolders, and he can't help but wonder what it all means.

How had Miller missed it? That flash of righteous indignation across Folson's face when he questioned Miller's leadership. Miller should have headed Folson off at the first mention of the distance they had to drive. Used to be, a soldier would beg to go outside the wire. At least Miller's soldiers. Always the team builder. Always the guy whose platoon seemed tightest, inseparable as Siamese twins in a Mason jar. Recalling it now, Miller isn't even certain who lunged first. Later, after Yak sent Folson to clean the shitters, too-proud Rachmann informed Miller of the real mess. Folson's wife had instant messaged him: *P.S. I'm asking for full custody.*

Miller gets out of bed and shoves his body into clothes. Outside, the air feels as good as it gets this time of year in Oruzgan Province. A humid eighty degrees with a slight breeze, the hum of FOB Copperhead droning in the background. Copperhead's been on blackout in the past, but not during Miller's time on base. No such thing as complete darkness or silence now, and by tonight's first glance, the FOB provides little relief. Security lights cast yellow halos across the sand. Generators offer their pitch-perfect hum. Doors slam, engines rev, tools clank, and dogs bark at the fence near the dumpsters. Miller walks to the far end of the FOB and sees a platoon just returning from a mission, no doubt ricocheting between amped and exhausted. Behind their convoy, a late-arriving supply truck is waved through the gates, and Miller gets a brief look at the driver: an English-speaking Afghan, talking with the guards as if this were just another shift break. Meantime, Gawri has been taking a cut for every vehicle that moves through. Probably has enough money to install a sprinkler system in his courtyard and host elaborate parties with guards like Unibrow, effeminate boys stationed like wall art just waiting to be adored. But wasn't Miller—in his own way—getting paid to keep the war machine moving along as well? He'd never felt so simultaneously powerful and powerless. He had access to some of the most effective technology and machinery history had ever seen, yet there were still things the Americans couldn't touch: tribalism, honor codes, generations of loyalties, the devotion of suicide bombers. Gawri, for all the needs he routinely presented to Miller, had, in fact, maintained an upperhand in Oruzgan all along.

The driver waves to the guard and slowly pulls his rig around the back of the dining facility. Light pours from the dish room where a few custodians attend to the moon dust coating everything from silverware to door hinges. Along a small outbuilding, Miller spies a small huddle of soldiers near the entrance of a storage cooler, perhaps readying to pull a prank or steal some grub.

He peels off the main pathway and moves toward the Ammo Holding Area. FOB Copperhead uses three inconceivably large storage lockers to inventory and house captured enemy ammunition. Over the course of his nine-month tour, Miller has seen them fill to capacity. He walks alongside the first, running his fingers across the corrugated edges. The fifteen-foot-high steel side casts a long shadow. At the end of the row, Miller rounds the corner and turns again, pacing down the aisle. Walls rise on either side, radiating heat from the day. Darkness takes on a deeper tone. The structures are supposedly safe, though any succession of RPGs lobbed on target would surely set off the munitions inside. The containers have been slated for removal for months, yet no one seems attendant. Miller stops in the middle of the row and faces the side of one structure. Slowly, he raises his knuckles and raps the steel. A metallic pinging calls back, barely audible. He raps harder this time, as if knocking on a castle door. Sound echoes as vibration travels through the steel, into the trapped air.

"Anybody home?" he whispers. "Anybody?"

Further along rests a significantly smaller Conex shipping container set aside for rifles. Miller leaves the dark alley and traipses to the Conex, settling onto the ground. He leans his back against the door and starts in on his lower lip, nibbling a new flap of dried skin. He wouldn't mind getting his hands on the rifle collection, claiming a few trophies for his firing range back home. He spits out a piece of skin and thinks about Folson. Miller is too smart to believe that his own return home will be smooth. But if he and his men aren't getting it right here, on duty, they're not going to get it right at home either. Miller has experienced enough not-getting-it-right to know. You can't leave loose ends untied on tour, then act surprised when they trail you all the way home and tighten like a noose.

Overhead, the stars appear to fade in and out, brightness waffling through the amber glow of the FOB. A pair of soldiers passes the holding area a dozen meters from Miller's perch but take no notice of him. He doesn't mind being unseen here, though back home, the experience grates on him. "Do you even need me when I'm gone?" he remembers asking Tenley after their argument at the park. It hurt to say it. Her reply stung more. "We manage."

That tone—so clipped and resentful. As though his wife and daughter were already living the way they'd have to live if he were dead. When Miller realized they were functioning like binary stars without him, anything he offered when he was home felt peripheral. Unnecessary, more like, and though Tenley hadn't used *that* word, it became a sticking point for Miller.

"Cissy will be half-grown," Tenley had said. Their daughter was napping in the downstairs bedroom with a cool cloth against the goose egg on her forehead. Miller and Tenley stood in the hallway upstairs, facing off. "Half-grown and half a family without her daddy here. Goddamnit, Nathan, what do you want? To be here or not?"

Was it her frown or the way she sounded so ungrateful that hurt the most? He wanted her to see him as capable, of course, and the more he seemed to prove himself in his career, the more it seemed to cost him at home. But he didn't have words for that trade-off yet, and besides, she is his wife. Couldn't she see how she and Cissy were at the center of all that want? That they always had been? In a flash, he crossed the living room, eyes set on the front door. He could already feel Tenley reeling away. Cissy too. The way a jump plane becomes so suddenly small as you fall back, fumbling for the parachute release. The way it's startling how easy it is to let yourself fall out of that plane in the first place.

"Maybe you'd be better off without me here, if that's how you feel about it," he said. "You and Cissy both. Just stick with the wives' club."

He knew that last part would get her. Tenley had tried to connect with the Guard's support networks, but he could tell then that she didn't quite fit in. Miller felt responsible somehow, as if his service meant more than just a missing husband and father; apparently, it screwed up Tenley's chances for friendship too.

He zipped his Carhartt vest to his chin and reached into the coat closet for his rifle and ammo. He didn't know where he was going. It didn't matter. The hollers were so impossibly maze-like, even Forest Service guys got turned around sometimes. Outside, he stomped around the house and crossed the yard. He didn't look back.

It wasn't long before he started climbing. Their two-acre lot was mostly slope anyway, and from there, Miller quickly crossed onto public lands, a Pisgah National Forest boundary marker rusted onto a tree and circled with red spray paint. It reminded him of an exit wound from a bullet. He picked up his pace. Cool air bit at his fingertips. Alert, he scanned the mixed hardwoods for anything out of the ordinary. Occasionally, he looked down, letting his eyes trace the narrow game trail he'd picked up. Flecks of mica glittered atop the soil. He used to find hope in that, the way mica winked at him with promise. But how could a man used to endless Indiana pasture relax surrounded by land like this? Pin-holed, creek-jambed. Ridge after ridge stretching down from high peaks to form a series of cuts deep enough to suggest the whole mountain range had gotten into a bar fight.

Time passed. An hour? Probably longer. He'd followed contours along the hills surrounding their property, the house dipping in and out of sight as he traced a creek to its source or shimmied under outcroppings. Heading loosely back toward home, Miller stumbled upon a scar of land open to the sunlight, an anomaly amidst these peaks. The space would make a perfect firing range, and he made note of his surroundings in hopes of finding the spot again. The wind hissed, and a few territorial squirrels chattered, quarreling over their middens. He considered targeting them but thought better. He had never believed in killing for its own sake. During Officer Candidate School, he quickly realized what a man believed could be far from what a man did. Across the clearing, an old hemlock had fallen across the ridge, its trunk the width of a man resting sideways on his shoulder, as if taking an afternoon nap. Fading sunlight illuminated the back of the decaying tree, its centerline stripped to the cambium so that it almost glowed.

He loaded his rifle and took aim. The wood sprayed.

Echoes of the single shot sang through the hollers below. He loved that. The way the world always felt doubly silent afterward, a sensation strong enough to snap him into clarity before tuning out again. Tenley would have heard that shot and begun to worry. He took his time. Loaded another round.

Firing without reply was a luxury lost on most civilians. The crack and pause. The power and suspension. If he repeated this action, maybe he could normalize himself. Maybe both Millers—the one serving and the one quietly watching—could reconcile and let the silence feel true. He fired again and shouldered the recoil. On the other side of his vision, The Korengal Outpost waited, vivid as reality: There sat Shrouder, strapping flea collars around his ankles to keep away the itches. There sat Babyfat, writing his blood type on his combat boots with black Sharpie. Miller could even smell the outpost. How piss and sweat and salt-stiffened DCUs mixed with the hot air, pureeing the musk of war. He loaded and fired another round. Felt the silence that followed. Braced himself for the interruption. Which flashback would hit him this time? Specialist Martin's Humvee, the IED that carved up his fire team like so many sides of beef. Miller had to carry severed limbs in a plastic bag over his shoulder and hand them off at the FOB morgue. Afterward, he retched into the thirsty dirt.

So many unexpected indignities. So much gone wrong in the name of something right. So much red tape, hierarchy. But that moment in the meeting house with the elder—that was all Miller's. No one had told him to ignore his own conscience. He lost so much after that moment and admitted now that he struggled to trust himself to make the right decision ever since.

Don't fire. Let the man speak. He had heard the words as clearly in his mind as if he'd spoken them out loud. Heard them and fired at the elder anyway, marveling at the pink mist bursting into the air with the quickness of a popped balloon. That was the millisecond he could have acted quickly enough to save Mercer with, but he was too shocked by his own actions. And by the time he realized the imminent danger, Mercer had been killed. How could that same man sit down for dinner with his wife and child? How could he prove dependability? Capability? Tenley didn't know about Mercer or the elder. She'd never understand that by going to Tarin Kowt for one more tour, Miller was claiming his chance to lead again and get it right. How he believed that then, and only then, he could still come home to her. To whom he'd always thought he was.

Her question had been entirely fair: *What do you want?* Yet he couldn't even begin to open up. His absence while on tour caused problems—no denying it. But being home didn't seem to help either. He knew Tenley would have her arms crossed when he got back to the house, waiting for an answer, but he couldn't face her yet. Knew the gunshots would deeply unsettle her. But he couldn't get himself to move. He couldn't get himself to do anything.

Dusk fell into darkness, and Miller had not left the clearing. He had a vague sense that the house was within a 500-yard radius of the firing range; following the drainages downhill would get him where he needed to go eventually. It wasn't until the call of a barred owl pulling him from his trance that he actually began to walk. He put his rifle on safety and left the small clearing, bushwhacking through a rhododendron thicket, then following a seasonal drainage until he got oriented. He looked down on his house at the bottom of the holler, its porch light glowing, and realized how long he must have been gone. The forest was completely black.

He walked silently across his yard and pushed through the front door. A roasted chicken with lidded side dishes cooled on a set table. But it wasn't Tenley's husband or Cissy's father who ate dinner that night. Miller watched himself, a fiberglass skin held at arm's length from this untrusted thing within. He studied Tenley and Cissy as they chewed their food. He imitated them, forking bits of meat onto his tongue. He chewed to the rhythm of two syllables in his mind. *Mer-cer. Mer-cer.* It felt as if he were consuming himself bite by bite. Maybe if he called out, maybe if he screamed, Tenley and Cissy would be able to hear. *Mer-cer. Mer-cer.* Chicken skin and roasted potatoes slid down his throat. He took another bite. *Mer-cer. Mer-cer.* He'd promised he wouldn't close off like this anymore. He'd promised so much. *Mer-cer. Mer-cer.* Say it! But each time he tried, his voice curled back on itself, reverberating off that shell in a cacophony of sentiments that meant only one thing. He had to go back.

And here he is, a Conex full of weapons at his back. Not one Spartan has been sent home in a body bag. Not one has lost a limb under Miller's watch. Not one civilian has fallen at the end of his sights either. Not this time.

He rises to his feet and looks again at the ambient stars. He dusts off his camis and begins the slow walk back to the barracks. The supply truck has parked near a loading dock at the back of the chow hall. The steel holding containers rest behind him, leaded to the ground, but as Miller moves farther away, he believes he hears something tick—a gun cocked, a cell phone button pressed. He can almost see it. The whole goddamn holding area exploding into the next galaxy, the next lifetime. But no. There's only this: the low-level hum of the FOB in the middle of the night and his own heart beating its way toward tomorrow morning, toward home. He heads back to his barracks despite the suspicious tugging from behind, as if he's tied to an undertow of magnets. He struggles forward, but he will not look back.

Day Three

10

Caught

There's always a moment before Rahim opens his eyes each morning when his body forgets its habitual cinching down. His breathing doesn't feel as if something inside of him is constantly drilling for oil. In that moment—before he fumbles for clothing, before stale air stirs through the room—his limbs feel lighter than clouds. Each breath cycles easily into the next. And sometimes, like right now, he's gifted with a soft memory: Aaseya's warm wetness, her smell from the night before. He parts his lips and opens his eyes, but the moment is gone.

Why must each day feel like falling behind? Rahim imagines the sun cracking, full over the horizon, moving double time toward the middle of the sky. His heart pounds in his chest, unappeased. There's only one way out. Work and work and work before his circumstances self-destruct, before anyone—himself included—traces those dollars back to their source. He leaps from bed, taking the stairs two at a time. And in the alley, he sees this—a boy.

Unforgivably thin.

Curved into himself, almost fetal.

Tangled hair as thick as a rug.

At least four years old. Maybe six. His body is frail, almost impossible, and Rahim is immediately struck with the thought that the boy is dead.

He bends down and holds his palm near the boy's mouth, waiting for breath. He studies the child further. Clearly orphaned, half-starved. Cut feet, useless clothing. The boy may as well walk into a meeting of mujahedeen generals and offer himself, head to toe, for the taking. Oh, they would like this one—his clear face and wide-set eyes, his remarkably small waist. They'd pluck him like fruit from the streets, there and then gone. But here it is— evidence of life as the boy's breath moves steady and dry across Rahim's palm. He ought to spare him, to save him from such a sick fate. He presses his hand over the boy's mouth. Feels the cracked lips and hot breath. Such easy sleep. Such peaceful quiet. He could make it stay this way forever.

The boy stirs, wrinkling his brow, and it's too much for Rahim to bear—even more to take away. What's gotten into him?

He pulls his hand back, ashamed, and jogs quickly onto the street.

Years ago, he had been sold out of poverty to a wealthy merchant recruiting along the poorer outskirts of Tarin Kowt. A small portion of the proceeds were sent to Rahim's family with the promise that their son was being housed, fed, educated, and even featured professionally for respected generals in Kabul. While the mujahedeen generals feasted from platters of saffron rice and lamb shank, fingering fried crepes or mutton stew into their mouths, chasing it all down with cups of frothy buttermilk, Rahim and the other dancing boys took center stage. Later, each boy learned which general he had been auditioning for and just what kind of sexual favors that man preferred. Why wouldn't he save a boy from that? Then again, why hadn't he saved himself?

Within minutes, Rahim arrives at the schoolhouse at the far end of town. He can't say exactly how he got there—walking, surely—but his mind had carried him elsewhere. He tries to calm himself, tries not to think about that tiny man in his gut, the one who never stops pounding his fists. He steps through the schoolhouse door, into the large classroom. The shady air chills him immediately. The room smells like old socks, worse, like ashes. A forgotten cave. It's hard to imagine children here, hopeful hands raised high, a teacher pointing to equations on the chalkboard. Insects dart across the floor, as skittish as Rahim felt the first time he entered this quietly minted Taliban headquarters. Fighters' laughter filters downstairs, tinny and typical. Most are high on hash. They've come from afar, borders Rahim will never cross. The infelicities of his life just a freckle on the broad body of war. These are not the same generation of fighters he remembers, not the Afghan Taliban he'd seen at work under Khohistani as a boy. This time around, it seems, hiring locals is simply one business transaction in a series of bigger deals. Rahim's insignificance ought to ease the clenching below his waist, but it does not.

Four fighters wait in a small classroom on the second floor. Rahim has met the leader once before. Obaidullah—uncharacteristically tall, chin like the tip of an arrow, a missing pinky finger on his right hand. His black robes dangle thinly, several inches shy of the ground, and the dark color paints his face in contrast, inexplicably pale. His *keffiyeh* is meticulously wrapped, mirroring his persona. Clean, calculated. The other fighters squat along a row of cushions against the back wall, fingering clumps of fresh bread into their mouths.

"Badria's already come and gone," says Obaidullah.

"Without me?" Rahim asks.

"Allah rewards the eager in heaven. But you know that, don't you?" Obaidullah smiles as he speaks but not out of friendliness.

"I only mean that it's less trouble for you when Badria and I get instructions at the same time."

Rahim's stomach tightens, sending a slight quiver down to his bowels. He blushes, as though the others can see his discomfort. Moments like this, it's hard to imagine a world as beautiful and compelling as the one Hafiz portrayed. "I can come earlier tomorrow."

Obaidullah shrugs. He runs the four fingers of his right hand through the long, loose end of his *keffiyeh* as if playing with strands of hair. "That'll be fine," he says. "I have plenty of work. But bring your sons with you tomorrow. If they focus as well as you do, they'll be good workers."

"I don't have any sons," Rahim says. "And besides, I can work four times as much as any man. What do you have for me and Badria today? I'll leave now and catch up with him. He's slow, you know. Easily confused. He can't do much without me."

Obaidullah appears unmoved.

Rahim walks to the window and scans the loop road beyond the edge of town, looking for his fellow brickmaker. Not that they've made bricks recently. How long now—four weeks? Five? Soon after their first chance meeting with the Taliban, when the fighters made their offer, Obaidullah checked on Rahim and Badria during a brief rainstorm and found them soaked and sopping as dogs. He laughed, mocking their brickmaking. "Enough is enough," he finally told them. "If no one comes down this road for you to hassle, it means our work has been effective. You don't have to bother with this petty labor in the meantime. Your bricks should be proof enough that nothing here ever lasts."

Rainwater ran down their bodies in rivulets and doubled Rahim's vision. Their clothing draped across their bodies like old bags. Obaidullah nodded at their sorry efforts. The bricks—half-formed and scattered along the banks of the creek—had already melted back into the desert as if by magic. For a moment then,

Obaidullah appeared almost godlike, a wavering shadow amidst the downpour as the rain slowed. Rahim envied the assured way the leader carried himself, the steady path that seemed to spread beneath his feet. Within minutes, the desert transformed into curtains of white steam, swallowing Obaidullah into the hills. The sand crackled, breathing, already dry.

Obaidullah confers with his three fighters now and returns to Rahim with instructions. "Badria will be waiting for you at the main bridge where the road leads out of the valley. He knows today's plan. If you really think he's slow, why do you want to work with him?"

"I've spent enough years working alone," says Rahim. He'll say whatever he thinks will end the conversation quickly and get him back to the street, back to the open arms of the desert. It's strange, loving this thing that taunts you with its insufficiency; most days, the desert is the only constant, as dependable as a dear friend. "Badria's amusing. That's all. And besides, he's got five sons. Any man blessed enough to have five sons is worth spending time with. Maybe his luck will come my way."

Obaidullah frowns. "The sands are shifting. We'll see a lot of movement today. I'll be too busy with my men to be bothered by anything on your end. Understand?"

"Yes," Rahim nods. He couldn't care less what Obaidullah does or doesn't do with his fighters. In due time, he imagines, the desert will probably swallow Imar entirely. Shape itself anew. Maybe even cast him and Aaseya into a different life with deeply buried pasts and futures so far from wartime that the world, as he experiences it now, will cease to exist. Soon enough, he'll leave Imar. Soon enough, he'll take Aaseya to a Western doctor in Tarin Kowt, even as far as Kabul, and he'll get her woman's problem fixed—whatever it is, this thing that won't start making babies—and then, there, with clarity and a new home, they'll start a family. She'll give him a son. Her demands will be quieted. With all of this, it's possible Rahim could eventually say he lives in the world Hafiz describes.

He catches himself. Who could be so foolish? Afghans have fought for all of time. Even not fighting ends up being a kind of fight. Hafiz's world seems as impossible as a flood and almost as dangerous to believe in. What man has ever thanked *hope* for his survival? It's the hard skills—the well-aimed rifle, the callused hands, the savvy negotiations—that make a man into what he must become.

At the window, a slight breeze lifts the lapels of Rahim's dark gray vest, bringing with it a thin cloud of dust. Bells jingle from a shop door on the street below and a man enters the cigar store. He steps away from the window and walks across the room, gazing out the back of the classroom windows toward the overflow trailings of the bazaar. In the distance, he notices a few nomads huddled around a cooking fire.

"There's a delivery into the valley expected today," Obaidullah says. "Doctors Without Borders—red insignias—two Humvees and a white van. I've explained this all to Badria. It's your job to make them turn back."

"Just deterred?"

Obaidullah nods. "Anything more will bring too much attention."

"I should go," Rahim steps away from the window.

A younger fighter from the side of the room stands. He moves awkwardly, the way a lunatic might approach a child, a slight limp each time his left foot touches down. He waves Rahim forward with a gesturing hand, but Rahim stays put. The soldier worries him slightly, that look of insane confidence plastered across his face the same way a corpse's expression pulls tightly into a smile days after death, heat bloating its features into clownish proportions.

"Look here," the fighter says. He shifts on his feet, wincing slightly. He opens his palms and taps a modest pile of powder onto his hand. Opium, so fine it appears grated from sheaths of silk. The fighter raises his palm and brings the stash to eye level, but Rahim declines, shaking his head. He glances nervously at the door. Even at forty, he's never seen opium so loosely offered, as though this soldier expects Rahim to lick poison from his palms. Rahim will take their intel. He'll take their money. He'll borrow their weapons and follow orders. But he won't ever be so faithful as to offer the Taliban his mind. For so many years, there's only been this—survival, choices no one wants to make, the warming sun as constant as his own breath.

> How did the rose ever open its heart
> and give to this world
> all its beauty?

Hafiz couldn't have known how the world would change.

When Rahim works for Obaidullah, he aims at the dirt. The sideview mirrors. Tires, bumpers. Any vehicle suggesting non-local commerce is a chance for five more dollars. It's not a question of loyalty or consequences. How many more years will the Americans keep up the fight anyway? The fighter limps toward Rahim, and there it is again—a zing of pain across Rahim's gut like a snakebite. He clenches his stomach and lunges out the door. Shuffling down the dank stairwell, he leans against the wall for support, feet falling quickly in place down the steps. The rose took what the desert could offer. The rose took it and opened its heart anyway. He reaches the bottom step and careens into the main classroom. Rows of abandoned desks stare at him like soldiers at attention. He drops his pants and squats. Shit pours in a stream between his legs. He closes his eyes, gripping the cool metal legs of a desk for balance.

Rahim finds Badria waiting beneath the shade of the bridge, its wobbly piers and half-rotted wood. Most drivers just plow through the dry creek bed instead of risking the bridge. Makeshift routes crisscross the sand, joining again in the tight valley. Badria lifts himself from the ground in a huff.

"Gimme some help?" he hands Rahim their buckets and brickmaking supplies—just a cover.

"Where are the weapons?" asks Rahim.

Badria dusts himself off and joins his partner along the road, arranging their supplies for easy transport. He's a short, somehow well-fed man, also in his forties. "I hid them," says Badria. "Obaidullah said to be especially alert today. I think the Americans are coming, but he wouldn't say, and then when I got here to the bridge, I saw a sitting magpie."

"The Americans? But…" Rahim trails off. He's never met an Afghan more full of suspicions than Badria. Making bricks, so little was at stake. Working for the Taliban, quite the opposite. Then again, maybe Badria is more in the know than Rahim once thought. He doesn't like the idea of a work partner playing favorites with Obaidullah. They get their orders and do their work. They go home. So far, it's been as straightforward as the passage of time and, suspicions or otherwise, in the past week, he and Badria harassed enough vehicles out of the valley to line their pockets with greenbacks. More than two months of brick wages earned in a fraction of the time.

"You know what the magpie means."

"Yeah, yeah. A message is coming to you. You're right, Badria. Here's your message: I don't have any energy to waste on your logic. Where are the weapons?"

"Over there," he points to a long tangle of shrubs and struggling trees at the base of a rocky upslope. Badria waddles off the road, and Rahim follows. The two men drop to their knees and begin digging and lifting, moving aside the mound of sand and sticks. Rahim reaches the weapons first, tugging the burlap sack by its end and hoisting it out of the ground. The sand feels cool deeper down, and for a moment, he considers fending off work. Surely the aid trucks aren't running early.

Badria picks up one of the Kalashnikovs. "I think seeing the magpie on the bridge means we're going to get our message from the road today. I think it means success."

"Inshallah," Rahim says, half-heartedly.

"No! I know it for certain," Badria stabs the spade of his shovel into the ground. "Just look at the sky! I can feel it."

"Uh-huh," Rahim pushes his cart along the two-track and laughs. "And I can feel that when we return to the village tonight, there'll be a feast waiting…an entire goat roasted in our honor."

"Mock me if you want," says Badria. "I've been praying. This morning, I woke to an alert feeling in the air," he raises his nose as if catching a scent.

"Maybe it's the clouds," says Rahim. They step into a large shadow spread across the road. The men stop to enjoy the anomaly, a dark cloth of momentary cool. Rahim tilts his chin skyward. "How long has it been since we've felt this—a month?"

"Nearly," says Badria.

Rahim studies the clouds, white puffs dotting an otherwise azure sky, their shadows like tattoos across the desert. Next to him,

Badria reaches down and presses his fingertips into the shady dirt, testing its temperature.

"Still holds the heat, though," he says. "It's always holding something. I can feel it."

They continue walking. Here, a small ghaf tree. There, a few spindly shrubs. Shell casings piled like anthills. The occasional heap of tattered belongings abandoned by nomads. It's all home. It's all a blessing. It's the only place, really, where the elements come together and remind Rahim there's something larger than despair and impossible decisions. Whatever that thing is, it infuses the air as much as the sunlight itself.

After a few kilometers, they wheel their carts and buckets over the ruts at a dip in the land. There, leaning into both downhill shoulders of the road, they've built their foxholes. Rahim settles into the hole and lies on his stomach, perpendicular to the two-track that's a few meters upslope. The hole is awkward but tremendously effective—this their best ambush spot yet, shielding his presence from oncoming vehicles. He stretches from head to toe and flattens out, then twists his upper body slightly so he can properly aim his rifle, ready to target anyone who gets too close. The pitfall is not being able to see the closest section of road over the berm without raising himself nearly out of the foxhole push-up style, then back down to safety.

Within an hour, the sound of moving vehicles punctures the silence. Rahim presses himself upward—the gesture has already become second nature—and steals a quick glance along the ruts. Three vehicles dot the horizon.

"It looks like all Humvees, but that's not right," Rahim says. "These aren't our guys."

"Obaidullah said there'd be three Humvees," Badria calls.

"No. He said two Humvees and one white van, Badria. Red insignias."

"No," says Badria, "Obaidullah made it sound like the Americans were coming today, all the way from the base. Didn't you listen? He's got big plans. He said three Humvees. He said we can't screw up. That's what he told me."

The vehicles rumble forward, kicking up clouds of dust and obscuring the view. Rahim feels suddenly lightheaded, uncertain. He'd been so comfortable moments ago, basking in the sun, flicking sand flies across the ground. Badria can't be right. Not the Americans. Not yet. Rahim is suddenly aware of his own tongue in his mouth—fat, dry, parched.

"Stop dreaming," he calls to Badria. "The Americans haven't been here since you last pricked your wife."

The insult calms him. There's nothing to worry about. Badria simply misheard Obaidullah, whose instructions were clear.

"I pricked my wife sooner than you realize," Badria says. "Your wife, though, seems altogether unpricked."

"I don't have time for you," Rahim says. "Put your weapon on safety. We're not messing around with whatever this is. Not yet at least."

He fishes through the burlap sack for the binoculars, groping the edges of the bag, keeping his gaze pinned to the road. "Where are the binoculars? Do you have them?"

"I thought you were going to get them this morning. I've been busy. I've been working through the night."

"Good God, Badria, you're useless," Rahim tosses the empty sack aside and peers through the sights on his AK. Still no telling. "I can't see anything. We have to let them pass. We can always shoot from behind, if we need to."

"That won't work. It'll be too late."

"You've got it backwards, Badria. Please, just—" Rahim pounds his fist into the sand. A few grains peck into his eyes. He paws at his face but gets no relief. "Forget whatever Obaidullah said. Just look at the road. Look at it, and tell me what you see."

"I never forget what he says. Obaidullah knows how many mouths I have to feed at home. That's why he gives me more work. That's why he tells me things he'll never tell you. It's a fact— the Americans *are* coming. You can ask him yourself. I heard him debriefing his fighters about it this morning," the whine in Badria's voice is notable, nearly like a helpless child, and Rahim feels a sudden urge to disappear.

"Maybe you're right, but Obaidullah still wouldn't want us shooting them. Not here on the roadway. He expects us to keep a low profile. We're just pebbles in the road, Badria. We're just a decoy. Don't you see that?"

"He told me to shoot at a convoy of three. This is a convoy of three. How much more obvious could it be?"

"We are not taking pot-shots at Humvees filled with US soldiers," Rahim says. "We're two men. Not even two soldiers. I'm not shooting. I'm not starting anything with them, not unless I see they've got red insignias. Not unless I see a delivery truck. Have you gone completely mad?"

Rahim squints desperately at the road, eyes watering. A mirage of wavering blue and brown meet at the horizon. He inhales a tight breath. Any second now, the dust might settle, the wind might blow, his eyes might cooperate and reveal clarity. But he can't get any relief. The uncertainty rattles him, his mouth throbbing, his eyes blinking back the wetness of irritation and blurring his vision further.

Until now, Rahim believed riding it out in the middle would safeguard him, even through the uncertain climate of wartime.

Even through the early years of marriage to a troublesome wife. Such foolishness. Such disillusion. He squints again through the scope, relaxing his breathing and blinking hard. The dust shifts. The rumble grows louder, close, and there it is, unmistakable: one, two, three Humvees charging forward. "I can see," he shouts to Badria, then lowers his weapon and ducks further into his foxhole. "They're not our guys. Just let them pass!"

Badria fires a series of warning shots, marking well in front of the first vehicle.

"Don't shoot!" Rahim calls. "What are you doing?"

Never before has his partner seemed so beligerent, so blatantly numb to basic protocol.

"Well it worked at any rate. They stopped," Badria loads another magazine into the clip. "Besides, now we have to finish and retreat."

Rahim looks again at the horizon, his vision fully returned. One vehicle has its door open, figures moving about. "You'd better start praying we see a red insignia. Obaidullah will skin us if we can't verify."

"Let them come to us."

"Now you say it?" Rahim kicks the wall of his foxhole and lets out a grunt. "NOW? Badria, we might as well tie ourselves up and sit in the middle of the road. Is that what you want me to tell your sons your last moments looked like?"

"No," says Badria. His voice is quiet, a whimpering shrew. "No, I don't want my sons thinking about any of that. I'm a warrior. That's what they think, and it's proving to be true. The war's coming back to Imar and Obaidullah's going to be ready. If you had any sense, you'd let him prepare you too."

Rahim scoffs. "Badria, you can't actually believe Obaidullah's concerned about you. You were right. That magpie did have a

message. You, me, your sons waiting in line for the next war—
we can never pick a winning side. Obaidullah's got us all exactly
where he wants us—doing his dirty work and leaving him poised
to choose who leaves Imar alive and who doesn't. The difference is,
you don't see it for what it is, Badria. You're not going to win doing
his dirty work. I'm not either. The only way to win is to survive."

His words cascade outward. The silence that follows feels
thick, like failure. Whether or not Rahim's rant inspired a single
conscientious thought in Badria seems impossible to know, but
as he looks down at his own fingers, limp against the trigger now,
there's no denying that, at the very least, he's talked some truth
into himself. It's not so much being used as it is the senseless cycle,
the endlessness of it. The sun will rise and set, rise and set. His
entire life, he's loved it for its constancy. Now, he worries it might
be the ultimate deceit, all the trappings of war carried out beneath
its unwavering watch.

11

When You Assume…

The Spartan convoy rattles along the blurry streets of Tarin Kowt. Seven thousand pounds of armored steel are boxed around each fire team like a gigantic "fuck you" to shrapnel. To RPGs. To buried explosives. To AK bullets fired from the hip of a ratcheted insurgent. To hand grenades lobbed like rocks. To soccer balls, plastic bottles, clods of dirt, anything aimed out of hate, confusion, freedom, righteousness, boredom, or insult. Nacho Supreme drives Spartan 1, mirrored Oakleys leading the way as he steers toward the city limits with monster-truck determination. Yak rides shotgun. Caldwell and John Boy are crammed into the backseat. Behind Spartan 1, Miller rides shotgun in Bean Curd, the center vehicle of the convoy. Reynolds sits next to him, rat-a-tat-tatting his ADHD thumbs in constant percussion against the steering wheel. A bottle of water is jammed between his legs. Folson and Huang sit awkwardly in the backseat, the bully and the runt. At the end of the line, Sparco, Rock, Taylor, and Romero make up Spartan 3, and just like that, this offshoot of twelve men culled from the full platoon moves in line like a chain of magnets.

They all know the risks. No front lines in this war. Enemies, ambushes, and IEDs popping up willy-nilly, a stomach-churning child's game of anticipation.

It could be now. Or now.

Now.

Within minutes, the three Humvees turn south along the highway connecting Kabul and Kandahar and settle in at a modest thirty-five miles per hour. Out here, the world opens into two colors: blue sky and brown desert, but mostly, sky—so much it could smother. The sun offers no escape from its burning eye.

On a good day, Miller can decipher a line through the glare and the desert that constitutes the horizon, an end zone he's always driving toward. He'd like to sit back and enjoy this view. He'd like to stretch his legs, for that matter. Soak his tight muscles in a hot tub or eat a fully hydrated meal that didn't give him the shits. Muster the will for an ounce of actual conversation on the phone with his wife. But this morning is not a morning for joyriding, and when is it ever?

Miller cross-references the GPS with the map in his lap and the lay of the land. To the south, the first row of mountains descends into the valley, perpendicular to the highway. Spartan will skirt that range, then turn west into the Imar Valley where peaks rise like knives out of the desert. They're mere foothills relative to the epic Hindu Kush, but they top out at about 7,500 feet. Notable enough. With ranges on either side of the tiny village, Miller can see why the Taliban chose that area as a stronghold in the aftermath of 9/11. The land seems perfect for rumble-and-run warfare, small factions dropping into the village or hiding between the folds of steep slopes as necessary. He'd be pretty stoked himself if he could run and maneuver across this landscape with that kind of ease. Not to mention his own Appalachian backyard—if you could call rhododendron thickets and steep-cut outcroppings a backyard.

Half an hour outside the city limits, Miller squints at a dozen moving figures fifty meters to the west. "Ease up," he calls through his headset. The convoy drops a notch in speed. "Spartan 1, can you confirm what we're looking at?"

"Yes, Sir. Male civilian herding cattle. Over," Yak replies. He speaks with the ease of a Buddhist monk. It's a wonder to Miller how the first sergeant so perpetually holds steady—one of those admirably quiet men who never calls attention to himself. More than once, Yak has caught crucial details others missed: a gray wire snaking out of a pile of abandoned clothing on the side of the road; a tap stand stuffed with disassembled weaponry, hastily hidden before a raid; an insurgent disguised in a woman's burqa.

Miller brings the nomad into focus through his binoculars and confirms Yak's assessment. "All right then, let's halt and let the cattle finish crossing," Miller calls. "It'll only take a sec. Over."

"Roger that," Yak signs off.

The crackling headset tickles the inside of Miller's ear. The feeling bores inward and angles for the source of his headache.

"Makes me hungry," says Folson from the backseat. "I'd kill that haji for a bite of a Big Mac right now."

It's Folson's first comment since they crossed outside the wire, and Miller's suspicions are confirmed. Folson is indeed still pissed about being forced on Aqua. Never mind the chance to end his tour with a good deed. Apparently years of military training are nothing compared to a slew of angry messages from a soon-to-be-ex wife when it comes to fueling a soldier's go-get-'em.

"Doesn't Micky D's have, like, flavor scientists and stuff though? That shit ain't real beef, whatever it is. That's for sure. One Big Mac makes my asshole burn for two days," says Reynolds. He brings Bean Curd to a halt behind Spartan 1. Miller hands him the binoculars, and Reynolds squints through the lenses. "These motherfuckers are so skinny, it wouldn't be worth eating them," he tosses the binoculars into the backseat. "See for yourself."

"Ow," says Huang, rubbing his elbow. "Watch where you throw."

"Gimme those," says Folson. He shoves Huang in the shoulder and brings the view into focus through the binoculars. "What's the matter Huang? Got a boo-boo?"

Huang rubs his funny bone. "Maybe we should give that guy an MRE."

Folson scoffs. "I am *not* parting with my vanilla pound cake."

"How do you know you got the poundcake?" Reynolds asks.

"He always gets the poundcake," Miller says.

In front of them, a small calf breaks from the herd and trots toward Bean Curd.

"Brave little guy," Folson says and points. "My girls would love this. Jenny did 4-H last summer and couldn't stop talking about starting a farm."

Folson opens his window and extends a few, thick fingers toward the calf's forehead. A cloud of flies lifts from its fur, and Folson brings his hand to rest behind its ear. "Bet you never seen a white guy before, eh little fella?" he says, and for a moment, appears almost tender, almost at ease. He reaches for his camera. "This is too cool. I want a selfie."

Reynolds taps the break pedal a few times, the vehicle lurching. "Fuck you, Reynolds."

The camera slips from Folson's grip. Quickly, he repositions himself, aims, and takes the photo.

"Gimme a break, Folson," Reynolds says. "You're nicer to that piece of steak than the rest of us."

He removes his Kevlar and leans forward, massaging his forehead. His mohawk lays partially flattened against his scalp. "This thing is still too goddamn small. I put in for a different size three months ago."

"You shouldn't do that," Huang says.

Reynolds yawns and leans forward, resting his head against the steering wheel. That a stopped convoy is like sitting ducks on opening day seems lost on him. That an unworn Kevlar, cast aside for a moment of comfort, could get him killed seems likewise unimportant.

"Man, I'm serious," Huang's whine fills the Humvee. "If you get hit, who's gonna drive?"

"If I get hit, you get hit. Remember?"

Ahead of Bean Curd, Supreme tosses his Mountain Dew bottle of spittle out the window in the direction of the haji and lays on the horn. The man and the cattle pick up speed, the calf returning to its herd. Caldwell shouts a few phrases in Dari, then something in Pashto, but nothing seems to register with the man, who may be unable to hear over the idling engines anyway. More cows trot past, tails swishing. Miller notices their fur, as black as charred bodies, and he feels his brain skip tracks: a civilian's corpse leaning against a skeletal tree, toasted along with the rest of his block during an air raid; then there was Captain Thompson, whose body melted into the steering wheel of a Stryker when an RPG cruised through the armored windshield. Astonishing, how the past can suffocate the present, something perfectly simple suddenly cast in morbid light.

"I don't like this," says Huang. "I don't like this one bit. We're totally exposed. Will you please just put your Kevlar on, Reynolds? Just put it on, and get us outta here."

"Relax, Huang," Miller says. "Ten more seconds and this herd will be past us. Ten more seconds and maybe this nomad will go tell a future generation of Taliban fighters that he met some pretty chill soldiers today out in the middle of bumfuck nowhere and that they didn't seem all that bad."

Reynolds cocks an eyebrow at Miller. "Really? I mean, LT—do you *really* think that way?"

Miller bites his lower lip. Most of the time, he finds Reynolds's queries are on the mark, an acceptable balance between defiant and goofball. But lately, the antics perturb him. "No, Reynolds. Nah," he says, "I'm just feeding you chocolate pudding for breakfast because I know deep down it's what you really want. That's all I'm here for, you know—to give other people what they want." He radios to Spartan 1, suggesting that Supreme rev the engine slightly to see if it will hurry the last of the herd along.

"Reynolds—" Huang pleads, "your Kevlar?"

"Dude!" Reynolds turns around and glares at Huang. "It's a war zone. Don't you get it? Chance of a lifetime. I'm trying to be patient here, but you need to chill the fuck out. Enjoy the show. Who knows, maybe one of these days you'll get to be the star."

"Huang's right, Reynolds," Miller says. "Put it back on."

The last cow crosses the highway, and Supreme hits the gas. Bean Curd and Spartan 3 follow suit. The convoy gains speed. Miller studies the side mirror, watching the desert curve back on itself, fortified by the horizon. He used to love the sun, the way it warmed the top of his head walking to school. How the end of each day came with the reward of a hard-earned meal. In the early years of marriage, the sun reminded him of Tenley's hair, the soft fluff across her forearms or the intimate clumps that gathered in the shower drain like tiny, golden eggs. But beneath this insufferable heat that drags the Spartans from one day to the next, his thoughts of Tenley waver like a mirage. Tonight. Tonight, he'll call her.

He wishes he could return to the summer they met: Seventeen-year-olds working their first time away from home as camp counselors in North Carolina. He'd never seen much more than the flatlander conservatism of Indiana, and she never so far from the grip of her North Carolina Baptist parents. With a woman like Tenley Baker, you didn't need to worry about getting your heart broken. She was as true as her roots from the moment she taught Miller to corral and ride horses. Her connection with the horses marveled him, a language he didn't know, though he recognized its intimacy. Could she ever speak to him in that way? She always rode ahead, just out of reach, talking to him about horse breeds and training methods. Or astronomy. The history of Appalachian crafts. You name it. Her curiosity and intelligence seemed boundless, and he craved proximity to such ease in the world. He could not calm his need for her. The lovely rolling of her spine as the horse eased along the trail. The bounce in her ponytail at a trot. Oh, and help him—the smooth settling of her hips in the saddle when they cantered. It was the most uncontrollable feeling he ever had. Like a drug. So far, that longing hasn't faded. Not on his part, at any rate. Who can speak for Tenley? He used to assume he knew her well enough, but if war and marriage have taught him anything, it's never assume.

His headset crackles to life. That awful tickling in his ear. That goddamn unending headache. Chaffen's voice registers, loud and clear, "Serpeant has been assassinated. *Do you copy?*" Serpeant is Gawri's code name for radio communications. Miller hesitates a moment. "You're our eyes and ears out there, Miller. You're reconaissance for the entire fucking provice now. Got it?"

And suddenly, all of it—the risks, the inadequacies, even the ROE from Higher—seem to have rightly brought him outside the wire, at the tip of the spear for this new kind of fight. One where patience and meticulous observation reign supreme. How could he have been so questioning? Finally, his most natural abilities are in high demand. Blind spots be damned. Self-doubt along with them. Whose war is it? Miller's war. Every aching mile after mile of it.

He remembers again those horseback rides with Tenley. How everything around them seemed to glow with light and permission. Once, they snuck two horses out of the corral, no saddles, not even halters, and headed beyond the camp boundary into National Forest. Crossing the Cane River at a deep bend, the horses reached their necks into the current as their legs kicked mightily under water. Nathan never forgot the feeling of floating just above the horse's withers, gripping the coarse mane, holding steady with his forearms against fur. He had never felt so carefree and so powerful in the same breath, virtually indestructible.

Midway through the crossing, his horse caught up with Tenley's. He wanted so badly to reach out and touch her. Her laughter echoing across the riverbank, the tips of her hair silky with riverwater, that water sloshing up her bare thighs. He wanted to be everything—the air she breathed between bursts of laughter, the water moving across her skin, the sun illuminating it all. High summer heat. Flies and chiggers and poison ivy. Rapids and rocks. Rules, regulations, camp policies, expectations, the unknowns of new love. None of it, none of it could touch them, and what made that possible—Miller believed, believes still as his convoy barrels ahead—was the sheer act of dissolving into it, of knowing when to let go. That's what brought it to life in the first place. That's what has kept it alive all these years later, and that kind of clarity is still within reach. It is, in fact, closer than it had been at any other point on this tour so far. All he had to do was know it when he saw it.

12

If Any Doubt Remains

Ghazél sets the pail at Shanaz's compound gate, and Aaseya nods, approving. She places her hand against the small of his back and guides him slowly in the direction of the bazaar. After a few paces, she turns around and sees Shanaz surprised into silence, then her black headscarf retreating like a shadow. Aaseya smiles beneath her burqa. It's delightful how easy it is to plant a seed, to let it grow. She can hardly wait to walk past the gate again, watering Shanaz's curiosity about the boy.

Aaseya has only been welcomed into that compound twice before. Once when Shanaz's father-in-law Quadir died and everyone in Imar came to pay respects. The boys flew kites from the rooftop, and Aaseya joined, shoving her way between muscled teens until one of them shared his strings, guiding her hands with his own as they sent two competitors' kites fumbling through the air. They won, but it was the feeling of that teen's hands on hers that she remembers most. Warm and free of calluses. As soft as an invitation. The second time came when she married Rahim. Shanaz insisted the new bride come to her home for a collection of items offered by relatives. The courtyard hadn't been vibrant then, dappled only with botanical remnants of better times, but Aaseya noticed the dry beds. The many garden tools stacked against the interior courtyard walls. By then, most villagers had realized that the Taliban falsely targeted Aaseya's family. Janan may have been openly kind to Americans in his past, but if that were true, he'd also been kind to Taliban fighters. His idealism didn't allow for holding back his heart, and maybe that, more than anything, was what killed him. Marrying was the best she could hope for—better, actually, than most fates an orphan would have earned. Aaseya recalls the marriage to Rahim—strange, how he'd been handed off almost as a gift when, by tradition, it was Aaseya, the beautiful virgin girl, who should have been viewed as the coveted one. She and Rahim took the odd arrangement of gifts from Shanaz and left her compound quickly. "I can hardly look at you," Shanaz had said as they departed. The sentiment made no sense at the time, though today it rings like truth. Shanaz must have felt guilty, maybe even repentant. But a sack of clothes hardly seems enough reparation for the damage done. Soon enough, Aaseya would collect.

At the bazaar, Aaseya and Ghazél shuffle between booths, searching for Massoud. It's possible he could ease her mind with information. She won't mind if the Americans are coming with a teacher, like last time, or if they bring water and school books. The shell casings could be older than she realizes, or the currency tied to an easy explanation. She continues following Ghazél's lead through the bazaar, past the fruit stands and ornate red rugs and tapestries. Farther, past a new vendor, his stacks of clay bowls and crooked hookahs precariously balanced. Just beyond, Massoud's stand sits intact. The shelves are empty. Massoud, nowhere in sight. Ghazél grows impatient, tugging Aaseya's hand. He looks at her, weary.

"There's one more place we can go," Aaseya says. "We're almost to the edge of the market. There's a tobacco shop there, if it's even open anymore. Massoud used to trade cigars for bread with the owner," she nods down the street. "Take me."

Ghazél agrees, his tiny palm pressing into Aaseya's. His feet move lightly across the packed earthen pathways, and he walks with an endearing little scoot at the end of each step. Aaseya loves the sensation of being guided deftly this way and that, soaking for a moment in the warm memory of her brother. Her fingers sweat against the back of Ghazél's hand, his knuckles like little conkers smoothed to perfection. The path widens into a street, and Ghazél stops. He shakes his head, refusing to move forward.

Across the way, a row of shops flanks the old schoolhouse—a place she used to love, a place she hasn't dared return to in years. Structures along the street rival each other in disrepair, the desctruction recent and unnerving. This was the school for boys before the war, a small outbuilding in its courtyard where Ms. Darrow taught girls. Just then, two men step out of the tobacco shop, exchanging greetings. The heavier of the two wears a burnt orange robe and nods goodbye, turning toward the street. Aaseya knows him in an instant, the waddle of a bread maker, doughy arms and legs outlined against thick folds of fabric.

"Massoud!" Aaseya cries out. She can hardly believe her outburst.

Massoud looks in her direction and pauses when he sees the boy at her side, but the moment is brief. Without signal, he turns his back and walks quickly away.

Did he recognize her voice? The burqa disguises her, and she's never been seen with this child before. Maybe Massoud was confused. The urge to give chase overwhelms her. She can't say Massoud is her friend. Not exactly. But sometimes he looks her in the eyes and takes her money without scorn. Sometimes, he even places the bread between her palms as if sharing a secret.

The door to the tobacco shop jangles shut. Through the glass, she can see the shopkeeper return to his duties. Aaseya studies the display window, defeated. Ghazél's presence does lend her some freedom, but even he seems to understand that a lot remains out of reach. On the other side of the glass, rows of cigars sit swaddled like miniature newborns, arranged in tidy rows. The shopkeeper taps on the glass and waves a cigar aggressively at Ghazél. Apparently the display window isn't for loitering. But it's hardly loitering or tobacco that holds Aaseya's interest. Just below the beveled shelf rests a small display of books and publications propped to draw attention. There are a few bright paperbacks and a stack of local pamphlets, then there—right there—words Aaseya knows in English: *The Merriam-Webster Dictionary*. She drops Ghazél's hand and brings both palms to the glass.

Ghazél pulls at Aaseya's burqa, restless.

"Wait one moment, sweet boy. Just wait."

Aaseya keeps her eyes on the tattered book, surely scavenged from the schoolhouse not long after Ms. Darrow left. Ghazél pulls again, this time upsetting the fabric so that the tiny screen misaligns over Aaseya's eyes.

"Ghazél!" she says, rattled. "What is it? What's your worry?"

He points to the schoolhouse and shakes his head, eyes wide with concern. She remembers when Alamzeb looked like that— terrified with the soldiers at his back, frozen in fear until she was able to persuade the Americans of his innocence. She'd been able to do so much more then than she can now. Ghazél stomps his feet, pointing again. He scrunches his lips into a circle, face painting a picture of disapproval.

"We won't go in there, if that's what you're worried about," Aaseya says. "I need you to go here, though," she nudges him toward the shop door. "Can you do that? Can you go inside and get this for me?" she points to the display. "This one right here. The red book. Ok?"

Ghazél crosses his arms. He forms his lips into a pout and huffs, as helpless as a desert cardinal.

"What is it, then?" Aaseya asks. She crouches down to bring them face to face.

Ghazél steps backward half a step, then flattens his palms together, crossing the bottom three fingers through one another and aiming his pointer fingers together like the tip of a gun. He brings the tip to Aaseya's forehead and twitches his thumbs to pull the trigger. Aaseya bats Ghazél's hands away from her face.

"What're you doing?" she says.

His shoulders slump in defeat. He points one more time to the schoolhouse and frowns.

"OK," she says, "that's fine. We'll never go in there. You don't ever have to go in there, ever. Is that what you're trying to tell me?"

She glances up and down the block. Very few villagers are within sight, as though avoiding this end of town. It's been years since she's ventured this far, and the space seems somehow different, closed off. As if it's holding its breath. She looks at the boy again to confirm his meaning, but he only stares with his mouth agape, paralyzed by what he can't say.

"Here," she says, "take a look at this."

She reaches into her pocket and hands him a five-dollar bill. Ghazél's eyes swell. He takes the money, awestruck. Aaseya hums a little tune, barely audible, and Ghazél finally smiles. She reaches for him, and he lets her pat his shoulders and kiss him lightly on the cheek. She turns him around for inspection and dusts off his shorts with a few firm swipes of her hand.

"Go on," she says. "I need you to buy that book in there and bring it to me."

Ghazél nods and folds the money into his fist like a wafer. He flees through the shop door, bells ringing as it slams shut behind him.

Aaseya crosses the street and waits on the corner. It was her fortune to meet Ghazél. It had to be. It's her fortune to have a husband earning money too. If life allows, Rahim will oblige; they'll adopt the boy, and she'll be able to wander freely again. She gazes at the sky, cloudless and anemic blue. Mourning doves balance on nearby rooftops. The birds look dull, brown, the same color as the alleys, the side roads, the brick walls that are built and then blasted and then built again between regimes. The same color as the dirt beneath Rahim's fingernails after a day working creek beds. The Americans have been known to hire locals. They must approve of her husband's business. For all she knows, they might have even hired him a crew. She paces alongside the street and pinches her forearms. The mourning doves lift in flight, and she follows them with her gaze. Silhouetted against the sun's rays, the birds turn black, beautiful. Within seconds, they're swallowed by the sun.

She looks past the schoolhouse to the outbuilding in its courtyard. Two short years and she had imagined herself an educated girl. Ms. Darrow called her to the blackboard for sentence diagramming, and that's when the Taliban came with their guns. Aaseya squeezed the stick of chalk between her fingers until it broke. That chalk was so expensive, so difficult to come by. Wouldn't Ms. Darrow be disappointed? Aaseya tried to hide it, but then the fighters were shouting, and Ms. Darrow put herself between Aaseya and them. They struck Ms. Darrow across the face with their guns, her hands reaching behind to hold Aaseya's shoulders and keep her safe while she took the blows. Ms. Darrow's headscarf fell to the floor, blond hair igniting the room like an insult. Then, all at once, one of the fighters pressed Ms. Darrow into the blackboard with Aaseya behind her, sandwiched against the wall. Aaseya could see the other students' faces, the way they covered their eyes, ashamed to witness. Then the fighter did something with his hands that made Ms. Darrow shrink—Ms. Darrow, so special—but Aaseya couldn't help her. She could only breathe, her face pressed sideways into the small of Ms. Darrow's back, and she hadn't smelled real laundry detergent before, but it must have been right for a Western woman. She smelled like flowers, even when that man was doing something, and Aaseya felt Ms. Darrow's knees buckle. Her teacher. Her teacher smelled like flowers.

Ten hours a week of language lessons. That's how much Aaseya studied before the Taliban banned education for girls again, before the war picked up its mighty pace, before the explosion thrashed her family and, likewise, all her possessions. (Odd, the things she misses: a sequined, green dress worn for an older cousin's wedding—the way sunlight played off its stitched, round discs like the skin of an emblazoned lizard—or her mother's wooden spoon that hedgehogs chewed into one winter, splintering the pulpy wood until its only use could be for Aaseya's pretend pots of sand stew.)

"Each word is a link in the chain," Ms. Darrow had told her. She never returned after that day with the Taliban, but Aaseya treasured the teachings. "The more words you have, the longer your chain can be."

Aaseya hoarded terms voraciously, the end result a vocabulary of two or three hundred words and playground conversation. *Ran, run, run, ran, run.* Aaseya mouths the words as she waits on the street corner, fingers stuffed into the folds of her elbows, pinching, pinching. *I am, you are, she is, we are, they are. I am…I am…*Even

Shanaz, who is illiterate, knows the power language can bring. There's no reason Aaseya can't benefit from that currency. With a little effort, Shanaz will keep talking about Aaseya's friendship with the boy. *Has she adopted?* the neighbors will wonder. The more speculation about Ghazél, the better. Rahim will be obliged to let the rumors prove true; Shanaz will readily see to that much, reparations paid Godspeed. *Ba haya* dissipating like a breeze.

Fueled, Aaseya rushes back to the window and presses her face against the glass. The shopkeeper's hand, the red dictionary—both of them at once, then both of them gone, out of sight. Aaseya stands on her toes but can see no farther into the shop. Let the villagers scorn her for her impatience. Let them throw potatoes. Let them toss her onto the ground—let them! Right now, there is only this swollen feeling across her body like so many words trapped within.

A motion in the schoolhouse catches her eye. There, in the upper window, a Taliban fighter comes into view. She's caught him mid-stride, a hawk striking. She freezes, likewise caught. How long had he been watching her? Did Massoud somehow tell him? Ghazél dashes out of the shop and grabs Aaseya's hand. She squeezes his palm like a lifeline. Ghazél wasn't kidding when he brought his fingertips to her forehead and fired his makeshift gun. He was trying to warn her. He shoves the book at her excitedly, and she pulls him around the corner, out of the fighter's line of sight.

"What do you know about the schoolhouse? What have you seen?" Aaseya asks, short of breath. She squats down so that she's at eye level with Ghazél.

The boy reaches into his pockets and hands Aaseya several shell casings plus the change from the shopkeeper.

"Guns? Have you seen fighters with guns in there?"

Ghazél nods, yes.

"Were they Taliban? Like the men we saw in the bazaar the other day? Like that?"

Again, a nod. He points to the shell casings in her hand, then to the narrow perimeter around the schoolhouse. He motions with each hand cupped, as if digging through the dirt, then mimes placing the shell casings into the imaginary hole. And if any doubt remains in Aaseya's mind that this child is trying to tell her Taliban fighters are planting IEDs in her own village, it dissipates with Ghazél's final gesture—a few, stiff swipes of his hand as though covering the hole, buried explosives and all.

"Listen," she says, "we're going to stick together. Is that OK with you?"

Ghazél wrinkles his forehead.

"I want you to stay with me. I want you by my side, living in our home. Will you just try it? Just come for the afternoon to see what you think. Later, you can meet my husband, OK?"

The questions come like statements, but even as she pleads, she worries her plan is surely flawed. She holds the book to her chest and waits for his reply, hopeful.

Ghazél shrugs and smiles shyly, apparently agreeable. He seems interested, but the trappings of Aaseya's worry are clearly beyond him. That he'll have a cool place to lie down. That she'll feed him regular meals. These things, Aaseya suspects, are what the boy agrees to, for now.

13

Duty Bound

Halfway to Imar, the Spartan convoy slows and passes a small pile of trash. The men scan for loose wires. A few MRE wrappers flap in the wind, entangled against a teal, linen *dishdasha*. The scene looks like a still-life painting, relics of war eddying in the powdered sugar dust of this landscape where everything turns on its head. Out here in the open, the ground moves like water—water isn't there at all—and the blue sky burns like yellow fire. These still-lifes hint at real people, real stories, a co-mingling of objects that Miller believes his old art teacher would have appreciated. He can almost see it—a gallery exhibition on the lost art of the desert: burned utility vehicles from an ambush recontexualized to suggest shelter, the way rust can resemble the ticking of the clock, or small arsenals of litter nestled into a rare and dying shrub.

The desert. Miller has certainly had his share.

"Hey, LT?" Huang leans forward so that his query can be heard. "Did you guys really write your blood types on your boots when you were in the Korengals?"

"Sounds like you've been talking to Rachmann."

Miller's headache thrums. He grabs a bottle of Aleve from the dash and swallows three pills. "Reynolds, gimme that water bottle."

Reynolds grabs hold of the bottle between his legs and tosses it to Miller. The rest of his mohawk has finally flattened in the heat, and the dark strands topple in clumps against his bare forehead.

"Rock said the Korengals were the real deal," Huang continues. He adjusts his Kevlar, pushing it higher on his forehead so it cants toward the roof of the vehicle. "He said there was nothing like it. It sounds like you really got in there."

Miller bites his bottom lip. He can feel the edges of his teeth meeting the flesh like little toothpicks breaking through tender skin. He can't fathom any rendering of what actually happened that will fit into the fable Huang has likely conceived. A tiny bubble of blood rises to the surface of his lips, salting his tongue. "I just did what I had to do," he says. "We all did."

"Huang," Folson says, "the only thing *real deal* about war is shooting a haji. It makes it real in ways you don't even want to know. Besides, you don't need to interrogate LT. Didn't you watch any war movies growing up?"

"Plus you guys," Reynolds adds and bats his thumbs against the steering wheel. "You guys are the real deal. I mean, most of the time, you know? It's good to be a Spartan."

"Hoo-ah," the men chorus.

Folson looks out the window, his puffy black eye straining against the light. The bruise lends him a Popeye look, but there's also a tenderness behind his armature. Miller hasn't given up on him yet. With a good-natured mission like this under his belt— and now the significance of it with Gawri offed and gone—Folson might even start acting human again, or at least forming sentences like those he'll need back in the civilian world.

"I really want to meet McChrystal someday," Huang concludes. "Or at least be in the same room with him, you know? My brothers would never believe it."

Miller wants to tell Huang his brothers would never believe what went down in the Korengals either, but he's still too stuck there to speak. He can almost see Rock pawing at his goddamn patch of eczema while addressing a huddle of Spartans, painting himself into a star role—the mission in the Korengals a success except for Miller, the rattled soldier who got it all wrong.

"LT?" Reynolds asks. "The new ROE are all McChrystal. Aren't they?"

It isn't a question so much as boxing Miller into a corner. Reynolds should know better, but Miller's jaw creaks open, and his chapped lips finally part. "We're following orders, Reynolds. That's the way it's done...and it's likely for reasons we'll never fully understand. All I can tell you is it may be screwed up in some ways, but it also feels right. We have *got* to slow down and start watching more closely. The ROE force that and, in the long run, might make history."

Reynolds cocks an eyebrow, unfazed.

"Oh, and Reynolds? Put your damn Kevlar back on."

Reynolds rolls his eyes, then reaches into the footwell for his helmet. Retrieved, he fiddles with the fittings and steers with his knees. "Just one more question, LT," he says. "Why would McChrystal risk getting his hands dirty by making grunts like us hold our tongues instead of our weapons? Doesn't he know we're the ones who actually get shit done? You know, by fighting on the ground...where the war actually *is*?"

"That was three questions, Reynolds. And three questions too many."

"Forget I brought it up," Huang says. He scratches his face. A hangnail snags on a pimple, which begins to bleed. "Just watch the road, Reynolds...the road! Could you just drive? For once?"

Reynolds grabs the wheel and steers Bean Curd completely off the highway, crossing the ditch. "We're taking orders from Captain Huang, everybody. Captain Huang is in charge here, so listen up!"

His voice bellows, filling Bean Curd with angry tones. The vehicle rocks and tilts as Reynolds steers up, then parallel to a wavering dune. The binoculars slide across the dash and crash the floor. Folson is knocked off-center, leaning into Huang.

"The heck?" Miller barks. "Reynolds, fall back in line right now! That's an order!"

Reynolds steps on the gas, nearly passing Spartan 1. His voice cracks as he shouts to be heard over the roar of the engine. "What's the difference, LT? What's the difference if we get shredded right here for no reason or if we wait to let some bug-eyed haji shoot us because we can't shoot first?"

Miller wrestles with Reynolds for the steering wheel, and the men are tossed right, then left, then right again. "The difference is that one way is a wasted KIA, and the other way is for the greater good. 'I am an expert. I am a professional. I will always place the mission first.' Sound familiar?" Miller quotes part of the Soldier's Creed. "Now get this vehicle back in line and yourself along with it."

Reynolds guns the engine, and a high-pitched rev cuts across the desert air. His disobedience hangs in the Humvee like a belch.

"Dude?" Folson says. He shouts nervously at Reynolds. "Hey, dude?"

Reynolds offers a quick salute and frowns. "I'm done now, Second Lieutenant," he straightens his Kevlar. "Monkey see, monkey do."

A mess of chatter spews over the radio, straight toward the base of Miller's skull. He imagines a baseball there, worn smooth from years of play. If someone could just reach inside of him, just take it out. "Spartan 1, this is Bean Curd. I copy. Forget about it. Our cue's up ahead," Miller calls. "Should be about 500 meters. Turn west into the Imar Valley. Bean Curd over."

"Copy that, LT. But we're not going to be alone up there," Yak says. Any hint of the percussive laughter typically lining Yak's voice has drained away. Miller presses the headset into his ear, awaiting more. "We've got three friendlies ahead of us, about ten klicks into the valley. I can see them now on Blue Force Tracker. Looks like they're stopped."

"Let's pick up the pace then. Get us there quickly so we can see what they're into. I've got intel from the TOC that says we're in for more than humanitarian efforts today too."

"Roger, over and out."

The convoy turns, and within moments, walls of ridgeline rise alongside them. Miller can't mention Gawri over the radio now—code name or otherwise—which might be for the better until they can figure out what's going on with the friendlies. The valley narrows into loose piles of scree and boulders, sunlight a scant wash of yellow amidst the shady corridor. The road fades into a slight impression of two-tracks, estimated and recalculated every few meters as Nacho Supreme leads the convoy toward their destination. Dung-brown desert dust gathers and lifts around them, accumulating in foggy clouds above their Humvees as if part of an independent weather system. Small creeks cross the roadway here and there, most moving at a slow, sandy trickle. Wide beds suggest more plentiful times, but for all Miller can see, the entirety of space and light seems to diminish with each kilometer gained. At the vanishing point of the valley, the citizens of Imar wait.

The next kilometer passes with heady silence. Yak radios Blue Force Tracker updates to Miller, indicating that the three friendlies have rolled forward a little, then stopped again, locked in place in a way few convoys should ever be. Supreme guns Spartan 1, and the convoy speeds ahead. The wind kicks up, and the ground seems to move with them. It's easy to feel hypnotized by that sand, the way the topmost layer suddenly lifts and glides like a creamy brown, horizontal waterfall. Nothing will stop that sand from blowing over the steep rims of these mountains all the way to the next continent. Who's to say there's nothing to stop the men from such disappearance either?

The valley tightens, and Miller feels short of breath as they head toward that point in the distance. *I am an expert and a professional. I will always put the mission first.* But there was more—*I am a warrior and a member of a team.* He thinks again of the Afghan elder he shot, then of Mercer dying so unecessarily. No matter what Miller does today or the next day, all his actions stem outward from that one frozen moment in the timeline of his life. He longs to succeed. To have something tangible he can show Tenley when it's all said and done. Forget medals and rank. He wants something she can count on. Something *he* can count on too. That light the day they rode the horses through the river. It's the same light that shines on all of them now. It always has been. Something will always go wrong, one way or another. *a2 + b2 = an elephant, a grapefruit, a goddamn spaceship.* The fact that war never works in balanced equations means that Miller can't either. Can Tenley ever see it that way?

They'd been out for two nights on a remote mission in the Korengal Mountains. Short on food, short on water, short on intel, and short on patience. They had gut-crawled over rubble and restlessly camped amidst clouds of biting flies. By the time the elders' meeting they'd been sent to watch concluded for evening prayer, Miller was ready to make something of the mission. They all were, he reminds himself. When a foot messenger approached the hut where one village elder remained, Miller and his men moved in. Their orders were clear: if a messenger arrives, the one who stays behind to speak to him is your target. Hasim Babur—a low-tier Tajik warlord in the last war, an embittered Taliban supporter this go around. Miller had seen the photograph on file, blurry and dated eight years. He entered the hut, Rock flanking him and another half-dozen soldiers hiding with the target in their sights. The elder kept his back turned, and Miller watched as he lifted a dusty, woven rug to reveal a grave-deep stash of ordnance buried in the ground. The elder and the messenger conferred, and Miller took aim. The elder turned, a slight gasp escaping his lips. Miller remembers the surprising pink flesh of the old man's tongue as his mouth caught in an "O" of surprise.

"Hasim Babur?" Miller said, and though he initially detected a momentary ripple of recognition across the elder's face, thinking of it now, he's no longer certain. Was it simply fear? Confusion? The messenger made a move as if to run, and Miller looked his way—saw the same hooked nose, the same chiseled cheekbones. Both men were also tall with wide-set eyes and full beards. Then, the elder thrust his hand toward the inside flap of his long vest, and Miller jerked his focus to that hand and whatever hidden object it reached for. He squeezed and exhaled, a millisecond frozen in time, then, all at once, arriving at its horrible end.

The elder slumped to the floor. Miller ran to him, fumbling through the man's vest for the weapon that could have turned on him, his men. The messenger lunged for the backdoor, ramming headfirst into Corporal Mercer, who wrangled free, but only in time to expose himself to the darkened blade of a farmer's knife. Mercer fell like a sacrificial goat, not even enough life left to grip his own throat. The soldiers moved in, Rock among them, and cuffed the messenger. Miller looked at Mercer. Looked at the messenger. Looked at his hands, which fished the elder's Afghan-issued ID card from the vest pocket. Tamim Shah. A nobody, by all records according to the brass. A civilian. Unarmed. An innocent man blackmailed by thugs who had overtaken his village.

That fast, a round-faced boy leapt from behind a pile of cushions where the elders had sat during their meeting. He screamed like a crow and stumbled across the small room, falling into the pile of weapons. He righted himself a few feet from Miller's steadily aimed M4.

"*Ghal!*" the boy said, meaning *thief*. He pointed to the messenger, seized by two of Miller's men in the back corner of the meeting house. "*He* is *ghal!*"

When Miller thinks of it now, it appears almost as a Callahan cartoon. The sick irony of this small child standing in the meeting house, a clattering of weapons at his feet. His narrow limbs looked as straight and rigid as a rifle. His eyes as dark as the opening at the end of the barrel. Was this how children in war zones came to be? Birthed out of graves and weapons? If Miller crossed his eyes slightly, the boy could in fact be made of weapons, could then disappear entirely as he twisted into a whirlpool of movement magnetizing every object in that fucked up meeting house, Miller too, tornado-ing through that hole in the ground, down, down into something hot at the center of the earth that would melt them altogether and put an end to the mess of who's who, once and for all.

He could not turn his head. He could not look again at Mercer, the darkening pool spreading, horror-movie thick. *I am a warrior and a member of a team. I will never leave a fallen comrade.* It must have been the heat. The days of dehydration. The dizzying months of his deployment. All of it spinning at that wrong moment to produce that wrong decision, an opening in time that stole Mercer in a ripple effect everyone said wasn't Miller's fault. But Miller knew better. He'd cast the first stone. Hadn't there been a moment when his own voice tried to steer him another direction? *Don't fire. Let the man speak.* But the damage was done—two innocent men dead.

"*Shar!*" the boy screamed in Miller's face—*evil*—then brashly swung his tiny arm at Miller's weapon, tipping the barrel off-center. Miller stood back, shocked. Then the boy turned his back to the soldiers and wailed, tossing his arms around the fallen elder. Miller stayed rooted to the spot, watching as the boy burrowed his tiny fingers into the man's beard. Rock gagged the messenger— the real Hasim Babur, Miller would later learn—fumbling with his square knot, while another soldier radioed for swift airlift to interrogation. Leading the prisoner out the door, Rock looked back at Miller, and the two exchanged glances. Miller expected Rock would look sheepish, caught in self-doubt about whether he could have saved Mercer himself. Instead, Miller was greeted by a look of pity. Apparently Rock had already cleared his conscience and now saw Miller as the one to blame.

Miller must have helped them clean up. Must have at least righted the elder's limbs, moving him out of his own pile of brains and blood, closing his eyelids respectfully. Must have stood by and saluted when the Black Hawk came to carry Mercer's body away. But whenever Miller thinks of it now, his memory stops at the boy's small, brown fingers clawing into the elder's coarse beard, reaching for something he would never find.

Surely, Miller isn't the only one who feels betrayed by his own abilities, how they fray even on this last mission outside the wire. Promises are greedy, inexplicable things, haunting like ghosts. Imar beckons the convoy forward, the chance for good deeds and intel enough to keep these twelve bodies of flesh and bone rolling across the desert, heartbeats from homeward bound.

14

The Entire Desert

Aaseya holds the dictionary in one hand and Ghazél's palm in the other. Every step has felt like a gamble, and here, along these final blocks toward her apartment, fear nearly paralyzes her. A few passing clouds offer little comfort. The tease of cool shadows, there and then gone. Merely ghosts sliding over another block, another village, more desert extending all the way to—does it even matter? She might be walking Ghazél straight into flying scrap metal. She might be walking herself into that mess too, both of them lifted from life as quickly as a shooting star sparkles, then fades.

Aaseya attempts to retrace their steps home. Every few paces, she stops and scans the ground. From afar, her meticulousness would look like a child's game—"I Spy," which she learned from Ms. Darrow, or "Flea Stomp," Alamzeb's favorite. She could teach these to Ghazél. Could and will. But first, their safety.

"A likely pair, you two!" Shanaz shouts at them with her hands punched into her hips, glaring from the entrance to her compound. Behind her, the gate is swung wide open like the mouth of a vulture. "That boy steals from my garden. That boy doesn't know the difference between right and wrong!"

Ghazél leans into Aaseya's side and looks up at her. "We want her to notice us," Aaseya whispers. "Trust me."

But Ghazél doesn't look convinced. He purses his lips, trailing behind.

"This is Ghazél," Aaseya says proudly. She reaches behind and gives the boy a little shove. "He can hear you, but he can't talk. He's been helping me today. We've already been to the bazaar together, and he purchased what I asked him to."

Ghazél stares at his feet.

"This boy—this Ghazél—well…" Shanaz bends down to look at his face. "So, you're the neighborhood thief? Pathetic!"

"Shanaz," Aaseya pleads, "he's been starving."

Nearby, several neighbors come to their windows to witness the fuss. A few men linger along the sidewalk, staring. For a moment, Aaseya indulges the thought of shaming Shanaz right here to anyone who will listen. *This woman is the one*—she'd shout—*who doesn't know the difference between right and wrong.*

"Get in here," Shanaz says, then shoos her hands at the neighbors. Gate closed, she hurries Aaseya and Ghazél toward the interior of her family compound. "This boy might be mute, but he isn't stupid," she continues. They follow her through the short, narrow corridor built to protect the expansive courtyard from public view. Aaseya's own family compound had a space like that too, and with Ghazél's soft palm in her own, she can only think of Alamzeb. The many games they'd played in their similarly shaded, quiet space. "What did you say—Ghazél? That's his name? Well, *Ghazél* has been stealing from our garden for months. He's a slave to the devil. He hasn't been shown anything proper. He's not going to learn it from you either."

"I—" Aaseya stops herself. There's no point in arguing.

In the safety of the corridor, her nervousness fades. She removes her burqa and wraps it around the dictionary, then adjusts her headscarf over her hair. The air smells exquisite, a perfume of flowers altogether too rare. She steps into the fullness of the compound and blinks. Shanaz's courtyard has always been special, but years have passed since Aaseya has seen anything beyond the compound gate. Now, the sheer variety of plants and flowers before her would seem indulgent—suspicious, even, in wartime—if it weren't for the fact that they're so immediately calming. A surprising comfort at the hands of a woman she swore she'd never trust again.

"Oh, Shanaz," Aaseya says, "it's so—alive. But how?"

She drops Ghazél's hand, and he runs to a tall stand of soft shrubs, then ducks into hiding. He peers out between the thick stalks and risks a smile. Several of Shanaz's young daughters follow him as if to stand guard, but Ghazél seems unfazed.

"None of this was easy," Shanaz shrugs. "But tell me something that is, and I'll say you're living in a different world."

She walks toward the cooking fires, and Aaseya follows. They pass a row of vibrant roses. An almond tree. Through an archway, more berry bushes are visible, and a pomegranate tree appears heavy with flowers against a back wall. The deep pink petals hang like clots amidst leafy branches. She'd love to climb that tree, to feel its sturdiness. Recalling that afternoon with the kites, she had thought for years this courtyard might be a place she would return. Why hadn't she noticed Rahim at gatherings here in the past? All relatives came, especially to funerals. But she can't place him in her memory.

The cooking station is long and low, with various pots and bowls arranged atop stands that straddle low-burning fires. A small child feeds twigs into the coals, humming to herself. She looks up as Aaseya and Shanaz approach. A fly lands on her cheek, and she brushes it off. Wide coals smolder beneath the pot of boiling water, and the child feeds more twigs into the heat. Another pot steams steadily, containing a dark broth of some kind. A few bones float at the surface. The air tastes rich and earthy—marrow mixed with blossoms and dust.

"I remember when the first flower bloomed after the war came to Imar. The pomegranate blooms came later that summer. The gifts of Allah are endless, but you have to open yourself to them. You have to oblige."

Aaseya sits on a low clay bench built into the compound's perimeter wall.

"I'm not good at that," she says.

Against her back, she can feel the mottled surface of the mud shaped by generations of sitting. Aaseya imagines Shanaz's entire family passing through this same seat—Shanaz's mother before her, a great grandmother before that—all of them with their wide backs pressed into this hand-shaped clay, leaning, leaning, never done with their work. And yet, here in the peaceful quiet of this courtyard, Shanaz hardly seems fatigued. She actually moves lithely, round as she is, gathering ingredients for a meal.

"What I mean is," Aaseya takes a breath, "that I'm not good at doing things I don't believe in. I'm not good at it at all, and I don't know what my father would have said about any of that, but I suspect you don't care. You've made it clear what you think of me."

"Have I?" Shanaz asks. She raises an eyebrow, but keeps her gaze directed at the two pots. She stirs patiently, a ladle in each hand, the liquid moving in sync with each stroke. The little girl stands at eye level with the hissing water and broth. The pots could so easily tip and scald her skin, but she seems completely unafraid. Aaseya wants exactly that: ritual, ease. Even when the thing you need to keep you alive is also the thing that might burn you beyond recognition. She takes hold of a few dollar bills in her pocket, running her fingertips along the edge of a crease. It would mean so much to Shanaz. Not just the money, but the information—a chance to sort through the facts and rumors and decipher who's coming to Imar. Or who's already here and why. In Aaseya's other hand, she still clutches the dictionary, wrapped in fabric. Shanaz never let her daughters study with Ms. Darrow. Many families in Imar refused. Is it possible Shanaz still feels threatened by the suggestion of another way? The reminder that language, like schoolgirls, once had the right to move freely across these streets? Aaseya tightens her fingers around each talisman, money in one hand, book in the other, the thrum of possibility in between. But even as she balls her fists, she knows neither object will take her to the end of a story she can believe.

"I have something I can offer," she says. She unfolds the fabric wrapping and reveals the book. "It's small, but I couldn't have gotten it without Ghazél, so maybe you can say it's from him. To make things right between you two."

She opens the dictionary on a nearby cutting surface and tears out several sections, handing them to Shanaz. "For your fire," she says, nodding at the coals.

"Well," Shanaz's face softens, "we do need more heat if we want to do this right."

The little girl steps forward and takes the pages. She crumples several and tosses them into the fire. Inky smoke filters around her face, tendrils of words she'll never read, possibilities she'll never know.

"What are you making?" asks Aaseya.

"*Kofta.*"

Aaseya hasn't been able to replicate *kofta* for several years, not without her mother. Boiled balls of ground beef or lamb seem easy enough, but there has to be more to the earthy, rich flavor. The girl crumples another page and shoves it low into the coals. Dark smoke billows and stings Aaseya's eyes. She steps aside for a moment and turns her face to the sky. All those sentences, rising out of reach. Through a watery gaze, she looks again at her surroundings. Everything appears in Technicolor—cucumbers, legumes, squash flowers. Even green shoots climbing to garden stakes. Olive trees growing healthy and strong. Beneath the pomegranate tree along the far wall, a row of perennials puts forth a mighty effort, somehow thriving in the drought. A family may have nothing left to spare, but if it has its courtyard, it has its peace.

"What goes in first?" she asks.

"Fat," Shanaz plops four cubes of sheep tail lard into the frying pan and hands it to Aaseya. "Melt this slowly, and then we'll fry the onions."

Aaseya brings the pan to the hottest part of the fire. Yellow flames lick its sides. Shanaz squats to gather spices from a low shelf and stands back up, flustered.

"No," she says. "like *this*."

She shoves Aaseya with her hips and takes hold of the pan, raising it several inches above the flame until the loud sizzle mutes to a low hiss. The little girl giggles, but Shanaz shoves the back of her head firmly. "Shush."

Aaseya takes back the pan. The fat melts slowly now, spreading like dark fingers across the metal. Shanaz grips Aaseya's wrist and tilts it in a circular motion, almost motherly, almost sympathetic—though something in her gesture still remains disapproving. They watch the cubes skate across the slick heat.

"OK," Shanaz says. She lifts the darkened pan slicked with fat. "Balance it here, add your spices, then put it back over the heat."

Aaseya sets the pan on a brick stand over a low mound of ash and reaches for salt and pepper. Shanaz works her fingers beneath the skin of an onion and rotates it in her palms, peeling the golden-orange sheaths swiftly. The little girl has wandered off, and Aaseya can only hope Ghazél is staying out of harm's way.

"Don't let it scald," Shanaz says, nodding at the pool of warming spices. "You don't make things very easy for yourself, you know? You don't make things very easy for anyone."

Heat comes to Aaseya's face. She'd nearly forgotten her purpose, but now, with Shanaz apparently back on track with her opinions, it's time for Aaseya to act. Why is it so hard for her to speak her mind? Ms. Darrow had been open and worldly. What a beautiful, horrible gift. Her neck tightens, as though a long snake crawls down her throat. She stares into the sizzling pan and feels its heated, heavy power.

"Look at you—you're helpless," Shanaz looks up at the sky. "Praise be to Allah, the most merciful, the most compassionate, forgive me for what I'm about to say," she lowers her gaze and drills her eyes into Aaseya's. "You are the most obstinate woman I've ever known. You would have been stoned to death by now if everyone here didn't already feel sorry for you. A woman can't ask anything of her husband if she hasn't given him the decency of good behavior. I'm trying to help you see that. I'm trying to help you get what you want."

Aaseya should leave before she explodes. She tries to swallow, but her throat tightens further. She follows the snake down, searching for the right words, then curls her tongue to speak. "I want my family back. I want your mouth to stay closed. I want to tell everyone the truth of what you did."

Shanaz seems to be smiling. "Is that all? You wouldn't like the truth if you knew it," she shoves a spoon into Aaseya's hands, and Aaseya flinches, fearing she may vomit. "Stir. Just stand there, stir, and listen to me. I don't owe you anything, and you know why? The day you got married, I paid my dues. My brother's marriage to you was my reparation. You've been nothing but ungrateful ever since. And as for your family, as for the explosion—"

"No," Aaseya says. She throws the spoon and covers her ears. Where is her voice? Where's Ms. Darrow? Alamzeb? She should beat this woman with her bare hands. She should strangle her by her headscarf, then throw her down a well. But Aaseya has no strength—she never really has. She slumps toward the sizzling pan, then down to the ground. She moves her hands along her forearms, and there, where her fingertips meet the bruises, she feels Shanaz's grip, the woman's face just inches from Aaseya's. And if ever Janan has visited her again on this Earth, it's now, through these words, moving as clearly as water across Shanaz's lips: "People do strange things in war time, Aaseya. Before you were born, we'd already lived through decades of fighting. I was done taking risks. I was done being complacent. I finally did something, and it turned out to be wrong."

She pulls Aaseya to her feet, then guides her to the low clay seat against the wall. Returning to the fire, Shanaz quickly snatches the cracklings from the hot oil and sets them into a bowl to cool. She tosses the onions into spiced oil, adds a brick to the fire, and balances the pan back on top, now farther from the heat. Aaseya watches as if through a haze. She feels suddenly small, pointless. The only kind of men in her country who were given away, as Shanaz suggests, were those who had been dirtied by the mujahideen or those whose bodies were deformed or mutilated somehow. Does the trail of suffering ever end?

Shanaz studies her for a moment. "I can see you've started to understand. My brother's different than most, but he's still a man. I told you; I'm trying to help you get what you want. Rahim needs a son more than he needs a wife, but having both would be even better. So tell me—what are your plans with this boy?"

Shanaz sends Aaseya home with *kofta* to share. She also offers a few T-shirts, a pair of sandals, two palettes, and three pillows to fashion a bed for Ghazél. But as far as advice beyond the domestic, advice for life outside this village, Shanaz has come up short. Aaseya feels foolish for expecting otherwise, though there's still no mistaking the woman's hold on her. She needs friendship more than public proof. She needs an ally. With Ghazél, it couldn't be easier. With Shanaz, time will only tell. The boy sleeps peacefully in the gathering room. Rahim won't be home until sundown. For now, that seems enough.

Aaseya opens the dictionary and sprawls across her bed. *Battery. Below. Blue. Business.* The English words return with a rash of curiosity. If Alamzeb were still alive, he'd probably peer over her shoulder and tease her until she shared her treasure. Or her mother, her father, Ms. Darrow—if they could see this, if they could feel the way Aaseya's heart pumps blood through her body now like a living, fluttering thing. She traces her fingers along each crisp line of text, flipping the pages back and forth, searching for anything familiar. She stops when she comes to a proper noun: *Bagdhad.* The Americans are there too, aren't they? It seems unfathomable to her. She has never traveled beyond Imar. The half-day's drive to Tarin Kowt is like a fable. How far can the interests of one nation possibly stretch? She scans farther down the columns, but the words stack against each other, meaningless.

She stashes *The Merriam-Webster Dictionary* in her chest of belongings and walks into the gathering room where Ghazél naps. She studies the small space, its impersonal feel. Here, a row of cushions, red and purple fabric stitched loosely over the foam. There, a low table for candles, wooden trim cracked at the corners. Hardly a trace of anyone she longs to be, of anything resembling what is hers. Farther back she sees the pantry, its dusty shelves half-stocked. She ought to wave the flies off the *kofta*, ought to prepare side dishes. But the Taliban. Those dollars. Rahim would want to know—might even be able to warn the Americans if she can tell him in time. How far away could they be? A day's drive? Weeks from a battle? She's probably overreacting. The Americans have greater concerns than her petty village, and besides, what would she say if she saw them? Gunfire won't wait for her to look up words in the dictionary. True, the English words had startled her back to an earlier self—the ambitious girl favored by Ms. Darrow, so proud to have earned the right to an education, so naive about how easily it would be taken away. But the past had only proven to set her future up for loss.

She paces across the ornate rug. When she reaches the edge, she gathers her fingers into the crook of each elbow and pinches. A tender little secret, this pain. Its sensation like the desert melting through her skin. She pinches again and winces, forcing her breath into the talcum air. She pinches again, again. A little cave of soft belief, a little home. This much is hers. This much can never be taken away. With Ms. Darrow, a different life had seemed possible. Aaseya learned to trust the way the right word could assuage confusion. A year after language lessons, the words had come rushing back, like tiny candies held against the inside of her cheek. US soldiers had cornered Alamzeb on his walk home from a friend's house one afternoon. *Trash, metal, explosion.* Nevermind that Alamzeb was only four years old; Aaseya knew these words as they careened loudly from the soldiers' mouths. They jabbed the air with meaty fingers, repeating phrases. One soldier gripped Alamzeb's upper arm. Another reached for something to tie Alamzeb's wrists together, but then there was Aaseya. A soft-spoken voice in the middle saying, "Toys. Game. Peace. Child."

She persuaded them to follow her home where she knew she could show them Alamzeb's games were simply that—a child's dream, not a threat at all. With Janan's blessing, she led them deep into the courtyard and pointed at Alamzeb's stash of play fortresses constructed with shiny bits of shrapnel for people, discarded aluminum cans for vehicles, bright blue bottle caps for tires, and the occasional MRE wrapper as a tent for the nomads. Her father walked the soldiers to his front gate, shaking hands and apologizing, briefly united by Alamzeb's young imagination. Aaseya always viewed it as a moment that could have gone so wrong, turned so peacefully right. Now, she understands it was this moment that linked her fate to Shanaz. She can almost picture it: the woman's fearful eyes peering across the street, suspicious of Western presence. It didn't take long—a week? Her entire family brushed clean from the earth as if lifted by a sandstorm. There and there and then not.

But Shanaz isn't the only one who was wrong. When else has Aaseya ever felt so empowered? The grade school girl with the sounds of her family filling the courtyard, lamb stew sizzling over a fire, stuffed dates or her favorite, *kishmish panir*—the smooth cheese prepared with moist, round raisins that caught in her teeth and stayed sweet for hours. The women of her family cooked and laughed while they embroidered ornate trim along their robes. That girl had choices, in a limited sort of way, but choices nonetheless. A crack in the stone. A tear through fabric. Determination shining through. She had choices but acted before all the links in the chain could connect. Obstinate. Foolish. Shanaz couldn't be more right. Aaseya may as well have orchestrated the explosion herself.

I am…I am…

She paces. Pinches, pinches. Ghazél shifts in the corner, his skeletal frame dwarfed against the fluffy pillows. His breathing

169

is nearly silent. Will his presence save her from scorn, as Shanaz suspects? Even today, Massoud might have turned on her. The tobacco salesman. Any man, really, who decided her indecency went too far could have slapped her back into place. Pace. Pinch. Aaseya's arms tingle to life, possibility emblazoning her fingertips. Fantasy only brings disappointment. She can't take credit for anything, just as she can't learn to read on her own. A few language lessons are akin to a handful of sand. She wants a sandstorm; she wants the entire desert.

15

Lost in Translation

Four soldiers step out of the first vehicle and thud across the road, weapons aimed. Their walk is something to behold, weighed down with body armor and bulging pockets, burdens a wonder to Rahim: their clunky boots, their oversized helmets, their stiff stances. And now the barrels of their guns—Rahim can only identify one, the semi-automatic—pointing at him and Badria like an evil eye. The men shout loudly, words and gestures filling the air. Rahim digs into memory, searching for any English phrase that might slow them down. His heart drops to his stomach, pounding, and he can feel the boxing match down there, the tiny man giving it his all.

The soldiers move in a straight line, fifty paces distant. Now thirty. The way Americans walk has always struck Rahim as the most confident and cumbersome stride he's ever seen. They motion at him and Badria, an unclear series of demands, and a wash of kicked-up dust flows along the roadway. Instantly, they're coated in talcum. Lovely, how the desert can give something back that you forgot you loved. This landscape—it is completely his. His weapon is safely hidden within its folds, and even his tracks in the sand erase before his eyes as another gust of wind works its magic. Several of the soldiers cough, the barrels of their guns tipping temporarily off target. Rahim imagines the sand shielding his face and neck, his limbs, an unbreakable glass armor. He can wait all day on these men and their orders. He's got all the time in the world. But then the sun, that ever-present glare. Dust rises and settles again, and now the soldiers are upon him—a mere three steps away, fully stopped, bloodshot eyes pinning Rahim into place. He squints into the light.

"Put your hands up! Up!" the first soldier shouts in English. Rahim knows these words and intuits instantly that if these soldiers are anything, they're overwrought. As though yelling repeatedly will make the words translate mid-air. "Put your hands up!" the soldier says again, louder.

Rahim and Badria drop their shovels and do as they're shown, hustling up the slope of the creek bed to stand in the middle of the road. Hands overhead, feet spread—they know the routine. Rahim hopes there aren't any women in the other Humvees, tightly muscled figures cradling guns instead of babies—the humiliation.

"I. Am. Your. Side," Rahim says in English. "Your side, your side."

"Do you understand English?"

Rahim shakes his head, then speaks to the translator, who he knows must be the one who looks like an Afghan, despite the American fatigues; he is the only one without a weapon.

"Why did you shoot at our convoy?" the translator asks in Pashto.

"I don't know what you're talking about. We're digging to make bricks. We come here all the time to work," Badria says.

The first soldier barks a command at the translator. He's short with pink skin and a thick, black stripe painted under each eye. A crossed-arrow insignia in black and gold is stitched along the collar of his uniform.

"It's really best if you don't lie," the translator says. Rahim doesn't recognize his face, but the accent is undeniably Hazara. No telling where the soldiers found him. "I've seen how these things can go," he continues in Pashto. "Just do what they say, and keep your hands up. They're going to search you."

"Fine," Rahim says. "They won't find anything."

"Tell them they're perverts," Badria says.

The pink-skinned soldier barks again, and the translator looks momentarily torn between Badria's audacity and the throaty command. Like a helpless pig, that's what Pinky is. Grunting and strutting. And the Americans are supposedly here to help. Easy for someone like Janan to believe. Rahim stares at Pinky's temple where a ropy, purple vein pulses beneath the skin.

"OK, they know. Search…" the translator assures Pinky, and these phrases, too, fall on Rahim's ears with rough familiarity. The experience of a pat-down never pleases him, but he'd rather keep the soldiers' focus right here, on him and Badria. They've already drawn far more attention to themselves than Obaidullah would ever want, and while their shovels and buckets cast along the roadside do look to be of authentic use, nothing can undo the fact that these soldiers have been fired upon.

What does Badria think, that they'll take them at their word? That the soldiers can't do damn near anything that pleases them? Rahim has heard stories of wives being raped, sons being arrested, elders being beaten in the middle of the night—even prisoners, sometimes, stripped naked and fondled. Once, a neighbor told him that Americans masturbate together, all in a circle, where everyone can see. Rahim's never fallen prey to much more than a few tense searches before a team went on its way, looking for something else.

But he's also never found himself with weapons to hide, a wad of cash in his wallet, or an idiot partner, for that matter—one who, even with a gun in his face, can't seem to say anything right.

A third soldier approaches and begins the pat-downs, Badria first. A fourth aims his weapon at Rahim's face. Pinky eyes the situation fiercely. The quicker Pinky's temples pulse, the more Rahim wants to bring his teeth to that flesh and bite, just to feel it split.

"How are your children?" Badria says to the translator. "Are they well?"

He keeps his hands raised as the soldier pats each arm, then his torso, all the way down each leg. Working back up Badria's body, the soldier empties Badria's pockets and mutters something to Pinky, who nods firmly. "What about your mother?" Badria continues. "I haven't heard good things about her."

The translator ignores him. Pinky taps his shoulder again, voice demanding. The translator nods, then turns back to Rahim and Badria.

"He says you shouldn't be here," the translator says.

"*You* shouldn't be here," Rahim blurts. He feels annoyed, more than anything, seeing this fellow Afghan puppeted by the Americans. Who do they think they are, buying loyalties like that, waving money to make a man risk his life? His family's lives? Rahim puckers his lips and considers spitting at the translator's feet, then swallows a hard knot of realization. How different is that from what he does now, greedy Obaidullah waiting up in the hillsides to come down and give him his earnings? None of them should be here. Not even him. Not this way. His country is an open wound, a mess of parasites, everyone coming to dig in and take their fill.

The third soldier searches Rahim next. Not roughly but not kindly either. His wallet is confiscated within seconds. Rahim notices a thin, white line staining the armpits of the soldier's fatigues. He's heard that Americans have to take salt tablets here, that their skin is so transparent, the sun penetrates it and dissolves all the salt in their bodies.

Pinky barrages the translator with more commands, pointing toward Rahim and Badria's foxholes. As Pinky's tone shifts, a feeling tightens in Rahim's gut. These soldiers are not wasting any time. There's something about them, an energy implying blame.

"He wants to know what you're doing here? What are the shovels for?" the translator asks.

"We're digging in the creek bed," Rahim says.

"He says you can't dig here. Don't dig along this route."

The translator runs his hands through the air fluidly, indicating the roadway and the open desert beyond. Even through his gestures, the Hazara mimics the Americans.

"We'll move," Rahim says. The longer the translator stands within reach, the angrier Rahim grows. So many years working his mind away from the abuse of *batcha bazi*, only to find this new brand of traitor muddling yet another conflict in Afghan history. The truth of it sickens him, makes him clench his teeth. If he could just hope for less, there'd be less to lose. But his life is a checkerboard of misplaced desires, a constant arrangement of slivers under the skin, and what good is poetry in a world like that? What good is goodness, for that matter?

Pinky paces, mumbling to the translator. The translator explains something at length, then Pinky sends two soldiers into the creek bed to search the foxholes. They walk gingerly, clearly hesitant, thinking the road may be rigged. It's all too much—this bully squaring off with Rahim, and the sun betraying his every move. His stomach knots. All he ever wanted was to get through unnoticed. He thinks of his money stashed in the doorframe of his apartment, most of it in dollars he can't spend overtly. He thinks of Aaseya, the way she looks at him kindly, but enrages him with her *ba haya*, her dismissals. He's fooling himself. They all are. Even now. Snatching from one faction of society only to feed

175

it to another. Returning home to a wife who gives him nothing, costing too much in return. Cannibals. That's what these soldiers are. That's what he is. Filthy. Like Khohistani's hands reaching for him through the dark.

The translator waits for Pinky's litany to end and nods, then turns to Rahim and Badria. "They know you're lying," he says. "You're lying, and this soldier right here," the translator points to Pinky, "is not a patient man when it comes to liars. Brothers, I've seen this before. He'll shoot you where you stand."

"Brothers?" Badria says. "Your mother fucks dogs. I'm no brother of yours. You disgrace our country, you—"

"Shut up, or *I'll* shoot you," the translator barks.

"With what?" Badria asks.

"Those," the translator nods at the two soldiers climbing back up the bank, carrying Rahim and Badria's weapons.

Pinky grabs both weapons with one hand, his palm as large as a cloth, and shakes them in Rahim's face. He shouts words like "bucket" and "AK 47" and "raghead." Rahim imagines head-butting Pinky, knocking him back so hard his helmet snaps and rolls into the creek bed, decapitated. But no. Of all things, that will most certainly not keep these soldiers away from him.

"Sir?" says the third soldier, the one who searched Rahim and Badria. "Sir, you—"

"WHAT?" Pinky replies but keeps his eyes on Rahim and Badria. He refuses to risk a sideways glance.

The soldier looks Badria over again from head to toe, then explains something to Pinky, who seems affirmed now, interested.

"Yes," Pinky says. "Yes."

He gives the weapons to the third soldier, and in exchange, is handed a pile of personal belongings from the search. The third soldier walks back toward his Humvee, carrying Rahim and

Badria's guns. The fourth soldier remains as still as a tree, shifting his aim between Rahim and Badria as each of them speaks.

"What did they say about me?" asks Badria. He looks at the translator, almost pleading. "Tell me!"

Pinky holds up Badria's wallet, a tangled handful of wires, and some pliers retrieved during the pat-down. He hands them to the second soldier, who puts them into a plastic bag and holds them up to the light.

From the corner of his eye, Rahim can see exactly what these items amount to. If it weren't for this degrading posture, feet and arms splayed; if it weren't for the weapon pointed his direction; if it weren't for these men in fatigues and all those who came before them decade after decade, Rahim would very rightly turn to Badria in this instant and punch him in the jaw. Instead, he holds his neck ramrod straight, keeps his gaze pinned to Pinky's temple, and waits for what he believes will be the last moments of his life. Sweat trickles down his inner thighs. Salt dries on his tongue, and he wonders if that's it—the last taste he'll remember. Maybe it will be the desert itself, sand sticking to his tongue as he falls to the ground, executed without a second guess. They might shoot him efficiently, fearing the mess they'd have to collect if too much of his body is blown apart. Wrists tied, back turned, on his knees, and that last, heated glance across the desert as Pinky paces behind him. Then that final poke, the tip of an AK into the back of Rahim's head, and—

Whatever work Badria is into, he's into it deep.

"What now?" Rahim asks the translator.

"They're going to check you for explosive powder."

Pinky thumbs through Rahim's wallet as though it were his own. He removes several US dollar bills, stares at them for a long moment, then replaces them. He mutters something—"dollars"

177

and "haji" are all Rahim can make out—then looks at the translator and asks: "From Gawri?" The name means nothing to Rahim, though the translator perks up, exchanging a glance with Pinky.

"Where'd you get this money?" the translator asks.

"From the bazaar," Rahim says. He's heard that infantry soldiers are ignorant. That only generals with medals on their uniforms know what's really happening during wartime. Maybe there's still a chance to talk his way out of this. Maybe the dollars will confuse Pinky or, better yet, make him lust for a bigger prize. A real target. Actual Taliban. Anything other than him and Badria, just two little maggots on a donkey carcass. "It's from the merchants who come up to our village from Kandahar," Rahim continues. "I bought rice last week. That's my change. The merchants gave it to me."

"Tell that loud one not to touch our money," Badria shouts.

The translator turns to Pinky and reports.

Pinky nods slowly, his mouth curling into a frown so that his bottom lip protrudes slightly. A fly lands on his wet, persimmon skin. He spits and waves it off. The third soldier returns with a kit and snaps on a pair of plastic gloves.

"And the AKs?" Pinky says, all of them understanding now.

"One gun per household," Badria explains to the translator, his tone mocking. The second soldier grabs Badria's hands and swipes them with a piece of paper.

"That's the American rule," Rahim says. "Those are our only weapons. We're following the rules."

They wait for the translator to repeat their replies to Pinky. All the while, Rahim is also checked for explosive powder, a farce if he's ever seen one. The Americans will take or leave whatever they choose. The test, he believes, is merely a magician's sleight of hand.

"What's your name?" Pinky asks through the translator.

"Rahim."

"Rahim," Pinky says, pondering. The syllables sound strange coming across his tongue, long and flat like a piece of jerky.

"Enemy combatant," the third soldier says. Rahim can't tell if it's a question or an observation, but in either case, the English words do not appear to have been meant for him. Pinky nods and the third soldier cuffs Badria, who curses and spouts. The second soldier, still standing guard, turns his full attention to Rahim.

"Rahim, Rahim," Pinky says and his voice has shifted to a taunt. He continues, a ranting list of familiar phrases falling on Rahim's ears like slaps. "What's your last name, Rahim? Fucking Akbar? Fucking Rahim Allahu Akbar Jesus Mary Joseph Raghead?" Pinky shakes his head, apparently amused with himself. The second soldier chuckles along with him.

"I don't. Understand," Rahim speaks in broken English, the translator otherwise occupied with the third soldier, both of them cramming Badria into the backseat of a Humvee. "I am. Rahim. Yes."

"Hey," Pinky shouts over his shoulder. The translator jogs back, breathless beneath the weight of his fancy American gear. Pinky shouts a final command, then spits onto the ground. The glistening wad lands a few inches from Rahim's sandals.

"He's done with you," the translator says. "Your test came back negative. They want to take you in—I can tell—but there's no more room in the Humvees."

"What about my wallet?"

Pinky stops mid-stride, apparently able to understand. He turns and walks back to Rahim, stopping just inches short of his smooshed nose. "A gift," he says, another word Rahim has heard, although the context doesn't seem right. "For you, *Rahim.*" Pinky returns the money and the wallet, slipping them lightly into Rahim's vest pocket. The gesture is almost feminine—overly gentle—its meaning lost on Rahim. Pinky barks a final comment and returns to his Humvee.

"You can lower your hands," the translator says.

"What did he say?" Rahim asks.

"He said you're '*lucky*,'" the translator smiles oddly, somehow bolstered.

"What is 'lucky'?" Rahim asks.

"'Lucky' means if he ever sees you again, he's going to kill your lying *raghead* dirty dog ass. Now get out of here."

16

Even the Greeks

"I got my eye on it; I got my eye on it," Yak calls over the radio. Supreme slows the lead vehicle and brings the convoy to a halt.

"What do you got?" Miller asks. Their convoy is three klicks from the friendlies, five more past that to Imar. Whatever Yak has spotted, it surely blocks forward progress.

"The little shits," Folson says. He presses the tips of his fingers into the puffy flesh around his black eye. "Am I seeing that right?"

And now they all see it—a scattering of wires, the main charge of an IED hastily detonated, the wide tread marks of American Humvees continuing past.

"Can we back up?" Huang asks.

"It's already been taken care of," Miller says, looking through the binocs.

The Spartans spill from their vehicles, as if from overstuffed jars. Stiff legs, hunched shoulders. They dance in the heat—shaking limbs back to life, popping necks. Caldwell gazes up at the sky, wandering in a small circle of steps at the edge of the road. John Boy bursts into a set of angled push-ups propped against the side of Spartan 1. Folson, Supreme, and Yak go straight for the bomb, eager to get a look. At the end of the line, Romero and Sparco bust into a sloppy version of the cancan while Rock takes their photo. Beyond Spartan 3, Taylor and Reynolds have their backs turned to take a piss, scanning the hillsides while they're at it.

Miller crouches down to inspect what's left of the bomb and shakes his head. "Our road clearance team would have caught this yesterday," he says. He always hates this moment. The one where there's no denying American presence isn't wanted anymore. *His* presence. It's so personal. Another part of him feels affirmed. What if a child had tripped this? A farmer? Anyone, for that matter, who hadn't signed up for the kind of ultimate sacrifice a bomb can exact?

He'd felt proud after the US's initial invasion. "We did it right this time," he remembers telling Tenley that Christmas after 9/11. She hugged him and told him she believed in him, that she knew their future together could be assured. "I'll wait. You know I will. Then we can get down to this business of growing our lives together, growing our family."

Memories like that still bring a knot to Miller's throat, even across the months and miles, finding him again as he fingers a few of the loose wires, rolling them between his palms. He marvels at the IED's simplicity, the power and powerlessness it enacts. He can talk himself into and out of everything—life, death. Too good. He is too good at leadership in bad situations, yet he loves the way this gift forces decisiveness. The way it feels like family. How do you tell your wife that you love the very thing that took you away from her? That you kill in order to lie next to her again? You don't tell her. And even if you did, you'd have to get to her first. You'd have to make it home.

"What do you think, LT? Taliban?"

Miller turns to Folson, offering a nod. "It was planted late last night or early this morning. The friendlies Yak saw on the Tracker must have cleared it."

Folson crouches to get a better look at the set up. Reynolds clods over to join him, forming a close huddle.

"Definitely looks like Spec Ops work if you ask me," Reynolds says. "Quick 'n dirty."

"I know something else that's quick and dirty," Folson says.

"Diarrhea?" Reynolds says.

"Speaking of Spec Ops..." Huang says from the backseat of Bean Curd. His legs drape over the side of the seat, dangling out the open door so that his boots hover half a foot above the ground.

Miller glances up the two-track and sees dust rising above three Humvees headed their direction. Folson's laughter pulls his attention back.

"Look at him!" Folson says. He grabs Reynolds by the arm and points at Huang. "Just look at him!" Folson loses his balance and falls from a crouch into a sprawl across the ground. "He's..." Folson breathes between giggles, "he's...so...fucking afraid... he...he won't even put his boots on the ground!" he clutches his side and continues laughing.

Reynolds stands and walks toward Huang. "Do me a favor," he says, grabbing Huang and yanking him to his feet. "Save us from Folson's bullshit? If not for yourself, at least for the rest of us. Just like...cowboy up, man. Snap to it. Can you do that, Huang? For one day?"

Huang looks down at his boots. "I'll try," he says, barely a whisper.

The Spec Ops halt a few meters in front of the Spartans, whipping dust down the line. Miller falls in step along the makeshift road, a dirty, brown cloud swallowing him like a wave.

When the Spec Ops leader dismounts, Miller can't help but notice his perky show of muscle and brawn. It's as though Spec Ops made varsity, the Spartans merely JV. Nothing unusual there, as much as Miller might beg to differ, but what *is* different is that bellyful-of-an-Afghan cuffed in the backseat of the Spec Ops' lead vehicle. A fat Afghan must be something like an embarrassment in a country with thousands of starving civilians. As Miller approaches, he sees the man is more stout than round, wearing the expression of someone who would rather eat shit fresh out of a camel's bunghole than face interrogation.

Sergeant Major Williams holds himself bolt upright, as if locked into his uniform by a steal beam. His handshake is odd out here in the middle of the desert, but Miller responds in kind and asks for the low down. Sunburned and cocky, Williams explains that they've come from outside Kandahar, just out for a joy ride in the foothills. Miller takes that to mean there's no way Williams will tell him why these Spec Ops are actually out and about. But when he asks Williams about the dead Taliban, the sergeant major allows it was their doing, nodding in the direction of the discharged IED as if to say, *You can thank me for that too*. Both men want to keep things short—miles to go before they sleep—and Miller gleans enough from Williams's CliffsNotes to understand that the road ahead is thumbs up all the way to Imar. Williams says his convoy had taken potshots, but that one of the gunmen came up clean on the explosive powder test, and there wasn't any room left in their Humvees to cart him off anyway.

"But at least we got this other haji headed to the slammer, right?" Williams says, then claps his hand across Miller's shoulder.

Miller resists the urge to duck away. His men wait impatiently along the road. Spec Ops are the last thing any of them need. The work Spartan does together is a living thing, ever-poised for excellence. Miller prefers to keep his Spartans upbeat, and the more time Williams takes with his show of bravado, the more impatient Miller becomes.

Williams glances back at their prisoner, then confides in Miller. "I suspect we'll get most of what we need outta this guy during interrogation. Like visiting another fucking planet out here, eh? Anyway, we gotta beat feet," he says. "Catch you on the flip side."

Their Humvees pass, and Miller notes the pudgy Afghan once more, wondering momentarily at his fate. "Gentlemen," he says, "looks like our road from here on out is cleared, but be on the lookout regardless. Take it all in. We got a message from the TOC. The situation on the ground is changing as we speak. What you see or don't see may cost lives for the patrols in Oruzgan once we're home. Let's mount up."

"Hold on," Yak says. He stretches his long arm and points toward the boulders high above. "Supreme here thinks he can beat me to the top of that ridgeline."

"Enemy territory isn't the best place for the Olympics."

"Agreed," Yak continues, "but even the Greeks had their fun during wartime."

"Is that what we're doing?" Folson asks. "Having fun? Guess I didn't get the memo. Jesus. Will this day ever end?" He kicks the toe of his boot into the dirt and rolls his eyes, all frown and furrow. Miller is unfazed—all part of the trajectory from pissed to humbled to back home and setting things right. Folson will come around. Miller has no doubt.

The platoon huddles around the base of the hillside, shielding their eyes as they gaze upward into the naked, hot heat. There, at a point that seems nearly over their heads, perhaps fifty meters up, a gray slab of rock juts from the cliff like a picnic table.

"That one," Supreme points at the rock. "Got it, Yak? To the top and back."

"I'll put ten on Supreme," Rock says.

"Uh…Rock?" Reynolds says. "Hey dude—"

Miller catches the firmness in Reynolds's tone and looks at Rock, aghast. The butt of his gun rests on his boots, barrel pointed dangerously on target with his chin. It seems a soldier would have to work hard to be that belligerent nine months into a tour. Apparently not.

"OK, twenty. Twenty on Supreme," Rock shifts on his feet, the weapon now aimed into his crotch.

"Thanks for the vote of confidence," Supreme says, "but that's not what Reynolds is talking about. Check your weapon before you shoot your balls off."

"Oh," Rock says, obliging.

Miller elbows through his men, headed for the start line. He looks up at the boulder, then back down at his platoon. Sparco is doing jumping jacks, limbering up for his turn. Taylor superheroes his way behind him and sideswipes a leg, knocking Sparco halfway into a sprawl. Yak's face can be seen a head above them all, grin as wide as a child's before the first slice of birthday cake.

"I'll put twenty on Yak," Miller says.

"I want in," Romero says. He fidgets with his fly as his back stays turned to the side. A wet puddle races toward his boots, the soil so dry it refuses to soak anything up. He zips and turns around. "Twenty on Supreme."

"Twenty on Yak," Caldwell says. Heads turn as though following the ball in a tennis match. Caldwell offers a shy smile.

"Caldwell speaks. What the hell? That's omen enough for me. I'll second that. Twenty on Yak," Folson says, and now even he's in it, wagering the odds, glancing again at the distant boulder.

Smack. A slap and rumble cracks through the valley, and Miller freezes. *Smack.* The sound rips around them.

John Boy speaks first. "Just the rocks, guys," he points at a steep hillside opposite where they stand. A stone the size of a football rolls to the valley floor, coming to rest a few feet from the front of the line.

Miller scans the slopes and ridgeline. A smaller rock breaks free as well, sliding halfway down the slope. "Rock, you and I are on watch. The rest of you Spartans? Have at it."

"Game on!" Supreme shouts, springing up the hillside into a head start.

"Ah, hell no," Yak says. He cuts through the scree like a snow leopard, his strides effortless compared to Supreme's huffing and high knees. They're tied at the top, fat hands slapping down on the flat rock to mark the turnaround, then clouds of dust kick up as both men pivot and brace for the downhill. They tear into the slope, gravity and battle rattle pulling them down against the shifting Earth, and just look at Yak go: each stride like a leap for every three of Supreme's frantic steps. He propels ahead, and the Spartans shout: "C'mon, big money, c'mon!"

Smack, smack, whoosh. Supreme tosses forward into the air, catapulted by a misstep, and for a millisecond, he looks frozen, feet and arms splayed like a flying squirrel, before he tucks and rolls into a cannonball, landing on a smooth patch of dirt. A loud grunt escapes his lips, forced by the hard landing, then—"Weeee—a-hah-hah-hah—hoo-hoo-hoooo!"—Supreme rolls the rest of the way down, ass over teakettle, surpassing Yak by a good ten feet and coming to rest at Miller's boots.

Yak braces himself against his knees, catching his breath. He shakes his head. "Goddamn, Supreme. Just…goddamn."

Supreme looks up, dazed and grinning, a slow trickle of blood coming from his newly crooked nose. "Who's taking on the winner?" he says and pushes up to his feet.

A small voice lifts above the din. "I will," Huang says. "I'll race against you, Supreme," he removes his Kevlar and begins stretching his legs.

"Well, how about that?" Folson says, nodding.

Reynolds gives Huang a jostling slap on the back.

"OK. Just gimme a minute," Supreme gulps some water, pops his neck.

"We'll run next," Taylor says, shoving Sparco toward the start line.

The two take off while Supreme rests. Huang stands beside him, running his arms in windmill circles. They could be part of a circus act—Supreme standing there as stalky as a rhino and a smear of blood across his cut-up nose, four inches taller than Huang's lean, antelope frame. But as Sparco and Taylor come cross the finish line neck and neck, Supreme and Huang line up, and Miller can't help but watch. This could actually be a fair match.

"Twenty on Huang," he says.

"Ready? And..." Yak pauses, "*GO!*"

The two scramble upward, Huang moving lightly atop the loose ground, and Supreme slamming up the slope, arms pumping as if to hoist himself along some imaginary system of cables. Huang could almost be a ballerina, the way he leaps from stone to stone on his toes as his arms lift and fall, lift and fall, wings of balance and momentum doing exactly what they're built to do. Miller follows Huang's steps, a marvel of precision, and though the men are equally close to reaching the top, he knows that Huang will win this round just as surely as a zing of confidence assures him he'll make it home, so soon, to work on life and love in Appalachia with Tenley.

He watches Huang advance nearly twenty feet ahead of Supreme on the way down, leaning into the hillside and bracing himself against it with one hand.

"C'mon, little fucker. C'mon," Folson cheers.

"Yeah, Huang, *yeah*!" Miller hollers.

"Almost there, dude, rake it in," Yak says, and the men quickly form two parallel lines, extending one hand into the center so that Huang can finish the race through a victory tunnel, high-fives and ass-slaps all the way down the line.

"I did it," Huang beams. He watches Supreme cross the finish line, and the two bear hug.

"All right, Spartans," Miller says, smiling. "We're Oscar Mike."

17

Some Break Away

It's Ghazél's soft sounds of sleep that finally pull Aaseya's thoughts back into the room. She'd like to clean him, at least a little, before Rahim comes home. She squats at the side of his new sleeping spot and studies his face. Flecks of dirt line his closed eyelids, and she can see a few fleas in his shaggy, dark hair. His lips are chapped, his earlobes bitten and red. Scuff marks fall in a line down his torso, likely from belly-crawling over rocks or wriggling through shrubs. At the bottom of his shorts, each leg pokes through the opening of fabric like a tent pole. His feet appear large by comparison, blackened with dirt. Aaseya brings her hand to his shoulder and coaxes him from sleep.

"When you're ready, come into the gathering room."

Ghazél blinks and nods a few times, his eyes opening into the soft light of his new home.

Within minutes, he's devoured a serving of yogurt and several crackers. He eats mightily, smiling at Aaseya between bites. She wipes a creamy, white smear from his chin with the tip of her thumb. He finishes and thanks her with a little bow, then nods in the direction of the satchel from Shanaz. Aaseya brings it to him, and he begins to forage. She helps him adjust the leather straps on the pair of sandals, and he scuffs his feet along the floor, curious. Next, he snatches a red T-shirt and pulls it over his head. Arms through the sleeves. He inspects himself, picking at the white plastic lines that curve and loop across the front in semi-circular letters: *Coca-Cola.*

"It all looks very handsome," Aaseya says.

Ghazél smiles.

"I'd like to help you wash your feet, if our water arrives before my husband comes home. And maybe you'd let me cut your hair?"

Ghazél brings both hands to the sides of his head and grabs a few clumps of hair. He shrugs. Aaseya turns to find a pair of scissors and a sound catches her attention. A distant helicopter, perhaps. Ghazél rushes to the window and stands on tiptoe, fingertips curled over the bottom of the sill. Aaseya joins him, and the sound grows in intensity, an unbidden rumble—not at all like the thwapping of blades through the sky now but an earthy sound. The undeniable movement of a convoy.

"It's the Americans," Aaseya says. "It has to be."

A spiral of dust rises at the open end of the village, then hovers mid-sky. "Ghazél?" she says, and even as the last syllable rolls off her tongue, she can already sense that he's gone.

She eyes the bed. The kitchen. Returns her attention to the street and there he is, the back of his bright red shirt a full block away.

"Come back!" she says. "It's not safe!"

But there's no telling what he's thinking now and no time to guess. Aaseya grabs her burqa and tosses it over her head, cursing uselessly as the fabric tangles. She'll never save him. He'll be blown to bits, and she'll still be stuck inside, struggling to get dressed.

Outside, she adjusts the fabric of her burqa mid-stride, her jogging awkward and unpracticed. Through the alley one block to her right, she can see American Humvees moving past. She tiptoes carefully along a shortcut, as if only letting her toes touch the ground would spare her feet. Of course, stepping on a bomb would rip her open from the bottom up, flopping her wet torso onto the ground some distance away. She squeezes through an alley and steps onto the parallel street into the tread marks left by the convoy. If their Humvees don't trigger an explosion, she won't trigger an explosion—and there's no way they'll notice her if she runs in the dust trailing behind them now in a dense cloud. She picks up her pace again, scanning the doorways and corners for Ghazél, coughing and shielding the screen of her burqa. The sound of the engines is magnanimous, out of body. It reminds Aaseya of a beast, something wild and unpersuaded, insistent upon a meal. She runs faster, stumbling over debris, coughing, and she thinks of a gigantic, crazed dog, its jaw snapping open and closed, a five-armed demon, and finally, the image of a house-sized, tooth-lined mouth settles in her mind. She can see it there, wide-open, waiting at the schoolhouse for Ghazél to walk right into its jaws.

At the near edge of the bazaar, Aaseya stops to catch her breath. She shakes the dust from her burqa and coughs again. Her vision clears, and she can hardly believe her eyes. Almost everyone in Imar has come to greet the soldiers, herding themselves like cattle around the convoy, rushing to take handouts—no hesitancy about it. She wants to warn them. Surely it's a setup. Surely the Taliban have been waiting to take prime shots at these unsuspecting, iron-clad men in camouflage. Perhaps a few villagers along with them. But first, Ghazél. She'll run straight through those soldiers to get to him if she has to. They might be handing out bottles of water, but as far as Aaseya's concerned, every last one of them is a target just asking to be shot down. No way does she want Ghazél near that. She can't help but think of Shanaz, who'd seen decades of war before Aaseya even took her first breath. Or her father, who somehow never let this horribleness trespass into Aaseya's family courtyard. Who held her close but also let her fly. He'd never prepared her for something like this, and yet, with this feeling of desperation—that she must love Ghazél, must protect him—in fact, Janan showed Aaseya exactly what to do.

She approaches the scene smartly, sticking to the sides of buildings, scanning the crowd for that red T-shirt. With her back pressed against the cigar shop window, she peers over at the schoolhouse. She expects to see a sniper, but the building seems oddly placid, and it strikes her then that Ghazél wouldn't want to be close to the schoolhouse at all. Has he even seen Americans before? Aaseya guesses that he hasn't, and so she knows he must be trying to hide. She ducks along the perimeter of the schoolhouse, around the back corner, and into the open area where not a single soul can be seen. Some days, the bazaar is so full that additional vendors or passing nomadic groups gather here, a sort of makeshift overflow market. But now the space looks dull and flat, a plain expanse in the bright, midday sun.

She finds Ghazél in the shade of an abandoned, three-walled stall, his back pressed against the plywood. He looks at her, wide-eyed. He can hardly sit still, yet he appears likewise paralyzed with concern. Aaseya sits next to him and exhales a long, quiet breath.

"Ghazél," she says, "I need you to stay close to me. We need to be safe, together. Do you understand?"

He nods.

"Why did you run away like that? Were you curious or scared?"

The answer doesn't matter—only that she let him feel her steadiness next to him, let him breathe it in. They sit for a few moments in silence, and Ghazél reaches slyly into his pocket to reveal the tiny, pink-haired plastic toy. He flips it from palm to palm, almost playfully, then holds it up to Aaseya like a proof. But the gesture seems odd, unclear. She nods kindly but can't draw any meaning from Ghazél's expression.

Nearby, a flock of doves lifts from the steep slope, fluttering and disturbed. A few loose pieces of shale slide downward. Aaseya watches the birds lift and flap, then land farther down the hillside. A few tent awnings flap, and the bottom of her burqa unfurls in the breeze. She stares at the swirling sands in front of her, the framed view from their makeshift shelter like a window on a world she once believed in. The flock of birds lifts again, settling farther downhill. Some break away and fly overhead, out of sight. She can almost see herself a mother, almost see herself a learned woman. Yet the past can still weigh her down if she lets it, as exhausting as stones tied around her ankles. It's not a burden she can afford to live with anymore. There are other things to tend to, louder now. She wraps her arm around Ghazél, and she knows it without question: everyone will die someday.

Even this boy.

Even herself.

Right now, the only thing left to do is live.

18

The Beauty in It

At the opposite edge of town, a thin-chested man waves kebabs at Rahim. "Five *afghanis*," he calls. "Five!"

Rahim approaches the ramshackle cart. It's not that he feels hungry. Rather, disheveled, this new skin of the lucky-to-be-living oddly exhilarating.

"Sir?" the vendor calls. Branches of varying thickness form an awning above his cart. A thin rice sack tied at the corners creates a rectangle of shade over the sizzling meat. He works capably, turning kebabs over a low flame, then snatches one from the grill and thrusts it toward Rahim.

Rahim smooths his *dishdasha* and surveys the food. "Two, please," he says. The darkened meat smells smoky and rich, the end of each stick slippery with warm grease. Rahim fumbles with the money in his wallet until he finds his last remaining *afghanis*. Better to save the bills for another time. He pays the vendor and stands for a moment, biting into the beef and licking his lips. Maybe he should find Badria's sons and tell them of their father's fate. But what if Obaidullah persuaded the sons to work for him too? Rahim takes another bite, considering.

Across the street, two boys play santoors, their backs resting against a beige shack. They can't be more than eight or nine years old, barefooted with patchy Western clothing draped over their bodies. Singing along with the plucked notes, their harmony rings like only the voices of siblings can, filled with the pleading pride trademarked by most folk songs. *Benazum Chashmanet.* The notes rise like the memory of fog lifting from the valley, resonating with Rahim's feeling that this is a new day. A day he should have died. A day now freely given. He hasn't heard the song in years, but he feels it now, dancing in his belly, awakened from a deep sleep. The song reaches its apex, the boys' voices splitting into harmony for the final chorus, and Rahim exhales. He won't enslave himself to Obaidullah. He won't return to the creek beds anymore either. He sinks his teeth into the kebab, crushed tarragon and peppercorn filling his mouth. Possibility melts down his throat. He crosses the street and offers the second kebab to the boys, who accept it gratefully.

As he turns toward home, Rahim hears a rumble as resonant as thunder. Humvees, no doubt. He abandons the loop road and flees beyond the boys toward the surrounding slopes. Face to face with two convoys in one day? The improbability almost makes him laugh, but the uncertainty in his chest propels him forward. Did the Americans execute Badria and return for him? But he saw them drive toward the highway. He watched them leave. Fearing the worst, he follows side trails along the contours of the slope, staying high above the loop road and well-hidden amidst the terrain. He moves easily over the outcroppings and through shrubs, but his heart is an earthquake in his chest. Below, he sees the blueprint of Imar. Three Humvees cruise toward the edge of town like a death squad, but they're different than Pinky's. These Humvees carry boxes that say "water" in Arabic, Pashto, Dari, and English.

Badria had been right, in an odd sort of way. Magpie or otherwise, there can be no accident about this aid delivery to a village that now serves as Obaidullah's headquarters. Rahim presses along the game trails a few hundred feet upslope from the bazaar and overflow area, remaining hidden and alone on the hillside. Here, the dead-end slopes on either side of the Imar valley meet in a perfectly curved wall of mountains. The soldiers will have to get back on the loop road in the park. It's the only place this far into the village where such wide vehicles can turn efficiently. Rahim guesses they're not likely to linger long and let themselves get cornered. Still, it wouldn't take much. He'll be safest here, along the side rim, downwind of any strategic positions and just above any potential targets. He crouches into the hillside, and a few loose rocks tumble down, scaring up a flock of doves. He settles onto his haunches, then leans against the ground and remains completely still. He craves the cool cornrows in the Mirabad, the soft sounds of that other village, that other valley, that other life. He's lived too many lives for one man—made so little of each. The sun remains high overhead, a constant eye, and it strikes him how utterly sapping and selfish the sun can be. So eternally insistent.

Several minutes pass, and Rahim raises his head just enough to scan the village. The Humvees are still gathered at the schoolhouse, the soldiers busy posing for photos and emptying boxes. In the park beyond the schoolhouse, just below his perch along the side rim, he sees a boy step out from one of the sheds. He's wearing a bright red T-shirt, his back turned to Rahim. In his hands, he holds a pink-haired toy. A woman follows, standing behind the boy, both of them in the center of the road. Her back is also turned, completely anonymous in her blue burqa—if it weren't for the voice Rahim recognizes next.

"Ghazél!" his wife says. "We have to stay hidden."

For a moment, Rahim is remarkably unshocked. Of course his wife is out again. Of course she's going to want to get water when it's free for the taking, and perhaps there's no shame in that. Perhaps there's no shame in much of anything. His culture certainly has its faults. It's certainly betrayed him more than once too. Why perpetuate such rigidity? But then it occurs to him how foolish Aaseya and the boy are, siphoned off from the crowd, waiting in the exact spot an ambush seems imminent.

He descends from the side rim and approaches them from behind. He has no plan, only the feeling in his gut that something is about to go terribly wrong. As he nears the shelter, he sees the boy step farther from Aaseya's reach, offering a clear profile view. Rahim doesn't recognize the red shirt, but the boy—with that gnarled mop of hair, those grass-blade legs—is undeniably the orphan he saw at the bottom of his apartment steps that morning.

Aaseya stomps her foot impatiently in the road. "Ghazél," she says, "I know you want to see them. You'll have your chance, but we have to be safe. It's not as simple as you think."

The boy steps farther away, refusing to heed Aaseya's advice. She takes a few steps toward him, and again, he moves farther away. She looks at the sky for a moment, as if exasperated. It's a feeling Rahim knows well, but it looks different on his wife. Her tone captivates him, so focused and caring. She calls after the boy again, but he only moves farther from her, nearly ten paces distant now, carrying the pink-haired toy in his outstretched hand. Aaseya's blue burqa falls in folds over her head and down her shoulders, rippling along her back. It's beautiful to see her like this—hoping, longing—and Rahim steps forward into the light, whispering her name.

"Aaseya," he says. "Aaseya."

She turns to him, an ease spreading across her shoulders, and there is no scorn left. There is only the middle of this road. This husband. This wife. This tiny moment of two worlds meeting, new to each other again. In the distance, Humvee engines kick back to life, and the boy looks anxiously over his shoulder, eyeing Aaseya and Rahim in their tight huddle.

"Don't go any farther," Aaseya calls, and finally, Ghazél sits down in the middle of the road and waits.

19

Doing Something Right

The convoy nears the main part of the village. A vendor selling kebabs works frantically to hold his makeshift cart intact as the Spartans vibrate past. Miller can see actual residences now—mud-cooked family homes, the occasional two-story dwelling. Coils of smoke lift from several courtyards. Some homes have no windows or openings at all, just a hand-built wall surrounding each compound of small, interconnected dwellings. Others have cut tiny spaces to welcome the light and air, faded red or yellow curtains flapping thinly in the breeze. Three little girls hurry from a hiding spot behind an outbuilding. The oldest shuffles the other two away from the convoy and looks over her shoulder at the men, moving with the practiced hustle of war. Even here, at the far reaches of nowhere, they seem suspicious.

"Team leaders, remind your men of the directive," Miller says into the radio. The throbbing has magnified and feels like a hawk's nest being woven into the base of his skull. "Gimme some of that," he says, nodding at Reynolds's pack of chewing tobacco. Reynolds slides it along the dash, and Miller swipes at it, tucks a pinch-full into his mouth. He spits hard into the footwell.

Reynolds hums an obscure hip-hop tune, and Folson fingers the safety on his M4. Meanwhile Huang has apparently found himself ready for battle. Staring into the rearview, Miller sees him double-check the ESAPI plates in his body armor, tighten the strap on his Kevlar, then shift upward in his seat. He exhales and broadens his shoulders, on alert. Miller peers to his left through Reynolds's window. A few blocks on this outer ring of Imar have been totally obliterated, but he can't tell if the damage is recent. Rubble collects in steep piles that spill into the roadway.

Bean Curd cuts sharply around a pile of bricks in the road, and Miller feels the convoy's synchronized movement like a completed pass downfield. A few of his men stick their arms out their windows and wave. Dozens of families jog alongside them now, following eagerly. Miller opens his window and catches a few phrases: "*Ooba? Ooba?*" a mother asks, meaning "water," and he gives a thumbs up. The Spartans just want to help. This should all go quite smoothly. If only the army could figure out a way to complete humanitarian missions without appearing so bullish. They could really learn a thing or two from the Guard, but no room for that kind of talk—not with the brass on Copperhead. Miller wanted to believe Chaffen when he said Imar is stable. But, that freshly cleared landmine they passed on their way here. That dead body. Those dollars. The delivery trucks. Now, Gawri's assassination. None of it feels good, and who cares, at this point, about the difference between hunches and hard facts? Miller is running on instinct—the only way it should be—and hopes to be able to hand over a report chock-full of intel when this mission is complete.

Miller reaches for his clipboard for a last glance at the village map. A little less than one klick long. According to the satellite images, just beyond the schoolhouse, the road stretches a bit farther through a park—someone has labeled it Checkpoint Budweiser on the map—and what looks to be a few more shacks before rejoining the loop road that doubles back around the village toward the highway. Unless someone comes right at them screaming *"Alahu Akbar!"* there's not likely to be much reason to fire at anything here anyway.

At long last, the Spartans roll to a stop at the edge of the bazaar, the two-level schoolhouse before them. Businesses and ramshackle compounds squat on all sides, though it's a challenge to fully orient with so many civilians surrounding them now, shoving and chanting. One woman cries, holding out her deformed baby like an offering.

"It's too crowded here, LT," this from Yak, over the radio.

"I second that," Rock calls through his headset at the back of the line.

"Easy does it, gentlemen," Miller finds his voice. "Kill your engines. Once they see us open the boxes, there'll be no stopping them."

But Yak is right. Even without the rumble of the engines and the clattering of gear banging around in the Humvees, this tight little spot in the desert only grows tighter, like a blood clot about to break loose.

"All weapons on safety. All hands at the ready," Miller announces. "One man up top. Everybody else, out."

He sets his clipboard back onto the dash and pats it, as though touching Tenley's shoulder before leaving the room. Huang rises into the turret, no questions asked.

Miller gets out. Chatter and demands hit him like a sonic boom, an unending ripple of foreign sounds. So many desperate faces. He sees everything, poises himself to anticipate the unseen. He looks up and down the line of Humvees. The Spartans fall seamlessly into position: Folson with his grumpiness, Caldwell with his muttered prayers. John Boy, Supreme. Each reaching for boxes of water, scanning their surroundings. Taylor passes out a few packs of Ice Breakers Gum and MREs, inviting a momentary cheer. Miller can even see Sparco at the very end, teaching fist-bumps to a few children. Romero hops up into the turret to watch the convoy's back. Rock fiddles with something in his cargo pocket, eyes down, M4 leaning loosely against the side of his leg. Miller rails him over the radio, and Rock straightens up, back in the game. The civilians' cries pulse even louder, and Miller joins his men unloading boxes of water. A few satisfied smiles, thirst quenched, and that's all it takes.

Their last day. This lost village.

It feels so good to do something right.

There's a method to it, of course. Scan the rooftops. Look down alleys. Miller's eyes remain in constant motion, fingertips ready to click into action. He smiles and scans: *West side, clear. East side, clear. North...*he hands out more water and looks at the schoolhouse, its darkened window openings and missing front door. "Huang, keep an eye on that schoolhouse," he says.

More children materialize, arms flailing, voices laughing in their race to greet the men from America. The air fills with high-pitched cries. "*Ooba! Ooba!*" they shout. A few trip in the hustle, their small, brown bodies slapping onto the ground. That quickly, they're up again, dusty knees pumping toward the nearest open box.

One of them giggles when Romero passes him a water bottle. "You're brown, like us!" he says in strained English. A few children touch Romero's skin and try to rub the color off, convinced it's fake.

Sparco stands next to Romero and laughs. "Yeah, what's up, haji?"

Romero smiles and waves to a few kids from his position in the turret.

"Somebody tell those kids I got more brown than all y'all," Taylor says.

Behind the first wave of children come more. Civilians by the dozen pour around courtyard walls, clapping down mud staircases, pushing past one another. The adults are slower but no less demanding. They move in a wall of color. Gray *dishdashas* and baggy, brown vests. Ivory *keffeyas* and black sandals. Slate blue burqas and bare, cracked feet. Some men are without shirts. A few elders watch from the sidelines, long, white beards caught in the wind. One man leans heavily on his stick cane. A little boy dashes up to him and shares his water.

The women are pushed to the back and must elbow their way forward again.

"*Maata raaka ooba,*" they say—*Give me water.* Then, "*Tersha! Ma!*—Move! Don't!" as they get closer, pushing past their husbands, reaching with dark, dry hands for that clean, clear plastic.

Miller cannot believe the greediness of the men. The way they bully the children and hoard bottles in their shirtsleeves. "*Yaw yaw,*" he says, remembering his studies. "*Aaraam sha.*" *One at a time. Calm down.* The Spartans repeat after their leader, the message making its way down the line.

Within minutes, the crowd calms as everyone drinks. Very few sounds escape other than the small, slurping glugs of water washing down throats. Just watching makes Miller thirsty himself, but he won't drink. Not now. There are peripherals to scan and more bottles to be given away, and besides, this isn't about him. This isn't even about war. It's about one human being doing what's needed to help another, and damn if it doesn't feel like what he was born to do. Has been trying to do all these years since those earthworms in the road. Since his courtship of Tenley. Since enlistment, since Basic. Since first promotion, first mortgage, first child. His old self again, not bitter. Not uncertain. Just focused and content. Doing the good, hard work of a guardsman. Across the crowd, Miller sees countless water bottles tipped bottom-up, draining into open mouths. It's beautiful, the way the sun plays off the plastic, shooting beams of light across the tiny village center like little flares of hope.

Caldwell must see the red-shirted boy first because he calls out to Miller, and they both study the child's approach—a fast run, though light as air, gaining on the huddle. He's the only civilian without water. Caldwell calls out to him in Pashto, offering. The boy is thin, in a pair of baggy shorts, a Coca-Cola T-shirt, and a swatch of tangled black hair. Caldwell shouts again, inviting the boy closer, but when the boy sees that Caldwell signals specifically to him, he backs away, skittish.

"What's that all about?" John Boy asks.

"Dunno," Caldwell says.

"Keep your eye on that one," Miller calls down the line.

Folson looks up. "Which?"

"Red T-shirt. Ten o'clock," Caldwell shouts and returns his attention to the crowd, the houses behind them, the alleys between. Miller scans again.

Rather than going for water, the boy stops in front of Bean Curd and looks at Huang high up in the turret.

Huang swivels the turret away from center, so as not to aim at this small, curious child. "Hi," says Huang. "*Assalamu alaikum.*"

The boy points at the schoolhouse and frowns, stomping his feet. He looks back at Huang, expectant.

"I don't think he can talk," observes Miller. "He's trying to tell us something though."

Miller walks toward the boy. "Yes, we're here to help. Help," he says, then gestures with open palms. He wishes he could be clear;

207

there's only so much time. He reaches into a box. "*Delta*," he says. *Here.* "*Ooba.*"

And up close he can see it, how the boy is no more than five or six years old, no father in sight.

No father. Tonight. Tonight he will call Tenley. He will sing to Cissy over the phone. He'll read books on child psychology. He'll apologize. He'll laugh. He'll cry. He'll tell them it's finally time. Time to come home.

The boy takes the water and drinks.

"That'll do it," Miller says, turning toward his men. "Load 'em up. Let's loop behind the schoolhouse and around the village. See what we can see on our way out."

One by one, all the way down the line, the soldiers of Spartan Platoon begin their retreat. They leave the empty boxes in the road, of use to the civilians in Imar somehow, no doubt. Up front, Supreme revs Spartan 1, and Yak and John Boy pile in. Caldwell hops in last, genuinely smiling. Farther down, Taylor and Romero pose for a quick photo with children whose small, brown faces smile into the sunlight.

Miller would like to think he's going to miss the satisfaction moments like this afford, but more than likely, he won't. There is something about that last moment of looking though. As if by staring hard enough, he could see what's waiting for his men at the end of this main drag, in these next few minutes, at the close of this day, at the end of their tour. But he can't. No one can. He exhales and slides into his Humvee.

"Long ride back," he says.

"I'll stay up top till we get out of the village," Huang says.

Miller peers beyond the schoolhouse. A few empty water bottles dance in the middle of the road, caught in a whirlpool of wind.

"Folson, come on!" Reynolds shouts.

Miller looks at Folson's back and notices the awkward stance—the way he holds his arms slightly away from his sides, as if afraid to touch something. "Folson?" he says. "What the hell?"

Not eight feet from their Humvee, Folson stands rooted to the spot.

"Folson," Miller shouts again, "let's go!"

Slowly, Folson turns to face his squad, eyes locked between heartbroken and humored. A young girl stands on Folson's boots, her hands hooked into the straps of his body armor. Each time he lifts a foot she giggles and clasps herself tighter to his frame, as though he's a carnival ride. She appears delighted to feel so tall, so strong, and she can hardly help herself—mirroring steps with this lumbering man, the one who won't smile, but if he'll just play along, her eyes seem to beg him, surely he'll laugh and realize the game. Miller hops back out and rushes to Folson and the girl.

"Easy does it," he says, peeling her tiny hands from Folson's vest. "*Korta zah.*" *Go home.* The girl steps down, and Miller pats her on the head, her dirty pink headscarf slipping slightly down her forehead. When he looks at Folson again, he can see his face start to ease back into itself, that grumpy, gifted soldier just on the other side of a tight-lipped stare. Even his black eye looks improved, the swelling finally starting to go down.

"My daughter plays that game with me," Folson says. "The oldest, Sarah. She plays it, and we walk all over the house together like that, sometimes even down the sidewalk, and I sing this ridiculous song—*gahlump gahlump, gahlumpity lump*....She can't get enough of it..."

Miller is surprised at first. Surely, nine months into this thing Folson would have noticed by now—the way children still play, even in a war zone. The way they look at Americans with eyes that know too much for their own good yet still want to giggle and pinch and lead games of chase down IED-laced roads. How their presence can jerk even the toughest soldier into a nostalgic state of mind, surreal. But he hasn't. Not until now, and secretly, this is what Miller had hoped Folson would get out of today. A moment of reckoning. Something to bring him out of his self-pity and into the world of here and now.

"C'mon brother," Miller says and puts a hand on Folson's shoulder. "Time to go home." They mount up, and Miller calls through the headset. "Let's keep it at five miles an hour," he radios to Yak.

"Yes, Sir."

The convoy moves slowly, skirting the schoolhouse, headed to the trailings of the bazaar where they can turn around and gain back-access to the loop road. In the backseat of Bean Curd, Folson bites his fingernails, squinting out the side window. Miller can tell by his view in the rearview that Folson's disoriented by the rush of emotions, that mess of feelings he probably thought he could get rid of the day he shimmied up the flagpole in his boxers, ready to hurl his life down into a desert pancake. But it's good to feel things. It's OK to feel.

"There's that kid again," Huang calls down. "Sitting right in the middle of the road—what the hell? And there's a man and a woman standing behind him."

"Hold up, Yak," Miller radios, but Supreme has already hit the brakes in Spartan 1. "I've got this," Miller hops out. In four quick paces, he's at the tip of the spear, and Yak opens his door to consult. "Yak, you got your phrasebook?"

He yanks it from his breast pocket and hands it to Miller.

"Good man," Miller calls over his shoulder. "Folson! Caldwell! Get your asses out here!" Folson and Caldwell catch up. "Spartan

3," he shouts even louder. "Eyes on the back of that schoolhouse. If the civilians follow us, keep them at bay. Huang, stay in the turret. Watch the opposing ridgeline."

He points to the end of the valley where the U-shaped peaks huddle like spectators. Miller's voice is charged with purpose. There's got to be more to this boy than a simple bottle of water. He turns to Folson and Caldwell. "Let's give this the time it needs. It's our last chance. We're better off talking to a few civilians here than dealing with that mob back there. This is for the guys coming in after us. You with me?"

"Yes, Sir," Folson says. Caldwell takes up position in the middle of the road in front of Spartan 1.

Miller and Folson move toward the boy, who stands slowly and holds out a small, plastic toy as an offering. Beyond, the woman calls to the boy pleadingly, and the boy raises his hands above his head in surrender. The man and woman do the same.

"*Mawewga*," shouts Miller. "*Moong delta raghlee yu che staase sara maresta wukru.*" *Don't be frightened. We are here to help you.* Caldwell echoes Miller's plea, then adds a few more phrases of his own that Miller can't decipher.

The sun is so blinding against the bright road with so little else to spread itself across, Miller has to squint to make sure he's seeing clearly. Three civilians, visibly unarmed, and one of them trying to give him...*a present?*

"Stop!" Caldwell hollers.

Miller registers the click of a magazine locking into place.

"Don't move!"

"Caldwell, hold your fire. These people are not a threat. Not on the books, they're not."

"LT, there's a landmine behind the boy," Caldwell says tersely. "I can see it in the scope, eleven o'clock, just three feet behind him, a little to the right. Jesus Christ, don't let that kid move!"

Folson jerks into action. "Hey, kid! KID!" he yells, but he's too fast for his own mouth, feet already pushing forward, fatherly determination in his stride.

"Drop your weapon, Caldwell," Miller shouts. "Folson? Folson!" but he's already cut the distance between himself and the boy by half. "Don't go any further, Folson. Let him come to you. Just talk him forward. Bribe him with something," Miller fingers his radio. "Spartan 3, keep that mob behind the schoolhouse and out of the blast zone."

Folson stops about twenty feet in front of the boy. "It's okay. You don't have to run," he says softly. "Just stay right there a minute. We want to help you," he motions with his arms, moving them up and down. "You can put your hands down," he says. "It's OK. Safe. Hands down."

Folson motions again. Up, then down. Up, then down.

The man and woman seem to understand, lowering their hands. Folson points to the landmine behind the boy so that they, too, see the danger. Caldwell offers a few more phrases in Pashto, but his words seem to fall on deaf ears.

The woman calls out to the boy, whose hands are still raised, a plastic, pink-haired troll held high in one of his palms. The man shouts a few words as well, pointing at the schoolhouse.

Folson gestures to the boy to coax him forward, but he only giggles, moving his arms to mimic Folson. Up, then down. Up, then down—apparently delighting in this spoof of surrender.

"OK, kid. OK," Folson responds in kind, raising his arms, then lowering them, doing his best to smile. Miller and Caldwell have moved in, guarding from forty-five-degree angles off either side of

Folson's back. They scan the sheds, the flapping tent curtains. Even from a good thirty feet off, Miller can see Folson's concentration, the way he steadies his gaze on the boy as he inches his boots slowly across the dirt to try and get close enough to pull him to safety.

Up, then down. Up, then down.

The boy giggles, a little crinkle forming across the bridge of his nose.

"Would you look at that?" Folson says. "This kid's having a blast," and he glances over his shoulder, flashing a smile at Miller. Folson looks again at the boy and steps closer, closing the distance to about ten feet. He extends his hand. "It's OK. It's going to be OK, isn't it?" and the only mercy in the next second as Folson inches forward again—ready to save this boy, ready to save himself—is that his foot presses into a second landmine—hidden, imperceptible—and it detonates so quickly, Folson will never know what hit him.

20

Carry On

One moment, Aaseya is looking at the soldier with the bruise on his face, and the next, the soldier has completely blown apart. Ghazél flies backward, hurtling into her legs. Rahim pulls them into a nearby shed for safety, but she breaks free, trying to tell the soldiers about the schoolhouse. Ghazél closes his eyes. Opens them again. Aaseya holds him as Rahim brushes sand from the boy's face, his limbs, his fingers, his toes. She studies her husband. There's such tenderness in his touch, a gentle efficiency to his concern. Rahim leans in, embracing her and the boy. Warmth meets warmth, and he releases them, taking a deep breath. He inspects Aaseya, as well, for wounds or injury, and she notes the steady protection pulsing through his palms. He's nearly in tears, whether from shock or exhaustion, she can't tell, but he won't stop saying her name. Again and again, her name, as if it were a poem, as if it were a lifeline, as if it were the only thing he had left to believe in, and then there is this—

"We're leaving," he says. "There's nothing here for us we can't live without. There's nothing here that works."

Aaseya looks at Ghazél, the wet flap of flesh open along his thigh. Too many other cuts to count. The boy whimpers slightly and closes his eyes. "We have to let them help Ghazél first."

Rahim nods. "This is Ghazél?"

"Yes," Aaseya says, "but we can't leave him. I can't leave him. Rahim, he's—"

"Shhh," he says, "I understand."

Ghazél cries out, an odd, round-syllabled moan that sounds part animal, part strained. Aaseya holds him closer and begins to hum. *He came from the village of sun / my dearest, my jewel / my shining smart one.* Voices of shock bleed into one another, but Ghazél doesn't feel scared. Sunlight moves through his body. It's warm, like the gooey place in his leg where two slivers of metal have gouged his muscles. Warm, like the man's hand gently touching his forehead, whispering a line of poetry Ghazél won't understand until years from now: "This sky where we live is no place to lose your wings," he's saying. "…No place. So love, love, love."

Ghazél would like to close his eyes. He would like to carry on with his quiet whimpering. He would like to listen to what this man is saying—to love, love, love. To feel that palm across his forehead and be held forever in their arms.

21

How War Works

Slow down, slow down, slow down! It's Tenley talking, right into Miller's ear, as if she's running beside him, tugging at his DCUs trying to keep her husband out of the fray. *Goddamnit, Nathan, slow down*. But he can't. He won't. He puts her away. There's no justice in war and no one to blame except himself, and if he waits another second, that family up ahead might take one, two, three more steps any direction and blow themselves into a thousand fleshy splinters. The desert is a minefield. The minefield is the ocean. He is walking on water. There is no Jesus Christ. He is utterly unglued.

Four meters now, maybe five, from the family and he sees something meaty in the periphery of his vision. It's Folson's upper body—his head still attached, his left eye still black. Then the horrible realization that Folson's legs are somewhere else, completely unattached. The male civilian takes one look at Miller and pulls his family away from the blast zone toward one of the sheds. The woman breaks free and flails her arms, nearly stumbling, then shouts at Miller in Pashto. She points ferociously at the schoolhouse.

Miller turns around, scans windows, the back door. "Rock. Yak," he calls through the radio. "Caldwell and I will take care of the boy. All other eyes on alert."

A flock of birds lifts from the roofline of the schoolhouse, cooing and tittering through the air, and the woman is screaming, still screaming.

"It's OK," Miller says, trying to calm her. "I'm here to help," but his words are useless.

The man she was with dashes out of the shed with the bleeding boy slung over his shoulder. He grabs the woman and pulls back. She flees his grasp one more time and emerges, pointing again at the schoolhouse, her voice impossibly high-pitched.

Caldwell dashes past Miller and ducks into the shed, carrying an armful of medical supplies.

Miller turns again, checking his men down the line. "Rock, tell me what you're seeing."

"I got nothing, Sir. Just a bunch a birds shitting on the roof."

"Look again. Look closely."

Miller stands on guard at the entrance of the shelter, the boy's soft moaning in the background like an undertow of sound. He longs to scour the schoolhouse for anything that will explain the mess spread before him, but the ROE make this impossible. Around the blast site, Huang and Rock pull security, then eventually peel off to perch in their turrets and zero in on the schoolhouse. Sparco and Romero struggle into action, exacting KIA and landmine protocols through the syrupy efficiency of these fat minutes following the impossible. Slowly, they collect Folson's body parts. Taylor squats strategically behind the open door of Spartan 3, targeting the schoolhouse as well. Up front, Supreme is kicking the side of Spartan 1, cursing. Reynolds grabs at his back, trying to calm him. Supreme kicks again, and his Oakley sunglasses fall from his face, trampled in the scuffle.

Movement in one of the windows catches Miller's eye. Huang and Rock align in sync, targeting the upper left quadrant of the building.

"On it," Huang calls through his headset.

They wait.

Supreme has finally quieted, and Reynolds pulls him toward another shed opposite the side of the road from Caldwell, Miller, and the family. They crouch low, targeting the dead-end ridgeline at the foot of the valley, opposite the schoolhouse. John Boy rises into the turret of Spartan 1 and faces the same way. Yak's tied to Spartan 1 as well, confirming coordinates to call into the FOB, likely requesting a Black Hawk to carry Folson's body back. The seconds tick past, the sun notching its stubborn way across the sky. Nothing else moves. The black eye keeps looking at Miller.

He wants nothing short of battle now, to know the Spartans have done something here other than lose a good man. What will he say to Folson's children?

"The boy's gonna need an evac," Caldwell says. "Can we get him on the bird?"

Miller already knows the answer the brass would give, and besides, the Black Hawk won't have advanced life support equipment or medics. The Black Hawk isn't coming for the living. The Black Hawk is coming for the dead. He looks over at the boy, at Caldwell. He shakes his head. Caldwell is fast at work on a flesh wound in the boy's thigh. The Afghan male presses a pack of bandages to the boy's stomach, where it looks like the bleeding has slowed. The woman holds the entire mess in her lap, redness darkening the fabric of her clothing. With the exception of his leg, it appears the boy's wounds are shallow but pervasive, shrapnel peppering his body like freckles. Blood trickles in lines as thin as spider's silk from at least a dozen cuts down the boy's arms.

"We can fix this," Miller says to the family. "We can help. I promise we can help."

The man and woman look at him, confused, and Caldwell attempts to translate.

"We need to get him out of here, LT," Caldwell says, and Miller nods, calculating.

"Tell them they'll ride with us. Can you say that in Pashto?"

"I think so, Sir, but—?"

"In Folson's seat. We'll hand them over to the ANA at the gates. They can take it from there. That's the only way they'll let 'em through, but believe me, if we cart this boy all the way to Tarin Kowt, they're going to let him through. I'll personally see to it. How long until you can get him stable? We've got to move."

"Ten minutes, maybe? Fifteen?"

An eternity on the ground, but the Black Hawk will be another five or ten minutes after that, and there's no moving out until Folson is loaded up. Miller feels a tightening in his throat, an itch in the back of his brain. He peers around the shed and into the roadway. Sparco and Romero are wrestling Folson's dismembered legs into a body bag. This is how they will end their war. By putting it all into a bag. The plainness of it nearly fells Miller, and the day isn't even over yet. The sun looks down indifferently. The sands shift into dunes. The earth spins, and people die, and everyone still has to take a shit, and all the mess of everything carrying on at once burrows into Miller's brain like a mole. He hears Yak sign off with the FOB, but he's still spinning, acid burning his throat. He tries to hold onto the edge of Yak's voice, to the familiar scent of diesel, to the humdrum high-low of war. He spits onto the ground.

It brings him back.

Tonight.

Tonight he will call Tenley.

But first, he's got to help Sparco and Romero. He's got to pick up the rest of Folson—he can do this. His forehead sweating, his mouth on fire, his stomach dropped completely out of his body, his M4 glued to his palm, his salt tablets still not enough, his body armor wearing blisters over his collarbone, his balls coated in sweat, his knees stiff, his boots tied to dress code, the soles of them pressing into the ground, down, down, like drill bits trying to spiral Miller into his own fast grave, and he wants it. Wants that grave more than life itself.

Just one more day.

He steps into the road. Five paces. Ten. He crouches down, cupping his hands around Folson's head. Sparco grabs the torso, and Romero opens the body bag. They lower Folson inside.

Years from now, Miller will see the uselessness of blame. Every Spartan believed what they did mattered, that war served a greater purpose that couldn't be achieved without them. Miller taught them as much. But the one thing clear as daylight now, in this moment, is that war only works in service of itself. Miller knows this with certainty, and as the first bullet zings past his left ear like an angry wasp, like an old friend, he hoists the bag over his shoulder and hustles with Sparco and Romero into position behind Bean Curd.

The first boom of an RPG comes next, followed by fevered silence. When it hits—about fifty yards off target on the upper slopes of the sidewall mountains—the sound is deafening. No one is hurt, but the reverb from the impact jars Miller, who braces his headset in an attempt to hear whoever is on the radio now, spewing details through the cacophony of rounds being fired. For a long string of seconds, the Spartans seem on pause, the world tipping slightly off-center as Miller strains to bring his vision back into focus. Somehow, he registers the cries of the civilian mob growing distant, retreating away from the schoolhouse and back into the heart of the village.

"Copperhead Nine-Nine, this is Spartan 6. Troops in contact, over," he calls into the TOC.

"Spartan 6, Copperhead Nine-Nine, roger. Send SPOT report, over."

Miller leans into the dash, glaring through the windshield to try and get a count on the number of enemies. In the turret just behind his head, Huang fires several rounds at the schoolhouse, legs jerking with the reverb.

"Copperhead Nine-Nine, Spartan 6, we're taking accurate small arms and RPG fire from approximately four military-aged males, Checkpoint Budweiser, time now. Request close air support, over."

Message received, Miller imagines a junior officer hustling to get Chaffen on the line, the whole TOC buzzing into action.

All at once, Huang slumps into the turret, folded into himself and apparently unconscious. "Sparco, Romero—man down," Miller shouts, and they move from behind the Humvee to assist. One KIA, one WIA with two Spartans on, the medic tied up with a civilian, and already, Miller has calculated there must be at least two gunmen in the schoolhouse, two more on the opposing ridge. He hustles to Spartan 3, rounds pinging the dirt at his feet like fat raindrops.

"One on the roof, one in the upper left window," Taylor shouts when Miller arrives. Another boom sounds from behind, but the explosion never comes. The RPG lands, undetonated, about thirty feet from Spartan 3.

"Spartan 6, this is Company Reverb 6. We're spinning up the birds right now. Tell me what's going on, over," it's Chaffen, curt and clear through Miller's headset, and what a relief, to think of gunships parting the haze.

Taylor fires another round at the schoolhouse, and Miller, wrapping up the call with Chaffen, follows with a few more bursts.

"I think we got him!" Taylor shouts.

The window looks empty, no sign of activity. Miller thinks he can see the top of a turban-wrapped head just along the windowsill. It's canted slightly and unmoving, likely the gunner they just bagged. But he can't be sure.

"Rock, keep on the schoolhouse. Taylor, cover me," Miller says. "I'm going to the front of the line." With a dash and duck, he's at the rear bumper of Bean Curd in no time, a quick glance to see that Huang has his eyes open, and onward to Spartan 1 where Yak and John Boy are taking serious fire from the opposing ridgeline.

"Tell me what you're seeing," Miller shouts.

"At least two gunmen working that launcher at eleven o'clock, just behind the outcropping on the ridgeline," Yak shouts, "and more of them firing from ten and two. But they keep moving. I can't tell how many."

"Air support is on the way," Miller says. "Cover me so I can get to Supreme and Reynolds. You and John Boy stay on the launcher. I want that out of commission *now*. We'll take the gunmen."

Yak fires several rounds while Miller dashes thirty yards off, joining Supreme and Reynolds in the shed. "Yak and John Boy are on the launcher. We're on the gunmen. Gunships are on the way," he shouts.

"Haji just popped up behind that line of shrubs when you were running, LT. Eight o'clock," Reynolds says. "Little fucker gonna cook next time he gets that stupid."

Another boom and this one looks spot on, the rocket arcing in a terribly straight line. "It's on you, Yak," Miller calls through the headset and already, Yak is trying to pull John Boy from the turret, into the relative shelter of their Humvee, but something looks caught—or off; it's John Boy, injured, though Miller can't tell how badly just yet.

When the RPG lands—about fifty yards in front of Spartan 1—the reverb rocks through Miller's boots and up his spine, rattling his skull. Supreme leaps from the entrance of the shed and lets out an angry growl, targeting the shrubs on the ridge. A few quick bursts come in return, then abruptly stop. A large rock tumbles free, followed by a body, and both come to rest about forty feet down slope.

"Medic!" Yak calls. "Caldwell! Medic!"

He hauls John Boy from the turret and lies him flat on the backseat of Spartan 1. Caldwell dashes from the opposite shelter, a trail of bandage wrappings littering his path. The Afghan male slips out of the shelter as well, leaping upslope to a footpath along a contour headed back into the village. Within moments, he's cleared the schoolhouse and moved out of sight.

Miller covers Caldwell as best he can, but he can't see clearly around Spartan 1, and then there is this—almost wavering, an illusion?—with an odd limp and grin, a slow-moving haji steps from behind a row of low trees just twenty feet distant and fires an AK from his hip with the glee of a zombie. Before Miller can think, he's blasted two rounds into the man's gut, and there's Reynolds, gritting his teeth through a final burst to the head. The haji teeters like a Jenga tower, then flops dead into the dirt that made him.

The Black Hawk arrives first, and it takes every Spartan still standing to provide cover as Sparco, Romero, and Miller load the bag and duck out of the way. It seems an eternity before the gunships approach, and the sound, even before they're within sight, sends a jolt of anticipation through Miller's body. Their thwapping grows in intensity, and as the rounds continue—too damn close, too damn many—he knows those birds will blast the entire backside of that mountain range if that's what it takes. Huang is back in the game, the bullet cleanly deflected by his body armor. Yak and Caldwell tend to John Boy, a single bullet wound to his lower right shoulder and a whole mess of screams and curses. Taylor and Rock take cover in Spartan 3, armored doors and glass wrapped like a prayer around them, and two OH-58D Kiowa Warriors finally come into view. Beautiful, rising through the bronze dust like jeweled birds of prey.

"Little Bird 1, Spartan 6, we've got at least one gunman on the roof of the schoolhouse—the only two-story building at the end of the village," he radios. "Likely more inside, over."

"Roger, we have eyes on target and can confirm military-aged males with weapons. We'll take care of them while you disengage."

Miller slams the door of Spartan 3, bracing for the *whomp* and heat, and as satisfying as a wish made—three, two, one—the schoolhouse erupts into flames. The roof caves inward as a sidewall crumbles to the ground, the entire structure like a gigantic birthday cake lit in flames for the apocalypse.

"Je-sus-H," Taylor says, blinking.

Miller hops out of Spartan 3 and heads toward the front of the line. "Little Bird 2, we're taking small arms and rocket fire from the ridgeline north of our position. There's at least one squirter headed out of the kill zone. Two more manning a launcher."

"Roger. Mark the target with smoke and confirm no civilians in the vicinity, then we'll make our gun run."

Miller arrives at Bean Curd, then calls to Yak and Rock through his headset. "Spartans, mount up!"

Sparco and Romero hobble arm in arm toward Spartan 3. One of them is limping, though Miller can't be sure which just now. Supreme finds his way to Spartan 1. Reynolds hops into Bean Curd and revs the engine. Huang eases into the backseat and slams the door closed. Miller hustles to the shelter to get the woman and boy. When he arrives, he sees that the man has returned, a satchel of belongings slung over his back.

"You come," Miller shouts. "You all come. ANA! Afghan National Army! We'll take you!"

He shoves them out of the shelter, following fast on their heels. The woman and boy settle next to Huang, silent and shocked. Surely, Miller can salvage this, at least. A family. A child. A new life. The man slides onto the back platform of Bean Curd where the boxes of water had been stored.

Miller hops into the front seat. "Reynolds," he says, "pop smoke."

Reynolds aims his carbine and loads the M203 underbarrel launcher. "Spartans," he says, "what's your favorite color?"

Miller and Huang shout in unison. "RED, motherfucker!"

Reynolds fires.

"Home run," Miller says. "Nice work." Then, over the radio: "Little Bird 2, roger. All friendlies accounted for. Red smoke on target. Clear to engage."

The Kiowa Warriors are something to behold as they zip by, approaching 100 mph just fifty feet above the ground. They dance like dragonflies. Little Bird 1 pounds the slopes with .50-caliber machine gun fire. Little Bird 2 rises slightly, then blasts a string of 70 mm rockets at the ridgeline.

"Hell yeah!" Huang pounds his fist into the seat.

"Good glory God," Reynolds says. He leans into the windshield, awestruck.

The Kiowas zip over the ridge and repeat their gun run. "Spartan 6, this is Little Bird 1. Targets destroyed."

"Roger, Little Bird 1, objective secured. Thanks for your help." Miller looks at Reynolds. "One more thing," he says. Reynolds looks at him, confused. Miller opens the door and dashes to the back of Bean Curd.

"Sir?" Miller says, approaching the Afghan male. He appears wide-eyed, completely covered in dust and grime. "Sir, your bag." Miller points.

The man shakes his head, failing to understand.

"Your bag," Miller says again, this time touching the satchel and tugging lightly.

The man's face flattens. He won't let Miller take the bag but agrees to hold it open while Miller searches.

"What's the hold up?" Rock calls over the radio.

Overhead, the Kiowas lift out of sight, already clear of Imar proper and headed on the long diagonal back to base. There's no time to be wasted now, but what had the Afghan been so hellbent on getting? Miller isn't willing to take any chances.

"Spartan 1, you all set?" Miller calls through his headset as his hands work quickly, sifting through clothing and a few food items.

"Roger that, LT," Yak replies.

"Spartan 3?"

"Yes, Sir. More than ready," Rock calls.

Miller finds something hard, about the size of a book. He looks at the Afghan, then slowly removes the object from the bag. It's a small, hand-carved wooden box. Inside, a stack of US dollar bills is pressed flat. He flips through a few of the bills, Folson's blood still on his fingertips. At a certain point, it's all in plain sight, isn't it? Completely, utterly, backwards. Miller closes the lid of the box as if closing a coffin and sets it back in the bag.

22

Like a Promise

When Aaseya was a child, there were things she might have insisted on seeing one last time. Her school desk, to be certain. The one Ms. Darrow let her choose for herself. Aaseya had secretly written her initials in English block letters beneath its wooden lid. And the communal bath house, not just because her mother sang to her there but because all the women came together in that space with an ease Aaseya never felt anywhere else. Like a collective exhale. A shared burden lifting with the steam off the women's backs. The way the light fell in soft beams through the thatched roof was something to behold. But now, with Ghazél lying across her lap and the soldier next to her in this Humvee securing the bandage on the boy's leg, there's only one last thing she wants to see. The convoy is headed straight toward it.

She leans forward in her seat, careful not to disturb Ghazél, and peers out the front window. With Imar at their backs, the loop road arcs toward the intersection leading out of the valley, and here—a place she's stood so many times, a line she never dared to cross—the convoy carries her over the threshold as easy as breathing. The sidewall mountains taper into soft hills, the desert floor widening beneath her. Before long, there's only sky and sand, the distant ranges barely an interruption. The sight of it lets her heart loose. The more the horizon stretches, the more she feels herself soar.

Tarin Kowt is visible in the distance for quite some time before Aaseya actually sees any other Afghans. The compounds seem humble, at first, but as the city streets spread and the blocks grow ever-crammed, she's amazed. Children play openly outside, and already, she's seen three women wearing headscarves instead of burqas. Brightly illustrated signs mounted on buildings shout at her, advertising construction companies, doctors, corner grocers. Gas pumps, billboards, men pushing carts filled with sacks of grain—it all rushes past in a rash of color. Several ladders are perched on every block to provide roof access where families have set up more tents for shelter or commodity. Vendors sell dishware, produce, watches, bangles, plastic flowers. Teahouses pepper each block, seemingly endless crowds coming and going.

The paved roads feel strange beneath the rumbling Humvee, and Aaseya finds it hard to believe they aren't hovering. The convoy moves quickly, and she notes the way families dash out of their way. Some cheer and wave. Others laugh or throw trash, whether playfully or out of harassment, she can't tell. The Humvee slows slightly to round a corner, and down the block, she spots an open-air building at least six stories tall. Unfathomable, to think of a building that high—even more to realize the structure is full of parked cars. A house just for cars? An impossible luxury; it may even be a trick of her imagination.

A few blocks beyond, she catches the glint of metal running in a long line atop a fortress wall. She sees the flags next—her own, the Americans', and a few others she can't decipher. She leans toward Ghazél, whispering.

"Open your eyes, sweet boy. Help is on its way."

Ghazél blinks and stares out the window, then closes his eyes again, cradling into Aaseya's arm.

The wait at the gates is long. The lead soldier—the one who brought her and Ghazél into his Humvee and let Rahim ride on the back—shouts aggressively at the security soldiers dressed like himself, standing guard at the entrance to the base. They ignore him, one security soldier even shoving the lead soldier slightly as he brushes past and walks straight up to Aaseya and the boy. The security soldier stares at them through the dusty window and shakes his head, then goes around back to question Rahim. Aaseya intuits that their conversation isn't pleasant, but the lead soldier quickly rushes over, barking a string of sentences that sound like defense. The security soldier steps away and speaks into a black, hand-held radio.

When she sees the ANA soldiers arrive in their dark camouflage and flat, green hats, she understands that she, Rahim, and Ghazél are going to be passed off. Their uniforms are a patchwork of logos and emblems, and as all six men approach the Humvee, the familiar sounds of her native language ease her uncertainty. "You're safe now," she hears one of them say. "We'll take care of your son," another says.

With Rahim, they are equally gentle. There is no body search, no jostling, not a single gun tip raised. Just their presence at her back now as they encircle her and Ghazél and usher them through a side entrance, past the security soldiers. Rahim is two paces ahead of her and turns back to catch her gaze. They've gotten this far, and she suspects they'll go farther still into these next uncertain days, the unfolding months, across the new terrain and permissions of their lives together. Stepping through a final gate, she turns over her shoulder to look for the lead soldier. *Thank you,* she could imagine herself saying, *for proving my father right.* But his back is turned as he addresses his men, and she knows now that nothing is ever that tidy. Beyond the soldiers, the open streets of Tarin Kowt spread like a promise.

23

Tonight is Still This Morning

Back on FOB Copperhead, a huddle of soldiers waits in line outside the call center. Miller approaches, a stiffness to his gait. Everyone has already heard about the KIA, the whole mission completely turned on its head. The Black Hawk carrying Folson's body landed on base hours ago. But the real buzz—Miller knows without having to tap into the rumor mill—is the Afghan family he drove fifty klicks back to base, including a male civilian who reportedly had intel linking Gawri to a man named Obaidhullah Nabi, a Taliban leader on more than one FBI hit list. Never mind that Chaffen blew steam out his ears when he found out what Miller brought to the FOB gates. Never mind that the boy—stable now, on an IV drip with fluids and antibiotics—needed medical care Miller hadn't been sure the ANA could promise. As soon as that Afghan male started talking with a fully trained translator at his side, any possible demerit headed Miller's way couldn't touch him. Humanitarian to the nines, not to mention life-saving intel—and John Boy and Sparco stable in the infirmary, to boot.

But even these small graces can't touch Miller, whose skin has felt aflame ever since Folson. He takes his place at the end of the call line. Soldiers in wait wordlessly usher him to the front. Within moments, he's inside the air-conditioned room. The buzz of fluorescents, the scooting of chairs, the soft grumble of half a dozen voices talking to loved ones, and Obama still there, hovering over history in the making. He finds the only empty chair and falls into it, then props his elbows on the makeshift plywood table running the length of the room. Two square feet make up this little cubicle of privacy, an off-white phone with dirty buttons staring at him like a scarred face.

When Tenley answers, Miller can hear the coffee on the other side of her "hello." In North Carolina, it's still morning. Still hopeful on her side of the earth. Still a time of day when Folson was alive.

"Hello?" she says again, and Miller can hardly stand the swell of emotion pushing up from his feet, tightening the bottom of his stomach, gripping his throat. He could never survive without her love.

"Tenley," he says. The best word he has said all day. He's likely caught her moments before she has to leave for work and drop Cissy off at Girl Scout day camp. He waits to find the words, the starting point, but sentences slug each other on the other side of his closed mouth.

"Sweetie? Nathan, tell me. Nathan?"

She can hear it then, the way something has gone horribly wrong.

"I'm OK," he says. He's not. But he's upright. He's breathing. All his limbs are attached. He can hear her set her mug of coffee down, knowing the pattern in the grain of wood at their kitchen table where she likely sits. The *Yancey Common Times Journal* would be on the table too, loose pages a little damp from the humidity. Next to that would be the ceramic flower vase—the one her parents gave them as a house-warming gift, made by a potter down the river. *Can you hand me the obits?* Nathan is almost there, sitting across from her. *I need to make sure Folson's not in the paper, need to know if tonight is still this morning.* But he's disoriented, wires crossing. Wrong, that's what he is. Wrong, for wishing he could be home this instant when he still has his platoon to lead. Wrong, not to order Folson back, tell him to watch his step. He imagines Folson's funeral, but what would they actually bury? There was so little of him left, and the black eye hasn't stopped staring at Miller since the blast. He can't think about it. Not now. By Tenley's clock, Folson isn't KIA yet. That's a thought. That's a little better.

"What time is it?" Miller asks. But even this is insufficient. Tonight is something else, isn't it? Tonight is this morning. Tonight he will call Tenley. Tonight is now, but now is two things at once, and how can Folson be alive and dead at the same time?

"I can be late to work, honey, don't worry. Please. It's good to hear your voice."

"Tomorrow," he says. "I mean today. My today, your tomorrow. It's going to happen. I wanted to call you, Tenley. I wanted to tell you."

Miller scoots his chair as close to the table as possible, torso hunched over the phone, head down. The receiver shakes against his ear. He has failed his men again, and if he has failed his men, who's to say he won't also fail his wife? His daughter? Again, again, again. He bites his fist, then pulls it from his mouth and whispers.

"I lost one of my men. One of my men is dead."

He can't tell Tenley the details, the way Folson's eye won't let up. Next of kin get first notice, and besides, she's never met Folson. What she must know, though, is that it could have been any one of them. It could have been Miller. He hears her take another sip of coffee and imagines her walking toward the window, the one right above the kitchen sink.

"And I lost our baby," Miller cries silently, chapped lips cracking through the strain. A hot rash comes to his face. It feels as though his brain could seep through his skin and dribble onto the phone in front of him. "I'm sorry. I wanted to tell you everyday that I'm sorry for that. For not being there. For putting us through this."

He can sense she's searching, probably leaning into the windowpane to look for something far away. Something deep within the forest. It would have to be big, humbling. It would have to be large enough to make Nathan's pain seem small by comparison, manageable. He's just a tiny voice coming at her now, from so many miles away. He's just a sliver.

"Is that what you think? About the baby? Nathan, please don't...Nathan—"

"—and I'm coming home soon. But I don't want you to be mad."

"Nathan, I won't be. I'm not. Sweetie, the baby was no one's fault. Even I believe that now."

He doesn't so much hear her words as feel them, like someone pressing a finger into a fleshy wound, and he's there again: Appalachia, the soldier who feels suffocated by his own backyard. But it's different now. He's different. Tenley's saying something different too. *Not his fault?*

"Nathan, I need you to tell me. Tell me more. Are you still there?"

He wonders if Folson felt anything and, if he did, where he felt it first. At the seams of his limbs where they flew off? Maybe in the soles of his feet, the arches bursting as if struck by lightening from the ground up. But Folson is gone. Folson isn't feeling anything. There's only this thing Nathan has become, not quite animal, surely not human, the phone shaking in his hands and his heart pounding so ferociously he's certain he really has split in half. It's a relief to finally look at himself, this vulnerability. The bloody mess he's made of it all. How horribly comforting, that blood.

"When I came home last Thanksgiving…when I asked you for another child. Do you remember?"

"Yes," Tenley says. "Hush, Cissy," she says away from the phone. "Mommy just needs a few more minutes."

He imagines his daughter standing in the hallway, waiting. Even at six, she's learned when a phone call is one of the war ones.

"I'm sorry for that too. It was too much. It was too soon."

"I could have made things easier than I did," Tenley says. "I regret that I didn't."

"It's a mess here. Nothing's what it should be"

"What is? How should things be?"

"I am. I'm a mess, Tenley. Everything here is."

Miller lets his forehead sink to the tabletop. He wants to keep it there forever. Or maybe ram his skull through it so hard, he makes a hole big enough to hang from, snap his own neck. That might be interesting to see.

"What can I do? I want to help. It's so good to hear your voice."

He hears katydids. Tree ducks, he liked to call them when they first moved to North Carolina together. Tenley must have stepped outside onto the porch. The mountain summer morning would feel cool there, alert. A world away from the FOB, the desert. How long has it been? At least since the Korengals. No, before that. At least that long since he's let her in like this.

"Are you outside?" he asks.

"Yeah," she says. "I'm walking toward the edge of the lawn."

"I can almost see it," he tells her. "And you. I can almost see you too."

He'd do anything to stare into the woods with her, to watch the filtered sun gently light the world. But he knows better than to rush. So much waits for them on the other side of patience.

He's right at the edge. He's got to believe she sees what he sees, even though they're worlds apart. There's an opening through the woods. He swears he can see it clearly, unbroken. Can she see it, too? Can she?

"Tenley, just…don't be afraid of me when I come home. Don't give up on me."

"I never would," she says. "I'm trying. I'll try. I want to be more patient."

"I couldn't keep him safe. I thought I could, but I was wrong."

"No one can keep everyone safe, Nathan."

"But he expected me to. They all do."

"And they all expect to die, don't they? Didn't you?"

Nathan pauses. She's so good like this. So right, in so few words. "Yes," he says. "Yes, I did. Many times."

Epilogue

Tenley holds Nathan those first few nights in the beginning, opposite how they used to sleep. She keeps her body cupped along his back, her arm slumped over his shoulders, barely reaching halfway around. It makes Nathan feel uncertain, like borrowing someone else's boots. But if this is what it takes, he reasons. If this is how he has to ease back into the light. He's different now; they both know that. But he's still a husband and a father. He's still home. Done. Through his half-sleep he often shakes and shifts, as though jerking out of some horrible costume. Once or twice, he's even woken himself with his own eerie chuckle, as if deciphering the butt of a joke. Other times, he shouts wildly, scaring himself and Tenley awake.

For many weeks, there's still the Nathan living and the Nathan watching Nathan. Together, they present a man wound as tightly as the muscles in his throat. It works something like this: When teenagers drive past his house on Grove Road, engines backfiring like the muffled explosions he heard at FOB Copperhead and in the Korengals, he lets his mind make a movie of everything his cells tell him to do—Second Lieutenant Miller, diving beneath the dinner table; Miller, chin-tucked, hands reaching for the safety on his M4; Miller, sheepishly returning to his chair at the table, holding Tenley's gaze. If he focuses hard enough on the movie, he can keep still instead and let the moment pass. It takes tremendous energy. Unimaginable focus. He knows now what Folson meant when he confessed that war felt easier than home.

Two months out, he starts up full time at Mountain Hardware, working the six to two. The guys never ask what he did "over there." They're good like that.

Arriving home one afternoon from work, Nathan sets his keys on the counter and aims for the sofa. He doesn't have the energy to hike up to his firing range on the ridge. Not today. Not most days. But heck—he's done it. Gone to work and come home. Almost a pleasure worth marveling at if it weren't so utterly boring compared to the unpredictability of war. He unlaces his work boots and kicks them off, stretching his long body from one end of the couch to the other. When he closes his eyes, sleep isn't far behind.

When she gets home from school, Cissy quietly jostles Nathan's toes to wake him. He immediately prickles at her touch. Too light. Too uncertain. As if an insurgent has snuck into the bunkhouse and is standing there in his living room, the tip of his AK targeting Nathan's forehead. First response: every muscle in his body cinches tightly, right up to the air trapped inside his lungs. Part of him realizes almost immediately how horribly this might go—Cissy feeling Daddy toss her to the ground with the flip of his legs, then his chest slamming into hers as he readies for the chokehold, then no—wait. It's just his daughter. His only daughter.

Nathan opens his eyes and sees her there, blond pigtails and a toothy grin. "Sweetie come on up here, away from Daddy's feet, OK?" He might be whispering. The Nathan watching Nathan still can't be certain.

She slips her backpack off her shoulders and curls into Nathan's arms. He shifts to his side so he can cradle her there, his little turtle. He wonders if she feels his heart thump through his chest wall or his lungs cinch tighter, part of his consciousness holding court in a violent world.

"How was school today?" he asks. He's back inside himself for a moment, the good father on the sofa with his girl. He wants to cry at the simplicity of it. Tenley would like to walk in on this. He aches at the thought of her and feels a clutching of energy below his belt. They still haven't found their way back to all that. In time. But he does need her. Knows, too, that she needs him back.

Cissy's saying something. Her day. That's right. Nathan strains to focus, her voice so sweetly syncopated he almost forgets everything else. "Let's get up, my girl. Let's see what you've got for homework."

Tenley's handling of Nathan's return might look cold to anyone on the outside. That's the thing about small towns, as much as Nathan loves them. But she's simply giving Nathan the space he needs. He understands this without even having to think it. She's mostly there when he asks and leaves the rest to time. But she has confessed to him that even her closest girlfriends are dishing judgment, warning her about the way combat changes a man. As if they knew, Nathan wants to say in Tenley's defense. As if they wore body armor, marveled at bullet holes through pant legs, and lived on MREs. Not that Tenley had, but at least she's closer to it than any of them. By the time holiday season rolls around, just as everyone is hosting parties and cook-offs, Nathan could scream from all of the social saccharine, and there's Tenley in their own kitchen, suggesting a two-week vacation to Nathan's parents' house.

"Do you want to?" Tenley asks. She's prepping a pork roast around mid-afternoon, marinating, stuffing. Sunday dinner is her favorite, and with Cissy tall enough to see over the countertops, Nathan studies the mother-daughter dance they've developed in his absence.

"Let's go see Grandma!" Cissy grins, leaping into Tenley, who, in turn, bumps a pan of steaming green beans. Water hisses onto the stove.

"Everything all right?" Nathan calls from the nearby table where he sits, hunched over a Scrabble board.

"Nothin' doin'," Tenley says. "My turn yet?"

"You're not gonna like this," Nathan says. He walks over to the stove.

"Triple score?"

"Double. But I used a Q and added to your last word."

"Ditch?"

"Yeah. Sorry, baby."

He catches her around the waist as she walks past. He loves that. How his wide palms cup perfectly around her midsection. But his hands haven't found their way back to most other parts of Tenley's body. He feels her hesitation, as if she doesn't quite believe his desire. Nathan keeps telling her he feels empty. Exhausted before they can even begin. But it's not misleading just to touch her, is it? Just to say he loves her? When they do try, it embarrasses him greatly to fail, his mind darting to memories so far from the softness of her skin next to his that she'd be horrified if she saw the same images he saw.

She stands over the game board. "QUIDDITCH? That's so *not* a word."

"It's Harry Potter's game, Mama. And it's a word," Cissy hops over to the table.

They all encircle the word as Cissy flips through the Scrabble dictionary. "Here, Daddy," she says, proudly opening to the Q section. "Can you find it?"

"Let's see…"

He thumbs through the pages. He's very sleepy. Sometimes bored. But he's getting used to the feeling, and the less he fights it, the less significant it seems.

"Mama says we're going to Indiana for Christmas!" Cissy blurts. "She says maybe even for two weeks."

Nathan glances at Tenley from across the table. "Two weeks, huh?"

"It would make your mother so happy," she says.

Indiana. The one thing, he used to tease, he might have married instead of her. "Do you mean it, Ten?"

"I do," she holds his gaze when she says it, marking the promise.

"I remember those two words," Nathan says, and when Tenley blushes into a smile, for a moment the family looks like four tours never came between them.

The day before their trip, Nathan zips his coat to his chin and heads for his firing range. He follows his narrow footpath through the browned leaves, flecks of mica glittering atop the soil. He hopes the cold front is just that and won't bring precipitation. He wants good road conditions for the drive north. His mother has called twice this week already, asking what more to prepare, oh, and didn't I tell you? Your sister is coming! She hadn't said it, but Nathan knew that meant nieces, nephews, a brother-in-law as well. He tries to feel excited, but suddenly what seemed like it would be an easy Christmas—maybe the one he'll finally be able to convince Tenley they should make the move—will instead be a hustle-bustle negotiation of shared bathrooms and chips and dip.

Up top he hears the wind hiss. A pileated woodpecker sends out its syllabic call. In the Korengals, monkeys made the most racket, screaming day and night without reason. Memories of their cries are still one of the few things Nathan hasn't been able to sever. They chatter through his nightmares and sometimes follow him to work.

Nathan aims at the hemlock trunk and fires. Home for almost six months and he still struggles with the parts of himself he hates. There's also the unsettling fact that these are sometimes the parts he misses the most.—combat; that dopamine-crazed siblinghood where every move matters. He can't remember the last time he did something bearing that much immediate consequence for his own family. Slow and steady. He'll have to make this work. But can he ever tell anyone the truth? Everyday life pales in comparison to the constant presence of death.

Nathan loads two more rounds and fires, the sound like somebody slapping cupped hands over his ears. It feels good. He fires again, then walks to the target. The old trunk has nearly rotted through in several places, a few bullet ends visible in the mealy heartwood. He perches against the edge of the widest section and stuffs his hands into his pockets, fingers curling around the spare bullets like loose change. How many bullets had been aimed at him all those missions? How many landmines? He thinks of Folson, his two daughters. When they grow old enough, Nathan will write them a letter. Tell them how hard their father had tried to make it home to them. How much Folson loved them both.

Nathan slides a bullet from his pocket and slips it into his mouth. The taste of metal startles: cold brass beneath his hot tongue. His thoughts race. For awhile, he imagines the smell of the outpost (how strange to miss something so rank). He remembers the piles of rocks for protection, the hours of nothingness punctuated by the buzz of firefights. He rolls the bullet around in his mouth, and the metal clicks against his teeth. Few people can understand this kind of longing. He can. Tenley cannot. And there it is, a cracking admission of her imperfection. He feels relieved. She has limitations. They both do. Maybe he can let her in even more, after all. Maybe there's a way for her to taste his war, if only through words.

That night, after they tuck Cissy in and start the last load of laundry before the big drive, Nathan decides he'll try to talk. He can't be certain what he'll say, but he knows if he starts by telling Tenley about antics his platoon pulled during the days of boredom between missions, he'll stumble into a tale, and maybe they can both laugh. Tenley can't understand, but she can listen. Nathan owes her that chance.

He mutes the television when he hears her footsteps down the hallway. She walks into the bedroom. He hasn't looked at her closely in months, but he looks at her now and smiles. The best surprise is this: she hasn't changed. Thin tank top, flannel pants, and a slightly knock-kneed gait. Even the curves of her elbows appear smooth, the dip of her collarbone, the way her bright blond hair (finally down at the end of the day) teases the tops of her shoulders. She shuts the door and crawls into bed. When Nathan doesn't move to flip off the bedside light, she turns to him, questioning.

And then he feels it. His heart like a hard, cold thing stuck in his throat, stealing his voice. He might as well bleed out right here, all of him. There are no words for this. He moves his lips to hers instead.

Back before they were who they are now—Nathan offering Tenley his class ring after just eight weeks—neither could have guessed themselves into this house, this bedroom, these nervous hands fumbling with clothing, the sheets, the goddamn comforter.

Nor could they have guessed that what came so easily then, is now a quietly suffered re-education.

He wraps his arms around her and swivels her on top. He can feel the stiffness in her arms, her thoughts still clinging to the day. He feels good, but he isn't there yet. She must be able to tell how hard he's trying. Maybe he should have turned off the light, the TV screen. He refuses to entertain the hundred million other directions his mind is used to going. Fingers on a trigger, fingers in Tenley's hair. She closes her eyes and pushes back at his advances, lets him kiss her, then pulls away, breathing. He feels her hunger and rises up to meet it, clumsy almost, as he pushes into her.

What is he so afraid of?

There's got to be some lovely, messy peace waiting for them in this middle.

Tenley moves her hands to Nathan's hips and pushes their torsos apart, looking down the length of their bodies. He knows every millimeter of flesh and heart hovering over him, every place he wants to touch or nibble. Her smell. The heat of her. He closes his eyes and feels the past pulse at the base of his skull, demanding attention. He moves with Tenley between the sheets, but his mind keeps splitting, the Nathan watching Nathan getting in the way. His mouth. That bullet. Its taste of metal blood. Tenley's tongue swooping for it, wet and hungry and so close. What is this forcefulness he feels in her, this thing that keeps reaching for him? He kicks his legs free from the sheets and forces himself to look into her eyes.

The first time he thought he had been hit, he didn't wish for anything. Just lay there, face-planted in the middle of an IED-laden road, marveling at the blankness. Later, he felt ashamed. Shouldn't he have thought of his wife? His daughter? He heard someone holler for a medic, and that's when he realized he was clean. The blast knocked him out but didn't cut him up. He crawled his way to the medic and hollered: "I'm out of ammo, but I'm not hit." The medic handed him a magazine with one hand and kept firing with the other.

Tenley slides her hands from Nathan's chest toward his neck, angling her hips as they rock together. It's not a choke, but it's reminiscent in an accidental sort of way. The Nathan watching Nathan could have told her not to do that, but she wouldn't have heard him. She's in it now, and that quickly, Nathan hooks his hands around her wrists, jerking his legs to flip out of the attack. Every cell argues *No! Yes!* and Tenley senses it—the way combat might jumble everything inside of you: right, wrong, the swollen in-between. Her arms redden from his grip around her wrists, and she gasps.

"Nathan!"

Her voice, loud and quick as a shot fired. His fingers slip, and then there's her palm, so swift, coming down across his face.

The house holds still.

One breath, two breaths. Three.

Nathan feels it then. Open, clear, everything moving *outoutout*. He joins his voice with Tenley's, both of them now—laughing, loud; lovely enough to ignite the room with life.

Acknowledgments

I would like to thank the editors of *Wrath-Bearing Tree*, *Consequence Magazine*, *KYSO Flash*, and *Hypertext Magazine* who previously published excerpts of this novel and showed belief in my work. Likewise, the readers and judges in the following contests, for which *Still Come Home* received early recognition: The Lee Smith Novel Prize (Finalist), The Big Moose Fiction Prize (Finalist), The Dzanc Prize for Fiction (Finalist), and the Faulkner Wisdom Competition (Semifinalist).

A handful of readers, authors, and colleagues offered feedback and support along the way. Without their expertise and kindness, I may never have finished this book. Most immediately: sister Anne-Marie Oomen, Abigail DeWitt, Holly Wren Spaulding, Patricia Ann McNair, Claire Davis, Mary Kay Zuravleff, John Mauk and Des Cooper. You let me flail and fuss, dream and fall. You lifted me back up. You whispered in my ear across the miles. You never stopped believing, even when I did. I cannot imagine my writing life without your friendship and teachings. And notably, for their military expertise and valuable endorsement of my creative efforts: David Abrams, Pete Molin, Matt Gallagher, James Moad II, Helen Benedict, the United States Air Force Academy, and the commendable war-lit family. You welcomed me and treated me as an equal. You never said, "You can't."

Randolph College (especially Bunny Goodjohn), Interlochen Center for the Arts (especially Betsy Braun), and Arrowmont School of Arts & Crafts (especially Nick DeFord and Jason

Burnett) provided a creative haven for me to write, revise, research, and dream this novel into being. When my life changed to include my first child, your support did not waver. If anything, it expanded. Thank you for making these pages possible.

There are so many others: My family who believes in the beauty of books and coffee and old-growth trees; my writing students who keep my craft senses fresh; my project manager, Heidi Johnson, whose demeanor and skills afford me peace of mind; my publisher Kevin Atticks and publicists Deb Jayne and Jessica Glenn (MindBuck Media); the community members and running trails of Celo, North Carolina; my husband Brad, to whom this book is dedicated; and my son River Ramone Quillen, who makes the world new every day. *Thank you.*

About the Author

Katey Schultz is the author of *Flashes of War*, which the *Daily Beast* praised as an "ambitious and fearless" collection. Honors for her work include the Linda Flowers Literary Award, IndieFab Book of the Year from *Foreword Reviews*, a Gold Medal from the Military Writers Society of America, four Pushcart nominations, and writing fellowships in eight states. She lives in Celo, North Carolina and is the founder of Maximum Impact, a transformative mentoring service for creative writers that has been recognized by both CNBC and the What Works Network.

Apprentice House Press
Loyola University Maryland

Apprentice House is the country's only campus-based, student-staffed book publishing company. Directed by professors and industry professionals, it is a nonprofit activity of the Communication Department at Loyola University Maryland.

Using state-of-the-art technology and an experiential learning model of education, Apprentice House publishes books in untraditional ways. This dual responsibility as publishers and educators creates an unprecedented collaborative environment among faculty and students, while teaching tomorrow's editors, designers, and marketers.

Outside of class, progress on book projects is carried forth by the AH Book Publishing Club, a co-curricular campus organization supported by Loyola University Maryland's Office of Student Activities.

Eclectic and provocative, Apprentice House titles intend to entertain as well as spark dialogue on a variety of topics. Financial contributions to sustain the press's work are welcomed. Contributions are tax deductible to the fullest extent allowed by the IRS.

To learn more about Apprentice House books or to obtain submission guidelines, please visit www.apprenticehouse.com.

Apprentice House
Communication Department
Loyola University Maryland
4501 N. Charles Street
Baltimore, MD 21210
Ph: 410-617-5265 • Fax: 410-617-2198
info@apprenticehouse.com • www.apprenticehouse.com

CPSIA information can be obtained
at www.ICGtesting.com
Printed in the USA
LVHW081311200919
631714LV00015B/457/P